D0909004

THE STOCKHOLM CASTLE MYSTERY

A LUTE PLAYER MYSTERY

THE STOCKHOLM CASTLE MYSTERY

JOYCE ELSON MOORE

FIVE STAR
A part of Gale, Cengage Learning

GALE
CENGAGE Learning®

Farmington Hills, Mich • San Francisco • New York • Waterville, Maine
Meriden, Conn • Mason, Ohio • Chicago

GALE
CENGAGE Learning®

LIBRARY OF CONGRESS CATALOGING-IN-PUBLICATION DATA

Moore, Joyce Elson, 1934–
    The Stockholm Castle mystery / Joyce Elson Moore.
        pages ; cm. — (A lute player mystery ; 1)
        ISBN 978-1-4328-3078-6 (hardcover) — ISBN 1-4328-3078-3 (hardcover) — ISBN 978-1-4328-3087-8 (ebook) — ISBN 1-4328-3087-2 (ebook)
        1. Lutenists—Fiction. 2. Criminal investigation—Fiction. 3. Sweden—Social life and customs—17th century—Fiction. I. Title.
    PS3613.O5628S76 2015
    813'.6—dc23   2015008323

First Edition. First Printing: July 2015
Find us on Facebook– https://www.facebook.com/FiveStarCengage
Visit our website– http://www.gale.cengage.com/fivestar/
Contact Five Star™ Publishing at FiveStar@cengage.com

Printed in the United States of America
1 2 3 4 5 6 7 19 18 17 16 15

To my children, whose youthful exploits showed me that anything is possible.

CHAPTER ONE

Autumn 1649

A gibbous moon streamed patches of light on the old forest floor as Johan rode his horse northward, weaving among the beechwood trees. Already the nights were turning cool. Ice would be forming in the northern reaches of the Baltic Sea, but, with God's help, he could make it to the port at Gdańsk before the last ship left. If not, he would have a winter's worth of worry before spring. Even this far from the battlefield, some over-zealous musketeer, having seen a description posted on a barracks wall, might sniff out a deserter for the reward. The thought spurred Johan on, into a rapidly settling mist that moistened his clothes.

At a turn in the river, he stopped for the night. The mare, a Polish Arabian he had bought from a drunken Hussar for two hundred *zloty*, showed signs of fatigue. Her arched neck drooped and she had stumbled once. He dismounted, then removed the saddle and his belongings, fitted a blanket over her back, and tied her to a tree. Later, after monitoring her intake of food and water, he sank down beside the horse, his lute at his side, snug in its case. If his luck held, a month from now he'd have a coveted scholarship at a Swedish university and be studying under a famed musician. After that, he would join a group, or establish one himself, to play for special ceremonies. That would ensure a livelihood doing the thing he loved. With time, the guilt of his brother's death on the battlefield would no longer haunt his dreams. He could make a fresh start and earn a name for himself.

He rubbed his shoulders against the bark of an oak, purging the ache through his shirt and dark cloak. So what if the cloak tore? It was already well-worn, having been traded at a Jewish second-hand store for his blue uniform and telltale red collar and frogging. It had taken three weeks, working at the end of each day, to remove the tiny stitches that secured the Knight's Cross to the blue fabric, but, once completed, the uniform looked like any ordinary blue coat. Besides, removing the cross had given him something to do on the long ride from the Ukraine. The best part of the bargain, though, was the fine set of clothes tucked inside his bundle. According to the Jewish merchant, the clothes were donated by a nobleman and only worn once. They fit Johan well, and were perfect for his audition. The Jew was pleased with the trade and so was he.

Dusk settled in and from a distant ridge he heard the long, guttural howl of a wolf separated from the pack. A few moments later, howls pierced the forest, primeval echoes that made the hair on his neck stand up, not from fear, but from the ancient cry that stirred a man's soul like a haunting melody. The thought made him want to play his lute, a foolish move that would draw any two-legged predators from the woods behind him, men more dangerous than distant wolves.

After a sparse meal of cheese and bread, he put the remaining food in his saddlebag and realized the chorus of wolves had gone silent. They would be hunting now, for hares or nocturnal animals.

He spread a blanket on the ground and stretched out, using his hat as a pillow, one arm atop the lute case. Later, roused from sleep by something cold on his cheek, Johan opened his eyes. Moonlight illuminated metal on a flintlock. How long had he been followed? How long did he have to live?

"Who are you?" a male voice demanded.

Johan turned his head, careful not to make a quick move, then raised himself to a sitting position. The intruder, silhouetted in dim moonlight, squatted on his heels. Broad shoulders, lean, erect torso, and big hands. So they were evenly matched, physically. Johan, hardened by the rough life of a soldier, tall like his father, and grown muscular with good Polish food, and this stranger, just as fit, but with a pistol in his hand.

The stranger slowly withdrew the pistol but kept it trained on Johan. "What brings you into this wilderness?"

Johan tensed. He'd let down his guard, distracted by anguish and the urgency to leave his homeland. He should have known not to fall asleep without investigating the area first. "I'm only passing through on my way to the port. From there I go to Stockholm—to Uppsala University. I mean no harm, so could you aim that somewhere else?"

As the man's grip on the weapon relaxed, so did Johan. "Is this your land?" Johan asked, hoping friendly conversation would allow him time to plan his next move.

"All of it, and so is this riverbank, clear to the lake." Pride resonated in the man's voice. "Beyond that are the lagoons— useless for farming, good for fishing."

Johan tugged at his fur hat, wanting to bolt, knowing it futile. Any man living in this wilderness would know how to hit a moving target. Best to wait it out and learn the man's intentions.

"Where are you from?" the stranger asked. "If you're a student, why not study in your own country?"

Johan fought the temptation to spill out his thoughts. The telling might rid him of the memories that drained his spirit, but a stranger would never understand. "I had no ties in Warsaw. Decided to leave and head north, that's all."

"So, you're running from the Cossacks. Sensible, I'd say. Why stay and fight for the Polish king when he's bound to lose? A traveler coming through said the Turks and the Khan had joined the Cossacks." The man lowered his aim a bit more and chuckled. "Only a fool would fight for a lost cause."

Johan shrugged. Cossacks or Tatars or Polish-Commonwealth soldiers: what did it matter? Dead men on all sides. And even now, did his anguish still show? Did this stranger sense Johan's failure, like a stalking animal that knew its prey was wounded? He swallowed hard, his eyes on the gun barrel. "I have no quarrel with anyone."

"Well, I do. See this?" He lifted the pistol again. "I took it from a dead man. He tried to steal some of my fowl. And I've learned to use it well."

Johan saw that the sky had gone from black to grey. It would be dawn before long. "If it's money you want, I have very little." He slowly reached to his waist and untied his purse. Trouble was, this woodsman was no innocent, and would likely have him remove his boots. No traveler kept all his money in one place.

"Keep your coins. No place to spend them out here anyway."

Johan breathed a relieved sigh. He barely had enough to transport himself and his horse across the sea. He decided the best way out of this was to act as calm as possible. "So you live here year around? I saw no homes, nothing to indicate—"

"I have a shack back over that hill. I was checking my traps when I saw you riding and followed you here. You'll never make it to the sea unless you're more careful than you were last night."

"I'll mark your words, and thanks."

In the opalescent glow of daybreak, Johan saw that the stranger was eyeing the horse.

"Tell you what," the man said. "I'll show you a shorter way to the sea, because you're going to need it. I need that horse. Besides, it'll cost you a fortune to transport her." He rubbed the wood of the flintlock. "Consider it payment for letting you live, and don't worry. I take good care of my animals, especially a fine mare like her."

Johan's heart sank. They were partners, he and the mare. Besides, she had cost him dearly, almost everything he owned in the world, but there was no arguing with the flintlock. At least the man hadn't demanded the lute, too.

While the gunman gave directions, pointing the weapon towards a narrow lane leading from the main road, Johan gathered his belongings, careful to keep the lute covered. He hoped the man had told the truth about a shorter route, and that the last ship had not yet left port.

The ship's captain, a grizzled old Russian, kept his one good eye on Johan, while the other looked to the side, milky and useless. His grin showed a few stained teeth. "The crew don't like passengers, but seeing as mine will be the last crossing before winter, sure, we'll make room. One hundred *dinars* will get you right to Stockholm. We leave at first light."

Johan swallowed. The man couldn't be serious. A hired lutenist could only hope to make about five hundred silver dinars a year. Besides, he'd been told horse and all would only be around sixty. One hundred was more than he had. "I'll work. I can cook. No job is too hard for me."

The captain shook his head. "I've plenty of crewmen. Besides, they take not kindly to interference. That's my offer. Take it or leave it."

Johan grimaced, picked up his bundle and made his way back up the embankment. To his right was a mariners' tavern. Dejected, and fearing he'd made the biggest mistake of his life in assuming all would go according to plan, he followed the path to the tavern. A maid set a beer before him and tilted her head, smiling. "Herring tonight, with beans and biscuits."

Johan nodded his thanks and she left, returning a short while later with two heaping dishes. She paused and wiped the already-clean table. "You're no sailor. What are you doing in these parts?"

He was hungrier than he thought, and the hot food tasted good. What he needed was time to think, but the girl wanted to talk. He broke a biscuit into the beans. "I was hoping to get across the Baltic before winter, but the captain is asking four times a fair price."

She leaned forward and smiled. "You'd better pay him the price. He's likely the last ship this year."

Johan smeared butter on another biscuit. "So he said, but it's more than I have. Besides, I don't like being robbed."

She tucked a thick strand of her brown hair behind her ear, which gave her a worldly look, but he guessed she was not yet twenty. Dark, mischievous eyes peered at him from beneath long lashes.

Across the way, a man stepped from behind his counter, wiped a table, and kept one eye on the girl. Her father? A lover? No matter. Johan wanted no complications, not now.

She gave the table another swipe with the rag. "Want another beer?"

He nodded and watched her walk away. She returned a moment later and set his drink before him. "Mind you, I never said this, but there's other ways to cross the sea besides paying." She gave him a wink. "Store bread and water in your knapsack, then sneak on ship when the crew is busy. Others have done it." She turned away, collecting dirty dishes from a nearby table before crossing the room.

Johan finished the meal and paid, intending to thank the girl, but she had disappeared behind a swinging door.

He stepped outside. A porch ran the length of the wood tavern. Benches lined the perimeter. Bearded seamen huddled in groups, smoking and drinking. He rubbed the new stubble on his chin. He was well on the way to growing a beard, so why not? Also, he'd probably fit in better if he ever reached Stockholm. It made sense to have a beard that far north.

After laying his lute and bundle on an empty bench, he sat to ponder his options. A heavy fog had moved in from the sea. Was it possible to get aboard without being seen? And if discovered, what then? Stowaways were considered thieves and trespassers. He'd read stories of men hung from the mast with only a piece of bread and a knife to protect them from certain death. Some opted for a watery grave before starvation, and simply cut the rope and jumped.

He shook his head. He had to reject thoughts like that. Besides, what else could he do? Walk all the way back to Warsaw? Spend his dwindling coins on a ride? Out of the question. He dared not show his face in Poland, not yet, not until that fateful skirmish was long forgotten, relegated to war stories told by old men.

There was only one thing to do. Take a chance and hope it worked.

CHAPTER TWO

As night settled over the village, Johan crept from the safety of his hiding place, a thick tangle of shrubs. The steep embankment offered no cover, so he said a quick prayer and hurried to the shoreline, past the lowered gangplank and into the sea, wading toward the rope ladder that hung from the starboard side. Waves slapped the wood planks as he struggled for footing. The toe of his boot found the first rung. And another. As he ascended, the rope, slimy and worn, gave him new worry. Would it hold a man's weight, or was this only for pulling up fish nets?

He gritted his teeth, and holding his bundle tight with one hand, continued up the ladder. Up. Up. Only two more rungs to go. When he heard laughter from somewhere on deck he paused, considered going back down, but he'd come this far.

He reached the top and saw four crewmen squatting on the deck, tossing dice by the glow of a lantern. The hatch to the hold lay open. Somehow he had to get inside without being seen and take off these wet clothes. He shivered, watching the men, involved in their game. One lifted a jug to his lips, took great gulps, and wiped his mouth with his sleeve. His companion lifted the jug, cursed at the empty container, and a tussle ensued between the two. The others shouted for them to stop, and Johan, taking advantage of the chaos, scurried across the deck and into the hold.

After a few minutes, his eyes adjusted to the dark. Aside from a few barrels strapped to an upright, there appeared to be no other cargo. Further back, partitions divided the space, but here near the bulkhead looked as safe a place as any to hide, should someone come. He brought his hand to his nose. The place reeked of urine and vomit. He wondered idly how many men like him had crossed the sea in this hold.

He put down his bundle, removed his wet clothes, and wrapped himself in his blanket. Best to stay behind these barrels until someone came to close the hatch. After settling against an upright in the darkest corner, he waited and watched until he could no longer remain awake.

As dawn broke, he woke to the sounds of a ship getting underway. Someone slammed the hatch closed. Johan breathed deep, knowing this was the last fresh air for at least a week, but with luck, he'd be on dry land before long. The ship creaked and groaned, the pitch assuring him they were in open water and moving steadily. Holding the lute on his lap to ensure its safety should they encounter bad weather, he closed his eyes and imagined he was already at the university at Uppsala.

When he woke, hungry and sore from the hard board on which he sat, he broke some bread from a loaf and drank a swallow of water. Setting the lute aside, he paced a short distance, avoiding ropes and barrels that would trip him up. He had to keep moving or lose his mind.

Several days later, having lost all track of time and with his food supply gone and little water left, he contemplated going on deck and turning himself in. Just to breathe clean air again would be worth the risk.

As he rose to stand, he heard shouts from the main deck. Had someone spotted land? When a bugler sounded his horn, he knew they had reached a port. Pray the God that had brought him this far stayed with him onto dry land.

When a wedge of sunlight seeped between two planks of the hatch, Johan climbed the ladder and peered through the crack. A few paid passengers walked toward the gangplank. This might be his only chance. He unlatched the door from inside. It held tight. Someone had secured it from the other side. He put down his bundle and lute and pulled with both arms. The wood splintered and gave way. He froze in place, then realized the crew was occupied on deck.

After grabbing his belongings, he pulled his cap low, climbed on deck, and hurried toward the crowd near the gangplank. From snatches of conversation, he learned that indeed, this was the port of Stockholm. A child, waiting with her mother, looked up and smiled, then pulled at her mother's skirt. "Look, Mama."

The woman turned, put a finger to her nose, and quickly turned away. Johan stepped back. Of course. After a week in these clothes, the sickening smell of the hold would give him away, a sure sign he was no ordinary passenger. Would she turn him in? The line moved forward slowly, slowly, and when his feet touched the soil, he knew his luck had held out.

He hurried up the steep embankment, anxious for a glimpse of his new homeland, and paused at the edge of a carriage path. A city of islands lay beneath the layer of fog as if waiting for winter.

Approaching from the east, he saw that this section of the city wall passed between two defensive towers. Toward the north, parts of the wall had been demolished, replaced by newly built foundations. A few structures neared completion, what would clearly be rich men's palaces along the waterfront.

Johan went through the single gate and crossed onto a narrow street. Here, on the outskirts of town, ancient shacks with turf roofs competed for space with pastureland. Goats jumped across the road from one sod rooftop to another, looking for greener pasture, undisturbed by the shouts of an old woman selling eggs, her full brown skirt dragging the soil like a worn broom.

He ambled on, marveling at the curious mix of palaces so near a farm lane. Doubtless the shacks would come down soon. This was a town in transition. A few years from now it would look much like Warsaw.

He shifted the weight of his bundle and saw a vendor ahead, selling food from a cart. After handing over some coins in return for a piece of fried fish and bread, he set off again, grateful for his first bite in two days. Better than that, the bread was fresh baked.

As he made his way into town, he crossed into another world, as if the city had wakened from a long sleep. Here, stonemasons chiseled massive rocks, brick layers stood on a platform one story high to set alternating brick and sandstone in a semi-circle atop a row of windows. Perhaps one day he would play his lute for some nobleman behind these very windows.

He shared the last bite of food with a mangy dog and continued on, past clusters of new buildings lining both sides of the street. Beyond that, the path changed to a stone-paved avenue wide enough for two carriages to pass.

He reached the outskirts of town where peasant shacks again lined the path. The road sloped downhill, but evidently not fast enough to carry away the filth of the city. The odor of leather and dead fish, coming from the few flourishing businesses, assailed his nostrils and overpowered the smell of dung and refuse piled between wood shacks that lined the road.

He crossed a stone bridge. Below, the blue water looked inviting, a place to wash himself clean, but the refuse floating near the bank made him hurry on. He came to another islet, with nothing in sight but a shack and grazing animals. Beyond that was a wooden bridge. He pulled out the map, scarcely readable now after the long sea journey. Satisfied he was on the way to Uppsala, he folded the map and continued onto the bridge. Halfway across, the planks shook beneath his feet, stressed by a loaded cart approaching from behind. The driver slowed. "I'm not going far, but you're welcome to ride."

Johan heaved his burden onto the cart. "Thanks. I'm heading to Uppsala."

He'd no sooner sat down than the man started talking. "I'm heading home. Visited my sick brother. No telling where my wife will be by now. She has a tendency to wander from home. The neighbors find her and bring her back. Happens all the time. So I have that to worry about, plus the price of grain, dropping faster than a dead sheep. Bound to send the country into a famine."

Johan nodded, listening to the driver's conversation and watching the miles slip by, until finally they came to a fork in the road. The driver slowed the cart. "You'll have to walk from here. I take this path, up over the hill. Keep on this same road. It goes straight to Uppsala. There's an inn by the road just before the city. Good food and decent prices. You'll reach it before dusk."

After thanking the driver, Johan set off again. Before nightfall, he reached the inn. It was worth a few coins to wash, sleep in a bed, and eat a hot meal.

The next afternoon he saw a church tower ahead. Across from that would be the university, if the sketch in the Warsaw library could be trusted. He paused at a public fountain where children splashed and shouted. Careful to lay his lute and knapsack in a dry spot, he washed road dirt from his face, keeping one eye on his belongings.

Refreshed and confident, he boldly approached the university and entered the building through a freshly stuccoed arch. A bronze plaque with directional arrows hung on the wall, but he could read nothing of the foreign tongue. From here he'd have to rely on the good will of strangers.

A young man came his way, laden with a pile of papers, and Johan decided the boy was a student helper, in spite of the fine clothes. The youth wore a red silk doublet and brown woolen breeches. No doubt he was one of the lucky ones, a nobleman's son whose father had wealth enough to guarantee a place at Uppsala for his sons. "Bonjour," Johan said, hoping the boy understood French, since few outside of his homeland spoke Polish. "I am looking for the headmaster."

The student shifted his load of papers and pointed down the hall. "Third door on the left," he said, surprising Johan with his perfect French.

"Merci," Johan said, hoping all communication would be this easy. He'd been embarrassed more than once by his own mixture of Polish and French, a direct result of his French mother's stubborn refusal to learn proper Polish, but now it looked as though he might get by not knowing a word of Swedish. He smiled at the student. "I admire your spoken French. Are you from there?"

The student chuckled. "No, I'm Swedish, but our queen encourages everyone to speak French. The university is supported by the royal family, so you see . . ."

He looked down at the load of papers in his arms.

"Oh, sorry. I'm keeping you," Johan said. He thanked the youth again and went toward the headmaster's office. Outside the door, another young man sat behind a large polished desk. The boy looked up from his book. Johan greeted him with a handshake. "I need to speak with the headmaster."

"He cannot see you without an appointment," the young secretary said. "I can give you a time next week. What is it about?"

"I have come from Warsaw. I want to study music. My teacher, Teodor Akerlund, sent a letter earlier. I am Johan Sokolewski, the lutenist."

From behind a half-opened door, a gruff voice called out. "Charles, send him in."

The secretary straightened, forced a smile, and showed Johan into the headmaster's office.

The man behind the desk, wearing a robe in a shockingly bright shade of orange, pointed to a chair. "So, how can I help?"

"I am Johan. Thank you for seeing me, *Pan* Meistre Rudbeckius," he said, reverting to the Polish title in his eagerness to show respect.

The headmaster chuckled. "I'm sorry, but I'm the temporary headmaster until another is appointed. Meistre Rudbeckius left this earth over a year ago." He crossed his hands over his sizeable chest.

Johan swallowed. Had he come all this way for nothing? "I see. Well, months back, my lute instructor in Warsaw sent a letter of introduction on my behalf. Other things interfered and I was unable to come until now." No sense explaining how he'd felt drawn into the war, defending the king's cause, putting his own future on hold. He wiped his brow, as if he could wipe out the memories. "So you see, I had hoped to audition—"

"Much has changed here. But tell me. You have no patron—no money for tuition?"

"That is correct, but I was assured there are scholarships."

"Oh, yes, there are, thanks to our late king's generosity. However, there are more applicants than scholarships, and we have donors whose families must be considered."

Johan decided to be straightforward. "Do you have qualifying auditions to determine the most deserving scholars?"

"Yes, that is the way it is done. At present, Count de la Gardie oversees the distribution of scholarships." He frowned as if the thought was distasteful. "You must present yourself to the count and audition."

"But I was told I would audition with the teachers."

"Yes, well, as I said, things have changed. I will put your name on the list. The next audition is Friday. Let's see . . ." He shuffled through some papers on his desk. "Ah, yes, here's the list. Yes, there's room. Do you have an instrument?"

Johan nodded. "My lute is always with me." For the hundredth time he gave thanks that the man who took his horse had not wanted the lute.

"Then be at the Uppsala palace gate Friday. Come at noon, and you'll be shown to the count's presence." The headmaster paused, looked at Johan, and seemed about to say something else. Then he stood abruptly and leaned across his desk. "Good luck."

Johan rose and bowed, wishing the man had finished his thoughts. The unspoken words gave Johan a vague sense of unease. By the time he reached the arched doors and walked outside, his heart pounded, the reality of what had taken place settling in. He was here, in Uppsala, and wonder of wonders, would try for a scholarship before a nobleman. That was what worried him most: if the count would know good music when he heard it, or if he could recognize talent in a lutenist. He had to hope that the count was more conversant with music than most royals he knew, but he was here now and his fate was about to be decided.

If he failed to please the ears of this count, probably some displaced French courtier from the sound of his name, then Johan had two choices—to stay in Sweden, or return to Warsaw, where he would likely be arrested and hung. Berlin or Vienna perhaps, where no one knew his name. Everything depended on Friday's outcome.

CHAPTER THREE

The following morning Johan woke in his warm rented spot above a stable. The price had been fair, the meal, good. He brushed hay from the blanket and second-hand cloak, tucked them in his bundle, and pulled out the garments he'd saved for his audition. They were wrinkled from being so tightly packed, but by the time he reached the palace they'd be fine. He dressed quickly, shivering in the unheated stable. After putting on his leather buff coat and gloves, he climbed down from the loft, left the stable, and headed southeast for his appointment at the Uppsala palace. Snow had fallen during the night, and now a frosty white blanket covered the lane and nearby buildings, except the rooftops of homes and businesses whose owners had wood to burn. He hunched his shoulders against the cold. His breath came in white puffs, matching that from a horse's nostrils as a carriage passed by.

Johan stopped at a shop and purchased two warm cakes. He left the baker's and had almost finished the last cake when a young man wearing a long woolen coat fell in step beside him and grinned. "Going far?"

Johan raised his hand in greeting. "Only to the palace."

The stranger arched his brows. "To seek employment? I guess word's gotten out about the queen and her fondness for the French. Are you French?"

Johan shook his head. "I'm not seeking employment." Let this brash young man think what he wanted.

The stranger chuckled. "To see a maid, then. You're no royal." He looked pointedly at Johan's garments and smirked. "Myself, I'm returning home from a lady friend's house. Your first time at the palace?"

"Yes. What do you know of the layout? I suppose there's a servants' entrance. Where would that be?" Johan pulled his cap lower. His lips were numb from the cold.

The boy chewed on what looked like a piece of dried meat before answering. "How would I know? I've never been there. All I know is it houses visiting dignitaries from time to time. A few royals live there, families connected in one way or other with the royal family. Distant cousins, bastard children, and maiden aunts—people like that." He leaned to the side of the road, broke a twig from a bush, and commenced picking his teeth. "If you're hoping to get a glimpse of the queen, she won't be there. She's at the castle in Stockholm. She only comes here for special occasions."

Johan nodded. He had no wish to see the queen. What he wanted was for this count, who appeared to be in charge of all performances and musical activities for the queen in her Stockholm palace, to be a learned musician. Why else would she have appointed the man to the task of overseeing the expenditure of her father's grants to the university?

A blast of icy air hit his face. He shivered and pulled his leather coat tight. Thank goodness he'd kept it. His brother swore the military-issued coat protected against the blade, but this far north it was more valuable as protection from the weather. Still, even with two woolen shirts, the wind came through as if he were naked.

When the road divided, Johan's traveling companion waved goodbye. Johan shifted his lute and knapsack to the opposite shoulder and followed the path up a slight incline. Past a copse of fir trees, the palace roof came into view. He approached the symmetrical building that rose into a layer of clouds. Domed towers guarded each end of the building like weary sentinels.

Coming nearer, Johan saw that he must pass through a sculpted garden at least as long as the palace was wide. By the time he reached a guardhouse he had decided to simply ask one of the uniformed guards where he should enter. He gathered his courage and approached. "I was told to see Count de la Gardie."

The guard pointed to the main entrance, accessed by several stone steps, and waved Johan on. Two more guards stood by the door but made no move to question Johan. He hoisted his lute and walked bravely through the open doors. Once inside, a guard quickly approached. "What is your business here?"

"I am to audition before Count de la Gardie."

The guard nodded and led Johan down a corridor, up some steps, and into a room. "Your name?"

"Sokolewski. Johan Sokolewski."

The guard turned and disappeared down the hallway.

Johan set his knapsack on the floor and propped the lute against a chair leg. The room was eerily silent, adding to his apprehension about the audition process. How long would he wait? Would anyone know he was here?

He crossed his arms, warding off a sudden chill. This must be the palace waiting room. Pastoral scenes decorated the ceiling. A gilded border sloped to the walls which were covered with tapestries. Velvet-covered chairs and a gleaming wood table reminded him how far he was from home. The table held a jug of wine and silver cups. Did he dare quench his thirst? Was this for him?

Determined the time was better spent calming himself than drinking a questionable liquid, he removed his coat and gloves and wiped his moist hands on the skirt of his blue wool *zupan*, taking care not to soil his outer *kontusz*. Styled with open front and slit sleeves, made of fabric dyed a rich brown, the garment marked him as a proud Polish-Lithuanian. No one would guess he'd been a common fighter in a failed war. Right now, though, he was most grateful for the garment's heavy lining, another layer of warmth. If the auditioning room was this cold, the slit sleeves would allow him to keep it on while freeing his arms to play the lute. He removed his hat and smoothed his hair, wondering if he had time to tune the instrument.

As he bent to uncover the lute, a uniformed aide appeared. "Are you Johan Sokolewski?"

"Yes." Johan rose and shouldered his belongings.

"This way. The count waits and it is past his mealtime."

"Then I shall wait until after he eats," Johan protested. To audition before a grumpy royal was not to his liking.

The aide shook his head. "No, I suggested that. He wants to get this over with."

Johan hesitated, trying to conjure an excuse to postpone the audition, but the man stood in the hall, waiting.

Judging he had no choice in the matter of timing, Johan followed the man to a room near the end of the corridor. His heartbeat quickened. An hour from now he would know whether the long sea journey was worth it.

"This is Johan Sokolewski," the attendant announced, "the last of the potential scholars."

While the attendant took a seat on a nearby stool, Count de la Gardie gave a brief nod to acknowledge Johan. The count appeared not unkind, but preoccupied, as he made a note on parchment. Johan wondered fleetingly if de la Gardie's looks had anything to do with his powerful position. Not yet thirty, and dressed handsomely in the latest fashion, the man sported a heavy head of dark hair, ending in soft curls on his shoulders and neck. His carefully trimmed goatee gave him an appearance of culture and refinement, enviable traits in any court in the land. Johan bowed and took the indicated chair, hoping the man's knowledge of music was as refined as his appearance.

The count laid the paper aside. "So, I understand you traveled quite far. Why to Uppsala?"

Startled by the man's forthright question, Johan wondered what answer to give. Why had he come here? To leave the nightmares behind? To seek the peace he longed for? He settled on the most innocuous answer that came to mind. "My teacher, Teodor Akerlund, studied here. He thought it was possible that I would be awarded a scholarship. He wrote Master Rudbeckius—"

"Yes, yes. I understand. I know of Akerlund. He was here before my time, but I respect the memory of Master Rudbeckius, and we do sometimes have openings for newcomers. You know, of course, that you must compete with the sons of noblemen, Swedish born, who naturally have preference."

"I do," Johan said, feeling less confident every minute, but determined not to show it. "My playing, I trust, will raise my status in your eyes."

"Ah, well said." The count chuckled and sipped from a cup. "So tell me, what will you play?"

"Recercare de tutti li toni."

The count arched his brows in surprise. "A most difficult piece. Well, let's see how you do. You may begin."

Johan hid a smile. Apparently, the count recognized the music and knew its complexity, both of which would go in Johan's favor. He plucked each string, testing its pitch, and began. He felt the count's eyes on him, but the sounds were coming out right, and a moment later he forgot where he was and why he was playing and was lost in the music. When he played the last note, he closed his eyes. It was over. For better or worse, it was over.

The count leaned forward. "I want you to come to Stockholm, to the Royal Palace. I need to hear you again."

Johan felt a cold chill. The count was undecided, which meant he was not impressed, not the way Johan had hoped. And why should he play at the palace? The headmaster had said de la Gardie made the final decision. "Stockholm?" he asked, wondering if he had heard right.

"Yes. Do you have funds?"

"I—I have a few coins left. Is there some kind of charge for a second audition?"

The count laughed, showing even white teeth. He retrieved coins from his own purse, handed them to the attendant, and indicated they be given to Johan.

"Take those," the count said. "You'll need to hire transport to the queen's residence in Stockholm. Be there by Monday around noon."

Johan took the money, bowed, and left the room, wondering if he should feel discouraged or elated.

All that night and the next, he concocted multiple scenes of what might lie ahead. By Sunday evening, he lay in his small rented room listening to ice pelleting the wooden shutters while he tried to sleep. By this time tomorrow it would be over. He'd either be a scholar or be sent away. If the latter, what then? He pulled the cover close and shut his eyes. He would not consider that for a moment. If the worst happened, he'd worry about it then. What puzzled him most was why the count had not told him yes or no.

That same Sunday evening, Mathias Svensson, Swedish goldsmith, balanced his glasses on the bridge of his nose for the hundredth time and peered closer at the gold coin before him. Rare indeed, a dinar from the Fatamid period.

Icy rain pounded against the palace windows. Surely the clatter would wake the dead, but this late, even the dogs slept soundly. The goldsmith crossed his ankles, grateful for the empty library, the warmth from the fire, and the lack of distractions in this cozy corner. By day, even with the partition dividing the books and statuary from the reading area, one heard chattering courtiers and noisy servants on the other side, people coming and going, the ladder being slammed against the wooden shelves. It broke his concentration and after one hour of this, he'd politely told them he preferred to work at night.

He brushed back a strand of hair and considered how this appointment, though temporary, might lead to other lucrative positions. Lucky for him the queen's staff had recognized that the cataloguing of rare coins needed an expert's eye.

The Swedish queen, it appeared, had no idea of the value of these artifacts her army had brought back from the sacking of the Prague Castle. More amazing was what the Royal Treasurer had confided, that in spite of the persistent dissemination of much of Emperor Rudolph's amazing collection these three decades since his death, the Prague palace had still yielded up a treasure trove of antiquities. The young queen should lock up the booty, not leave it here in the palace library for a goldsmith to steal. He chuckled. Easier and wiser by far to catalogue her coins for the price she promised to pay for his services. Besides, what fool would risk the executioner's ax to steal a few coins from the royal treasury?

He made a note on the ledger, then laid the coin aside and reached for another. The gold, soft and smooth as a lady's cheek, reflected light from the tall beeswax candles. He turned the coin over, squinting to read the lettering, and heard a motion behind him. Before he could turn around, something crossed his shoulder. When the blade struck his heart, he fell forward, bleeding onto the coins and onto his gold-colored brocade waistcoat.

The sun shone but it was bitterly cold that Monday morning in Stockholm when Johan dressed again in his only set of fine clothes, the blue *zupan* and brown *kontusz*. After a breakfast of gruel and hot watered wine, he put on his hat, shouldered his belongings, and set out. He followed the signs through the Stockholm streets until he came to the vast open field sloping up to the Castle of Three Crowns. Climbing the hill, he was reminded of the importance of traveling light. Aside from his lute, snug in its leather case, his belongings were few—traveling clothes, toiletries, and the garments he wore. In an hour or so he would leave the palace, either as a scholar or an out-of-work musician. He could only do his best, and the rest was up to God.

A gatekeeper took Johan's name, left him standing in the cold, and returned. He pointed Johan to a cobbled walkway that led through an open gate and into a courtyard. Just then a side door opened and a woman, surprisingly agile for someone who looked to be about fifty, ran out screaming, holding her full skirt high so as not to trip on the stones. Behind her, in close pursuit, came a mixed crowd of uniformed guards and exquisitely gowned ladies. "My book!" she screamed. "My book. Help! The murderer took my book." She crossed the courtyard and ran past Johan. Before he could step out of the way, one of the guards pushed past him, knocking him to the ground. He hit the stone hard, heard a dog yelping, and realized that his belongings and lute lay scattered across the stones.

The excitement had passed and he found himself alone, except for a few curious onlookers. As he leaned to retrieve a red pennant flung from his knapsack, a man stepped from beneath a covered archway. In the next moment, the toe of a boot came down hard on the cloth pennant. "A Polski, are you?" The boot ground into stone.

Johan reacted fast. His fist flew to the man's shin. With a howl, Johan's tormentor drew back. Johan jumped to his feet, driven by a red-hot anger, and saw the man had turned his back and was limping away, a sight that gave Johan a moment of satisfaction. *Let it go, Johan.* The worst thing now would be to go after the man and make a scene, with the others watching who might not know what provoked the newcomer and would side with the scoundrel, probably a courtier. What kind of court was this, where acts of aggression to strangers might be commonplace?

He picked up the pennant, saw it had been torn, folded it carefully and stuffed it in his leather traveling bag. Did the man somehow know what the pennant meant to him? No. That was impossible. This was Stockholm, not Warsaw. A Swede would not recognize a battle pennant from a place across the sea.

After gathering the rest of his belongings, Johan reached for his lute. The leather cover was ripped. He ran his fingers beneath the leather, along the grain of the wood. The instrument's soundboard had suffered a crack.

He stood, shouldered his burden and started across the courtyard, determined to see this through. The onlookers backed away, pretending to be occupied, all but one, who fell in step beside Johan. From the man's neatly cut brown straight hair that fell just below his ears, a clean-shaven face, and athletic build, Johan suspected this was some royal courtier. "I saw it all," the stranger said, using eloquent French. "He got what was coming, but don't mind Henrik. He acts unseemly now and then, but it never goes beyond that. Everyone's on edge today." He frowned into the sun.

"I've come at a bad time?"

The stranger hesitated. "You haven't heard? You must not be from around here."

Johan shook his head. "No, I just came into Stockholm."

"Henrik said you were Polish. Do you know him from somewhere?"

Johan rubbed the back of his neck. Evidently this Henrik had a grudge against anyone Polish. Well, that was Henrik's problem. For now, there was more to worry about than some disgruntled Swede. More important was the broken lute, and his own sore neck. He decided not to comment on this Henrik until he found out more about how things worked here. Safer to change the subject. "Never laid eyes on him before. Tell me, what was all that commotion about?"

His new acquaintance lowered his already low-key voice. "That was the queen mother. She's easily excited."

"She said something about a thief. What was taken?"

"You are new to court, but everyone here knows that when something happens, it will only be minutes and you'll learn what it was." He shook his head and leaned close. "There was a murder last night in the royal library, and now a theft has been discovered. This will keep the palace police busy."

Johan swallowed. "A murder?" What a day to have come here. He wanted nothing more to do with violence, let alone criminal violence. How would all this affect his next audition?

The stranger nodded. "No one knows the details yet. The palace guards closed that wing and aren't saying anything." He extended his hand. "I am François Douchet—a dancer by profession."

"And I am a lutenist, Johan Sokolewski. You came here from France?"

François nodded. "Like many others. You'll soon learn our young queen has a fondness for all things French." He chuckled. "All the better for some of us. Now, come along inside. I have a rehearsal, but if you tell me why you came here, I'll point you in the right direction."

"I came for an audition."

"Then go that way."

Johan thanked the dancer and proceeded into a hallway. Torches, perched on the wall in carved and gilded wooden holders, lit the way. Tapestries hung between the torches, one more beautiful than the next, with patterns depicting mythical tales and battle scenes. The palace smelled of burning wax and perfumed oil. His boots made little slapping sounds on the colored tiles.

He passed a small group of men playing cards, speaking in low tones. A few paces later, two guards stepped from the shadows, blocking his way. "What is your name and why are you here?"

"I am Johan, sent here for an audition."

One of the guards crooked his finger. "Come this way."

They went to another part of the castle and the guard paused near an open door. "Wait in here. They will send for you." He turned on his heel and left.

Johan eased his knapsack and lute from his shoulder and went inside the room. Groups of men sat on benches arranged around the perimeter. As Johan approached they looked up, then resumed talking. Were all these men waiting for an audition? Surely not. That would take hours. Besides, they had no instruments.

He put down his belongings and sat. The room itself was sparsely furnished, but the walls were decorated with gilt leather, lush tapestries, and murals with scenes much like the tapestries in the hallway. Above, stuccowork with swelling, curving forms adorned the ceiling. Evidently this had once been part of the palace proper.

A young man, dressed in grey woolen breeches and a red waistcoat, approached the bench. He pushed back his hair and greeted Johan. "I'm Carl. You're a newcomer, am I right?"

"Yes. I am Johan." He glanced at his bundle and saw how worn the leather must look to the eyes of a courtier. He was suddenly conscious of the streaks of dirt on the sleeve of his *kontusz*. His boots were badly scuffed and needed repair, but

what could one expect after months of travel?

"Did you just arrive? Perhaps you saw the incide
courtyard."

"Yes," Johan said, running one hand through his hai
less he looked a little disheveled after the encounte
exactly was it all about?"

The man chuckled. "That was our regent queen. W
Eleanora, but you'd do well to stay out of her way. So
she is delusional, but I was told a thief took a book of l
the library. That's possible, of course." He shrugged.
may be upset over the murder." He drew his brows
"You don't suppose someone would kill for a book, do
you never know." His gaze slid from Johan to somethin
him. He called out. "Zofia. What's this about the queen
book?"

Johan turned as a young woman entered the room.
one of those women who glided when she walked, a nat
riage of health and good breeding. As she approache
saw that part of her hair had come loose from beneath t
lace cap she wore. The wayward strand, a twist of reddi
half-covered her cheek. If she were to dance with Joh
head would only come to his shoulder. He felt suddenly
tive, the way he felt for a fawn in the woods, but when
him a swift upward glance and settled her gaze on h
judging whether to reveal court secrets in front of this s
he knew she was no fragile child but a near-woman, inte
on sizing him up. She waved the courtier aside, took
closer, and fixed her eyes on Johan. "Who are you?"

A faint scent of lemon rose from her hair, mom
distracting him. "I am Johan. I—I am here for an auditi
count told me he wanted to hear me perform before he
decision about a scholarship. But first I must see about
ing my lute."

She tucked the errant strand behind her ear. "I am Zofia, the court astrologist." She reached for the lute. "I will take your instrument to our lute maker. We have plenty more lutes like this that you can use until he repairs yours."

He thanked her, deciding to keep to himself the fact that a Tichtold lute, considering their value, would not be lying in storage in a court this far from Germany. Besides, she was trying to be helpful.

"And you are in the wrong area for the auditions," she said. Carl, you should have told him, instead of gossiping about the royal family. Johan, come with me." She left in a whirl of heavy skirts. Johan, following behind, tried to keep his mind on why he was here and the audition that lay ahead, but could not keep his eyes from seeing the way the bodice of her gown hugged her midriff like a lover who would not let go.

By the time she reached the appointed room, he was uncomfortably warm, even in this bitterly cold castle. "You can wait here," she said. "The Ballet Master will be in soon. He will tell you what to do, but you have a few hours before you'll be needed. If you have not eaten, ask the attendant to get you something from the kitchen." She indicated a young boy snoozing on a bench in the corner. "That's if you can wake him." She shook her head. "Sleeping when he should be tending to his work, and he wonders why he is not promoted to royal page." She left the room, not looking back.

Later, having roused the boy and sent for food, Johan contemplated what he had just witnessed. Exactly what kind of an audition would have a ballet master in charge, and who was this bold and charming astrologer who seemed to know her way around a palace where a murder had just taken place?

Chapter Four

The sleepy boy handed a platter of food to Johan, retreated to his place on the bench, and within minutes was snoring. Johan balanced the platter on his knee. Sliced beetroot, preserved cabbage, a few fried herring, and a small, thick pancake topped with a cherry and clove sauce. As he ate the meal, he reflected on his curious situation. Here he sat, waiting for a ballet instructor, a curious turn of events. The French count, de la Gardie, was in charge of granting scholarships. So why come here, to the Stockholm castle, to audition again?

As if that was not unsettling enough, a murder had taken place last evening in this same castle, and the queen had instructed everyone to resume normal duties. Did that include nightly entertainment, a debacle he feared he had been drawn into? And then he'd been told by a lady astrologer that the ballet instructor was to advise him of what was expected during the audition.

An attendant burst into the room, interrupting Johan's musings. "The instructor is too busy to see you. He asked me to give you this." He thrust a costume into Johan's hands. "You are a shepherd in the field. Be backstage in the Performance Hall at seven o'clock." The attendant left in a whirl of perfume. The odor lingered in the room and Johan was left to puzzle over what smell the attendant had been trying to hide.

The drowsy would-be page, roused from sleep on his corner bench, sat up, eyed the costume, and lay down again.

Johan considered the costume, made of a thin brown fabric, rough, and of curious origin. He would wear his woolen shirt beneath. He slipped the tunic over his head, tied the rope at his waist, and waited with increasing apprehension for what would happen next.

At seven that evening, Johan stood in an alcove near the stage, a wooden rise at one end of a long performance hall. What kind of audition would this be?

Below the makeshift stage, people sat huddled in little groups, whispering. Were they talking about the murder the previous evening? Were they all to judge his playing?

What worried him most was performing on a borrowed instrument, thanks to the courtyard scuffle necessitating a repair to his own fine lute. Using a strange and inferior instrument was a calamity which would surely diminish his chances of winning a scholarship. As if that weren't enough, he had been instructed to wear this costume, an outfit not conducive to having his music taken seriously.

Attendants doused wall torches and the audience quieted. To calm his angst, Johan plucked one of the lute strings. Holy Mother. The inferior lute had already lost its tune. As he tuned the lute, the ballet master, Antoine de Beaulieu, a Frenchman who seemed to be in charge of all things musical in the court, thrust a piece of music before him. Johan stared at the score. The ballet was about to begin and he would be on stage shortly. Would he not be allowed to play the piece he had practiced? He opened the music, his heart sinking, and was elated to discover that he had seen the score before. In the time he had left, he read through it mentally, hearing the music again. Fine, he could play the piece without hesitation, but would he even be heard by the man who counted the most? From here, it appeared Count de la Gardie was nowhere around. Would he even be in the audience tonight, or was all this in vain?

When Johan heard his name he crossed to stage right as directed and played the song, singing the words faultlessly. His voice, while passably good, was no match for the regular singers, and he wondered if his playing would be overlooked. Nothing was working out the way he had expected. He was almost finished when he heard a commotion in the audience, but light from the candles at the front of the stage made everything beyond look black.

He went to the wings and waited, perturbed that he was playing a double role—one as petitioner for a scholarship, the other as an entertainer during a brief interlude to a ballet. Finally, as the dancers accepted their applause and the wall torches brought the audience to life, Johan saw de la Gardie seated directly behind two ladies, both of whom occupied chairs placed on an elevated dais. The younger lady, whose gilt chair sat above the others, must be the queen. She leaned to one of her ladies, then clapped loudly and laughed at something that was said, while the queen mother sat quietly beside her, looking morose. Did the young queen embarrass her mother? Had there actually been a theft and a murder, or was the regent queen, upset by violence of any sort, simply delusional, as the courtier implied earlier?

He felt a tap on his shoulder and turned to see two ladies, both dressed in rose-colored gowns.

"Her Majesty the Queen requests your presence in her anteroom within the hour," one said. The other hid a giggle behind her small hand. Before he could respond they fluttered away like twin angels. When he turned back, de la Gardie was nowhere in sight.

Johan returned to the practice room, removed his costume, slipped on his own clothes over his shirt, and made his way to the queen's antechamber. To his surprise, de la Gardie met him near the chamber door. "So," Johan said, unable to wait any longer to learn his fate, "did you approve of my playing? Do I have the scholarship?"

The count ignored the question, nodded to two uniformed guards, and the doors to the queen's antechamber swung open. Count de la Gardie steered Johan inside. The queen, seated a short distance away in a high-backed chair upholstered in crimson, looked up, her large blue eyes fixed on Johan. "I expected you earlier," she said, in perfect French. Her deep voice, though, took him by surprise. For a small woman, her words carried huskily across the room.

He remembered his manners and bowed. "Your Majesty," he said, wondering if Count de la Gardie somehow needed the queen's permission to award tuition money. Coming here, to Her Majesty's own antechamber, had been curious enough, but what was worse, he felt like an outsider, like there was something he should know and did not. "I hope I pleased you with my playing tonight."

"Exceedingly so," she said. "I know enough about music to appreciate the challenge of playing a strange instrument." She turned to de la Gardie. "You've done well, as always."

He inclined his head. "My pleasure to serve."

She looked back at Johan and offered a friendly smile. "The count, in addition to awarding scholarships, procures musicians for the court."

"But I—"

She held up one hand, and Johan, who took a particular interest in people's hands, the length of their fingers, noticed the queen's slim delicate hands, in contrast with her hair that looked unkempt, and her mannish way of sitting, much like a man in breeches sits at a tavern. Her full skirt kept it from being an immodest position, but her mannerisms took him aback. Her tousled hair, a thick mass of curls, would be becoming if properly groomed, but what did he know? This might be a new hair fashion in Sweden.

She tapped her fingers on the arm of her chair. "I would like you to be a court musician," she said, interrupting his musings and setting his mind spinning. "The Count is quite right—you have talent that should be encouraged. I have no quarrel with your taking lessons on the instrument, but if you agree to become part of my court, you can study with my lute teacher. He is associated with the university. As an employed musician of the court, you will be expected to play in the ensemble from time to time, but the lessons are free."

Her words washed over him like a Baltic wave. He wanted time to think, but she waited for an answer—and she was a queen.

She leaned forward, evidently aware of his discomfort. "I understand you saw a bit of commotion when you arrived. I'm sure by now someone told you what took place here last night."

Should he be truthful? Was she trying to question him? "I was told there was a—a death, and a theft, but since neither concerned me, I paid no mind."

She smiled broadly, her gaze on the count. "Ah, a man who knows how to stay out of trouble. That's refreshing, don't you think, de la Gardie?" She turned back to Johan, not giving the count time to respond. "The murder will be investigated, of course, as will the theft. I find the best way to handle things like this is to keep a sense of normalcy. The Burgomaster and Town Council agree, as do my advisors."

The count rose and retreated to a table where he poured himself wine. Was this permissible, in the queen's own quarters, to help oneself? Right then, Johan realized he had no idea about court etiquette, let alone court justice. He weighed his options. If he stayed at court, he would have much to learn. On the other hand, the offer to live in a castle and take lessons for free was probably better than a scholarship. "I'm honored, Your Majesty, at your generous offer. But what exactly would my duties be, besides the ensemble?"

"When not rehearsing or performing, your time is your own, for leisure activities—reading, studying. There is a game room, quite well supplied with tables and game boards." She studied him with her large blue eyes, as if wondering what more she should tell him. "You would live in the musicians' dormitory. It's quite a large room, next to the dancers' dormitory. You each have your own space, divided by wooden walls. It's your responsibility to keep it clean, except for the floors, which are mopped weekly. A laundress replaces the linens weekly, too. Does all this sound satisfactory?" Without waiting for his response, she continued. "I love lute music, and so I would ask you, from time to time, to play for my amusement, of course. That is expected of any court musician."

Clearly, she was expecting an answer. Johan took a deep breath, and somehow the words came out. "Then I would be delighted to entertain, Your Majesty, and I am grateful for your generosity—and the count's too, of course."

"Fine. We're agreed. So, since you're to be part of my court, you will find out soon enough, so I may as well tell you. The commotion in the courtyard, which set the gossips talking, was caused by my mother. She is unwell—has been since my father's death, as you may have heard. Everyone from China to England knows, I suspect." She lowered her chin a moment, then straightened, as if remembering she was a queen. "There was a theft in the Royal Library, a book my mother is particularly attached to—a special bible. Its absence was only discovered today. I'm sure my gossipy courtiers told you a man met his death last evening. That is under investigation but I'm sure the bible thief is the guilty party. Mother was there this morning, when the palace guards roped off the area for cleaning. She overheard my librarian speaking with his assistant. They had checked most of the valuables and found nothing missing, except the book she treasures. As Mother is wont to do, she flew from the room, exciting the entire palace." She sighed, and Johan suddenly saw a young woman who looked tired, tired of being a queen. "I would have preferred it be kept quiet until we found the murderer, but of course, that's impossible now." Her bow-shaped mouth, one of her finer features, curled into a pout. "It was a very valuable and unique book. Whoever took it knew that. I could have traded it for great diplomatic favors."

Johan wondered why he was being told all this, but he saw the count had taken a chair not far away, and the queen seemed anxious to talk about the crime in her castle. Perhaps even a royal could be lonely. He straightened his shoulders and tried to act interested. "What book could be so valuable?"

"The Silver Bible. Next to the Devil's Bible, it is—or was—the most valuable book in my library."

"I see. Well, perhaps the thief will be caught, along with the murderer."

"Oh, they're likely one and the same, so if we get one, we'll have caught both. We can only hope so." She covered her mouth and yawned. "So, we agree, then." She signaled a servant from the shadows. "Lars, get someone to show Johan to the musicians' dormitory."

Johan bowed low, knowing he had been dismissed. Later, lying on his assigned cot in the musicians' sleeping quarters, he relived the day's events and how his life had changed in a matter of hours, and prayed he had made the right decision. After all this, he would not receive a scholarship. Had he been awarded a higher prize? It seemed so. Taking free lessons from the queen's own lute instructor—living at court, with free lodging and food. What more could he have asked for? His future, for now, looked promising. Never had he dreamed of such an opportunity. And the young queen seemed enamored of his playing. Well, in the weeks to come, he would validate her trust in his talent. He had only to listen and learn in order to find his place in what appeared to be a maze of court musicians—singers, players, and ballet artists—a mix he hadn't expected.

The following morning, while Johan broke his fast in the dining hall, a small figure climbed onto the bench and sat beside him. Startled, Johan turned, expecting to see a child, but instead, he came face to face with a little man. He had seen dwarfs before, mostly with traveling shows and royal parades. The man beside him, though, unlike the others, was a perfectly formed miniature, fully developed and seemingly comfortable in his body. Johan felt instant respect for the person beside him, impeccably dressed in blue breeches and matching fur-trimmed doublet.

The dwarf broke bread from a long loaf set out for the table occupants. "Her Majesty, the Queen Mother, wants to see you— sometime midday, after she's finished her toilette." He leaned closer. "Her hair is thinning, you see, and the hairdresser takes half the day with it." He reached unconcernedly and buttered the bread. "I'm Gunner, by the way. Everyone calls me Gunne. And I know you are Johan, the new musician."

"Yes. Are you—part of the queen mother's court?"

Gunne grinned. "She has a fondness for dwarfs—and hunchbacks. But you'll see all that when you go."

"Have I broken a rule of etiquette? Why would she want to see me, I wonder."

"Who knows? Eleanora does as she pleases, even if it interferes with the young queen's rulings." He looked around. "I'm on duty and have to go now. Remember, before noon. Her rooms are in the west wing."

Johan spread jam on another bite of bread, washed it down with beer, and remembered his lute. "Could you tell me where to find the luthier's shop? He's repairing my instrument."

"It's on my way. Come with me."

Johan followed the dwarf out of the room and down a corridor. Gunne paused by a staircase. "There, just past the laundry. Next door on the right. His name is Noël Alliamez, if you're wondering. Remember, before noon at the queen mother's."

After thanking Gunne, Johan went to the luthier's shop and knocked.

"Come in," the man called.

Johan stepped inside and was surprised to find that Noël Alliamez had the warmest room in the castle, backing up the way it did to the royal laundry where fires were kept burning all day to heat water. "Good morning," the lute maker said.

Johan extended his hand. "My lute was brought here for repair."

The luthier wiped his hands on a leather apron. "Ah yes." He reached to a shelf and retrieved the instrument. "You are in luck. It was only a small crack and I was able to glue the wood." He handed the lute to Johan. "A fine instrument. I understand it landed on stones in the courtyard."

Johan plucked the strings. Better to be discreet. "Yes. Carelessness, pure and simple. It will teach me to watch where I walk."

"That's not what I heard. I was told the queen's mother created a commotion outside—was on one of her tears—but then, I can't say as I blame her. An unexplained death in the palace, and then her book goes missing. Those books are real treasures, and I think she feels as though they are hers, even though the king was long dead when the booty was brought to Stockholm."

Johan fit the lute into its leather case. He had quite forgotten the warning of how fast news traveled, as if Hermes himself lived within the castle walls, waiting to carry messages. The luthier took a hummel from the shelf, laid the pear-shaped instrument on his worktable, and returned to his stool. He sorted through a pile of strings lying nearby.

Johan, in no hurry to leave and face the queen mother, about whom he had heard only strange stories so far, sat nearby and watched Noël's limber fingers replace one of the three strings. The luthier kept his eyes downcast. "I mostly stay to myself here, but I'm curious. Have you heard exactly who died last night?"

Johan shook his head. "Some say it was a murder, but no one seems to know anything more. Everyone believes the murderer also stole the queen mother's bible." Johan shifted his lute to the other arm. "What was so special about the bible that was taken?" he asked. "Surely the queen mother could afford—"

"It is that particular book she treasures. You wouldn't know, of course, but months back, a boatload of spoils from Prague arrived here. Everyone in Stockholm knew about all the treasure that the queen's army brought from Prague. Old Rudolph II had collected anything and everything, and in spite of the rebels having sold most of his collection earlier to support their cause, our general found so much treasure at Hradany Castle that he had problems shipping it back here."

The luthier reached for another string. "I was told there were five hundred or so paintings, hundreds of bronzes, scientific instruments, along with jewels and ebony cabinets, but I've never seen the collection. There was a live lion, too, but he died. The horse doctor said it was old age, but I reckon he caught cold up here, don't you? I do know that the queen gave away several of those paintings—ones she didn't especially like. Now the rest are hanging around everywhere. Most of the coral and ivory and other valuables are locked up in the royal treasury, everything that's already been inventoried. The bibles went to the Royal Library. I guess that's what upset the queen mother, because she loved the Silver Bible and read from it every afternoon, if the Royal Librarian can be believed, and he has no reason to lie. It leaves me uncomfortable, though, knowing a murderous thief crept into the castle and escaped with the bible, leaving not a trace. I suppose it's possible the murderer walks among us." He rubbed a cloth across the lute's back. "There, another one done."

Johan remembered, with a start, that he was supposed to see the queen mother before noon. He jumped to his feet. "What do I owe you?"

Noël Alliamez shook his head and smiled. "I'm surprised no one told you. My repairs are free to anyone in the court. Our young queen believes this is an essential service. She supports the arts in every way—but you'll find that out for yourself."

Johan extended his hand, thanked the luthier, and made his way to the west wing to face whatever waited.

CHAPTER FIVE

Johan approached the queen mother's quarters, curious as to what this royal summons could mean. He turned down the final corridor to her rooms and noticed the palace décor had changed. Here, instead of colorful mosaics and tapestries depicting mythical figures, a series of imperial-looking faces stared down from the walls. He continued on, then paused near a painting surrounded by a circle of candles. The personage wore a high starched collar and sky-blue garment. A receding hairline above a noble forehead left no doubt as to the man's intelligence, but it was his piercing brown eyes that commanded attention. His carefully waxed moustache and neat goatee softened his expression. From the way the painting was displayed, Johan knew the subject was someone important. A little below and to the right was a portrait of a composed, elegant lady. Johan frowned. He'd seen that face before. Was that the queen? No, it was a younger version of the woman who had run screaming through the courtyard the day of his arrival here. That was the queen mother.

When Johan reached the queen mother's quarters, two ladies came forward, blocking his passage. "Who are you and what is your business?"

"I am Johan Sokolewski and I have an appointment with the queen mother. Gunne told me to be here before noon."

The taller of the two, her grey-green eyes fixed on Johan's lute, drew her brows together. "You are to play for her? You should have told us. Come this way."

Johan, puzzled as to when he could have told them anything, almost missed an exchange of smiles between the two ladies. Again he was reminded of how much he had to learn about courtiers—or was it the ladies here who seemed overly bold?

Before he could consider the issue further, he was taken into a larger room. Once inside, the shorter of Johan's two escorts slipped her arm through his. "You must wait here to be announced. Sigrid will tell the queen mother you are here."

At one end, sitting in a gilt chair on a dais and surrounded by chatting ladies, sat the queen mother. A small black curly-haired dog lay in her lap. Dwarfs sat in a semi-circle at her feet, Gunne among them.

The taller girl advanced to the throne-like chair. When she spoke, the ladies seated around the queen mother looked toward the door. Johan shifted uneasily and gripped the lute tighter. The bevy of ladies assessed him like a horse at the weekly sale.

After what seemed like several long minutes, the tall girl returned to his side. "You may approach. If she tells you to sit, take one of those side benches. And mind your manners. This is a royal court."

He nodded. This Sigrid was a bit rude. A little authority could do that sometimes. This all seemed like so much useless formality, especially after the informality surrounding his visit with the reigning queen. He felt his patience slipping away like an eel in cream sauce.

The shorter of the two girls, who'd waited with him near the door, now led him forward. When they reached the dais she paused. "Your Royal Highness, Maria Eleanora, Queen Mother of Sweden, this visitor, Johan—Johan—" She turned to him. "What was it again?"

"Sokolewski," he said, hiding a grin. "The court lutenist."

"Your Highness, Johan Sokuski begs an audience."

Johan decided to take charge. "Your Majesty, you sent for me?"

The queen mother leaned forward, allowing a shaft of light to fall on her face from the room's only window. In spite of her obvious age, he knew at a glance she had been quite a beauty. Her hair, gathered now into a fashionable bun, was turning white, but the face, with its strong nose and inquisitive brows, looked much like the youthful portrait he had seen in the hallway outside. He bowed low, only half-aware of the discreet glances he attracted from the ladies surrounding the old queen.

"*Mais oui,*" she said, "if you are the new musician. *Bonjour, Monsieur.* I will speak French, the language of the court, for now. In the old days, we spoke German, or some other civilized language." She sighed. "But that's in the past. Now, why did I ask you here?"

She laid one finger to her cheek, a youthful gesture, and a moment later smiled broadly. "Oh, yes. I recall. I do owe you an apology, don't I? Did they repair your lute? Oh, my, how silly of me. Of course it's fixed." She chuckled. "You'd not be carrying around a broken lute, would you?" The dwarfs near her feet grinned at her joke, followed by laughter from her women.

"You may not know," she said, looking straight at Johan from large blue eyes, "but for years I was responsible for making this court the talk of the north—bringing musicians from all over, even further than France. Now, though, my daughter sends one of her favorites to choose the players who will entertain. Bah— the music they play now. But you—I heard you last night. You have talent, so I am pleased that de la Gardie had the good sense to bring you here." She stroked the small dog with her ringed fingers. The dog kept one watchful eye on Johan. The ladies all looked his way.

"I thank Your Majesty for the compliment," Johan said, feeling uncomfortable under the gaze of so many eyes. "I understand the theft upset you, and of course—"

She broke into a wail, and Johan bit his lip. He never should have mentioned the bible. Gunne rose from his stool, walked to a nearby table, and brought a gold box to the queen.

She patted the dwarf on the shoulder, withdrew a linen from the box, blotted her nose, and asked for a glass of wine. While she drank, her ladies whispered. The dwarfs conversed among themselves, and Johan grew increasingly uncomfortable. He'd been told to come here, but it seemed a whim of the queen mother's. Should he apologize and make an effort to leave? Before he could settle his thoughts, Eleanora cleared her throat and handed the empty glass to one of her women. Composed from the wine and attention, she leaned forward. "I like you, lutenist. Play me a song."

Johan saw, from the corner of his eye, that Gunne was grinning. The dwarf could have warned him what to expect, but Johan was here now, and this was a royal command. After tuning the strings, he strummed a chord, then sang the shortest piece he could recall.

The song, evidently, had been to her liking, because she was smiling now and asking for more of her good German wine. When she nodded off, Johan looked around the room, but no one seemed surprised. Some of the women resumed their sewing. One of the dwarfs took some cards from his pocket and pulled his stool close to three others.

Gunne hurried to Johan. "She falls asleep like this from time to time, and that gives us all a break. Come with me. I'll show you a part of the castle you probably haven't seen." They walked in silence until coming to a flight of stairs. Gunne paused and looked up at Johan. "I know how you must feel. When I first came here I knew no one. It's difficult, but don't worry. For the most part, they're an amiable group." He smiled and started up the stairs.

Johan followed, thankful for this small man's friendship.

At the top of the staircase they entered a long hall, dimly lit by wall torches. A small window seat looked inviting, but Gunne kept walking to the far end of the corridor, then took a turn into a short hallway that ended at a wide window alcove. "It looks down on the courtyard," Gunne said as they approached. "You'd be surprised at what I see going on down there sometimes. It's how I found out my wife was cheating." He laughed, a deep, hearty laugh for such a small man.

Johan sat on the padded window seat. "An excellent vantage point, Gunne, though I'm sorry about your wife."

Gunne climbed up and seated himself on the red cushion. "It's over and done. When it happened, I asked Eleanora to transfer me—maybe to the palace at Uppsala. They have nightly entertainment there, and I knew I could always fall back on my ball-tossing skills, but she would not hear of it. Instead, my wife and her lover got sent by the queen mother to serve her royal German relatives at court." He grinned. "So I'm rid of a faithless wife, and better off now."

"You were a juggler?"

"Yes. I performed, like my parents before me. I tossed balls into the air like an idiot. One summer Eleanora saw me perform and took a liking to me. She asked my parents if she could bring me here. They were delighted, of course, to have one of their children singled out for such an honor. Besides, that meant one less mouth to feed. There were three others then, although everyone's gone now. I was the luckiest, for sure. So now I get to sit in the best seats, in the royal box at state affairs, and I dance once or twice a week when the queen mother gets sad and we have to cheer her up. I hated to see her cry today, but I doubt she'll ever see that bible again. Whoever took it knew its value."

"Who do you suppose would kill someone for a book, Gunne?

Someone from outside the castle?"

Gunne shrugged. "It could have been anyone." He glanced out the window. "Look, there comes Queen Christina, returned from the hunt."

Johan turned to peer below, trying to pick the queen from the line of riders entering the courtyard.

"She's riding the white horse, behind the standard bearer," Gunne said.

The flag, a smaller version of the large red and white banner that hung on one wall of the ballet hall, rippled in the icy wind. Behind the flagman a lithe figure dismounted the white horse. "Are you sure that's the queen?" he asked.

"Quite sure," Gunne said, grinning. "Don't let the clothes and man's hat fool you."

Johan gave a low whistle. "She can sure handle a horse."

"And no wonder," Gunne said. "She had the best teachers. Her father raised her like a prince. She was trained in fencing and riding much the same as the military."

Johan was no longer listening, instead watching the girl beside the queen, who was dismounting. From here, it looked like the court astrologist he'd met earlier. She removed her hat and a shower of curls fell to her shoulders. "Is that Zofia standing alongside the queen?"

"Yes. You met her?"

"Only briefly."

Gunne nodded. "She's the only woman the queen will take on the hunts. I think she only tolerates Zofia because she admires her skills and knowledge of science, but the queen has little tolerance for her women. She prefers conversation and board games with the men, just the opposite of the queen mother, who, if you ask me, acts more like a real queen, when she's herself. Other times, well, some think she's addled. I think she is sickened by grief, although King Gustav has been dead now over fifteen years." Gunne shaded his eyes, judging the sun's position. "I'd best get back. She'll be waking about now. And there's a masked ball tonight she'll want us to attend."

Johan followed him down the hall, and when Gunne turned to go to the queen mother's chambers, Johan went down the steps. Perhaps Zofia would pass this way when coming inside.

"Good day, Johan." Zofia's eyes shone bright, her cheeks flushed pink from the cold, and she smelled like the outdoors, mixed with the lemon. It must be the soap she used.

He swept a gallant bow. "My lady, was the hunt successful?"

She shrugged. "I only ride along. I have no stomach for the kill. For me, a successful hunt is when their prey escapes. Now, did Noël repair your instrument?"

"Yes, and quite satisfactorily. Earlier, I played for the queen mother, and she approved."

The corners of Zofia's mouth turned up and Johan knew she was hiding a laugh. "Eleanora's ideas of entertainment are sometimes at odds with those of others," she said.

"Are you saying my playing should not be admired?"

"Of course not. I only meant . . ." She gathered her skirts. "I'm sorry, I have to go. I've work to do."

"Wait. Tell me about your work. Are you the queen's companion?"

She opened her eyes wide, as if he had asked her to hold a snake, or swim in the icy Baltic. "I am the queen's scientific consultant."

"I quite forgot. Yes, you're her astrologer—a singularly important post, I'd guess." He fell in step alongside her.

She cast him a sidelong glance and continued down the hall. "I'm also the queen's friend. She has no patience with ordinary womanly pursuits, like sewing and gossip. Besides, the ladies cannot keep up with the hunt—few women could, unless they'd been raised around horses. She and I both learned to ride as children. Not together, of course." Her face softened. "I had a pony, a Christmas gift from my parents."

"Did your parents hunt?"

Zofia shook her head. "No, Mother was always a little afraid of horses, but Papa encouraged her, and she had just begun to feel comfortable on a horse when . . . when she died."

Johan broke in. "I'm sorry. Didn't mean to bring up sad memories." He struggled for something to say. "Tell me about your position here at court, as an astrologer."

She brightened. "I'm not only the court astrologer, I am also an alchemist. Like Queen Elizabeth's astrologer who wrote a book on alchemy, I study both."

Johan tried to hide his surprise. "I had no idea that royals believed one can turn ordinary matter into gold."

She quickened her step. "I see you have no idea what advances have been made in my field of study, but I will tell you this. Many courts sponsor alchemists, for various reasons, some of which have to do with medicine."

Johan's excitement in meeting so charming a lady faded. Why would someone who seemed to have high ideals be involved in magic? His thoughts went back to the villager, the magician who lived outside of Warsaw. If not for her, his mother would be alive today—but no use reliving all that now. He tried to focus on the girl in front of him, to separate her from the magician of his nightmares, but how did Zofia's experiments differ from those of the woman who killed his mother? He blinked, forcing the unwelcome thought to the back of his mind. "Are you work-ing on a cure?" he asked. "Is the Swedish queen ill?"

"I've already told you more than I should have. It's private information." She frowned and kept walking.

"I didn't mean to pry," he said. "I was interested in the sci-ence of it. If I understand, you are trying to change the state of a chemical."

She took a deep breath. "It is much more than that. You, like many others, believe an alchemist to be a charlatan. Few people know that alchemists study at the universities, alongside cartographers and mathematicians, but old beliefs are hard to break. That is why I never talk about my work. Most have little knowledge of science."

He felt his face color. She had just insulted him, for no good cause. He paused, thinking it best to leave, when she pulled a key from beneath her bodice. "Oh, come now. I meant no harm. Would you like to see my laboratory? It's this next room."

He hesitated. Did he want to see inside a magician's workroom? Did he really want to relive it all again? Still, she was waiting, her eyes wide and hopeful. In spite of a warning that rose in his breast, he nodded, feeling as though he had just passed some kind of test, some secret passage this young alchemist had devised for separating the worthy from the unworthy. No matter, he thought, as he followed her into a darkened room. She paused near a table, searching for her tinderbox, and he heard the sound of flint being struck.

The room came to life. An arrangement at one end of the table appeared to be a model of the known planets. Shelves lined the walls, filled with jars and bottles, books, and what looked like an apothecary's balance scales. In the middle of the room, neatly arranged on a long table, were pans and bowls with tubes running from one to the other. "There, you see?" She put both hands on her hips. "I do scientific experiments. There is nothing magic here—no glass ball to tell your fortune, or wax dolls to lay a curse." She teased him with her eyes.

"The queen is generous—to give you the space to work."

"It is a business, lutenist. I work with chemicals, trying to learn how they can be used to treat illness. I am convinced, along with many others, that chemicals can heal the body if correctly studied in relation to the position of sun and moon, barometer readings, and wind direction. Many scholars insist the planets are associated with certain parts of the body. I am particularly interested in the constellation Aries, said to be associated with the head. Perhaps all those elements have no importance, but it is worth investigating. The queen, thank goodness, is interested in scientific findings, so she supports my work."

"Then you must be from one of the noble families of Stockholm. How does your father feel about his daughter—"

"My father is considered to be a member of the bourgeoisie class, a respected businessman. A bookbinder by trade. He repairs items in the queen's library—has for years. When I was young, he brought me along when he came to the castle. When the queen learned of my interest in alchemy, she encouraged it, even bought me some books, which I could not afford myself." She took a book from a shelf. "This, by Ambroise Paré, documents his findings for treating wounds. He discovered the value of turpentine for preventing infections, and now physicians use his lotion—simple egg yolks, oil of rose, and turpentine—instead of boiling water that caused pain."

"And you—what are you working on?" He bit his lip.

She chuckled. "It's all right. I think you're genuinely interested." She sighed. "Most courtiers try to prod for court secrets. Somehow I trust you."

He opened his mouth to reply but she continued. "To answer your question, I do many experiments at a time—never just one. There's so much to be learned. At present, another alchemist is making astonishing advances in science. I have some of his writings, and no doubt he will be famous for his work. Already he has written of the effect of air on sound, and he is studying respiration. Do you know there is a gas without which all animals and birds—and man himself—would die?"

Her eyes shone, and Johan suspected Zofia's first love was alchemy, and always would be. Truth to tell, her passion was a bit like his, for music. How could he fault that?

As she replaced the book, he was reminded of the queen mother's fondness for the missing book. "Too bad the Silver Bible was not kept in a locked room like this," he said.

"Ah, yes, night before last—a violent death and a theft. It's upsetting enough to have someone killed, but the loss of her book broke the queen mother's heart, and sent her into another one of her bad periods." She brought her hand to her mouth. "Oh, I forgot. You may not know, and I detest court gossip. It's only that I feel badly for her. I wish one of my experiments would produce a potion to cure diseases of the mind, but I fear that is years away. Bodily wounds are easier to understand, whereas grief is hidden, like a secret known only to its sufferer. I hope they can find the thief, but I fear her beloved bible is already far from Sweden."

Johan shook his head. "To go to such extremes to steal a book, that must have been someone who knew about its value, and where to find it, of course."

"Yes, but that could be anyone. Trouble is, people believe the legend—although it has no truth in fact—that ownership of the Silver Bible gives that person, or ruler, power over others. It is not reasonable that a book, produced by man, would have such power."

He crossed his arms and nodded agreement. "Yes, but if there's a history behind the bible, that would make it worth more in the marketplace, whether to a collector or book trader."

"Exactly. So it seems logical the crimes were committed by one of the warring factions."

His puzzlement must have been evident, because Zofia poured them both a drink, indicated a stool for him, and sat down next to one of her tables. "How much do you know of court politics?"

He smiled. "Little or nothing. I have found that's always best."

"Perhaps so, perhaps not. But if you are to live here, you will learn soon enough. Knowledge sometimes is one's greatest ally."

"Then tell me, Zofia, how to guard my person."

She chuckled. "You are not in danger, no more than ignorance can be dangerous. Ofttimes, as you surely know yourself, religion divides men, and here at court, it's no different. Oh, there's no overt battle—more like a simmering tolerance. The queen's tutor, Matthiae, leans toward Calvinism, and hopes for one great Protestant faith." She sighed and leaned forward. "He will deny it publicly, but the queen and others know it. He has her protection, even though Calvinism, in Sweden, ranks up there with Catholicism as being the greatest threat to the Lutheran faith."

She leaned back and smoothed her skirts, obviously enjoying his rapt attention. "Have you met the Chancellor?" Her eyes twinkled. "Speak to him at length, and you'll soon learn that he follows the beliefs of the dead king; strict Lutheranism should be enforced in Sweden. Most feel that way, or pretend to. Queen Christina is titular head of the Swedish Lutheran Church. Catholics removed her uncle from the throne, and her father died fighting for the Swedish cause."

Johan frowned, digesting what he'd just heard. "Then it's understandable that some would have strong opinions concerning the bible being here in the queen's own library. So you think whoever killed to get the book believes its ownership ensures their faith will be dominant?"

She nodded. "It's possible."

"Then it could be anyone—a secret Catholic, perhaps."

She brushed back a loose curl from her forehead. "I doubt

there are many of those left in Sweden. Life would be too difficult."

Johan emptied his cup. "I have kept you long enough, Zofia, but have learned much. I admire your work, too. If I should get a pain, I will come here first."

Her friendly demeanor dissolved into a cold stare. "Don't bother, Johan. I do not treat illnesses. Seek out the court physician for your pain."

He instantly knew he had made the wrong jest. Damn his foolishness. "I meant nothing—it was only a joke, Zofia. I was going to ask if you would save me a dance tonight. I understand a masked ball is planned."

She shrugged. "I won't be going." She stood by the door, waiting for him to leave, and he had the sinking feeling that it would take days to repair the harm he had just done.

As Johan made his way back to the musicians' dormitory and his assigned cubicle, someone called his name. He turned to see a man of average build striding briskly. He wore modest court attire that contrasted with his bold countenance. His light brown hair was streaked with silver strands, and he held a music score. Johan knew instinctively this stranger was a man in authority. The man extended his hand. "I'm Antoine Beaulieu, the ballet director. You are the new lutenist—a fine one, from what little I've heard of your playing. And thank you for filling in last evening." He chuckled. "I'm the director, but from time to time unexpected things happen, such as your appearance as a shepherd. It was convenient, I suppose, and gave the queen a chance to hear you perform." He shrugged. "Ah, well, not your fault. And it added to the ballet. Sometimes the count's interference does not turn out so well. He has good intentions, though. I just wish they'd tell me ahead of time."

"I'm sorry if my—"

"Not at all. In fact, that's why I wanted to speak with you. You have excellent rhythm. I need men of your size, to play warrior parts and such. I'm offering you a spot in the ballet."

Johan started to object, but the dance master held up his hand. "Hear me out. The training is good for men of any age, especially anyone who wants to be better in fencing or riding."

Johan shook his head. Joining the ballet was the last thing he wanted to do. "I appreciate the offer, Monsieur Beaulieu, but I lost the only horse I ever wanted. I hope someday to own a carriage, and I have never learned the art of fencing. I must decline your offer."

Beaulieu chuckled. "Very well. I understand. But be sure to watch our new ballet two nights from now. Stagehands have assembled machinery designed to make ocean waves and cause the golden sun to rise in splendor over a beaming goddess." He grinned and lowered his voice. "That will be the queen herself. Count de la Gardie and the queen's cousin, Charles, have also been cast in prominent roles. But I must go now. Can't be late for the rehearsal."

Johan smiled. "I'll be sure to watch your ballet," he called, as the director hurried away.

That night, while listening to the snores of other musicians through the thin boards that divided their cubicles, Johan lay staring into the dark. From all reports, tonight's masked ball was a success. Perhaps he should have gone, instead of staying here to practice. But why, when Zofia would not have been there?

He turned onto his side. There was something about the girl, the earnestness in her voice when she spoke about healing a soldier's wounds, but she had strange notions. For all he knew, she might believe in chants and omens. Still, was it fair to judge her, to assume she was like the village sorcerer, when he knew so little about Zofia and what went on in her workshop?

He adjusted the covers and sighed into the night, struggling to reconcile his admiration for Zofia with the fact that she thrived on the unexplained.

Shortly after midnight, he fell asleep, only to dream again of the woman responsible for his mother's death. The sorcerer held a pot of something dark in one hand, a candle in the other, and when she touched the flame to the pot, a ball of fire erupted, rolling down her skirt and across the floor where it hit a wall, exploding the room in a ball of flames. He reached to lift his mother from the bed but she was nothing but a spirit, rising from his arms, ascending into the flames. He turned to the sorceress. She touched her white lace cap. A twist of reddish-gold hair covered her cheek. She walked toward him and as she came close, the scent of lemon masked the smell of burning wood. She smiled and reached out to him.

He backed away, choking. He had to get out. As he tugged at whatever held him back, he woke in the dark dormitory, sweating and cursing, and found the coverlet wrapped around his chest. *Thank God. Thank God.* But would he ever be free of the memories?

CHAPTER SIX

Following his restless night, Johan woke with a start and realized he'd slept late, exhausted from his peculiar nightmares. Strangest of all was that the sorceress no longer had the face of the lady he remembered. That was Zofia's face in his dream. He rose and dressed, unnerved by the turn this familiar nightmare had taken. Must have been last night's wine.

Sunlight slanted from the high windows, brightening the ceiling above, plain white plaster that contrasted with the other frescoed ceilings in the palace. Not a sound came from nearby cubicles. Even the adjacent dormitory, where the ballet dancers slept, was quiet. Probably they were already rehearsing for tomorrow night's production.

Grateful for the quiet, he decided to make use of the time to practice. He crossed the room to a corner where daylight filtered through a slatted window covering. After laying his music on a bench, he tuned his lute. Satisfied at the pitch, he bent over the score and concentrated on the music.

The main door to the dormitory opened. He looked up as a solitary figure came in and closed the door. To Johan's relief, it was not the dancing master or his troupe but the theorboe player, Alexandre Voullon, whom he'd met briefly. The man had come to court along with the French viol-players recruited by Count de la Gardie.

Voullon wore a carefully styled moustache, the ends of which turned slightly upward, giving him the look of a man pleased with himself and the world around him. His shoulder-length hair curled in neat rolls near the ends. A wide collar drew attention to the firm set of his chin. Of average height and build, Johan guessed Voullon was not yet thirty. "*Bonjour,* Johan. I see you have found a quiet time to practice. It's usually impossible in the dormitory, and everywhere else draws a crowd of onlookers." He shook his head. "Have you been questioned yet?"

Johan laid the lute aside. Alexandre was in the mood to talk. "Why no, about what?"

"Oh, I forgot. It happened before you arrived, so you cannot be suspect. The night guards are diligent. No one gets past them."

"Tell me about the questioning. Is it about the murder? Are courtiers being questioned?"

Alexandre Voullon nodded. "You don't know the queen mother well, do you? She is like a hound with a bone, and will not give up easily."

"So she, and not the queen, is in charge of an investigation?"

"You'll soon learn about our young queen, too. She has probably already dismissed the entire thing from her mind, having turned it over to the guardsmen, who turned it over to the castle police. As for the missing book, she will simply tell her librarian to have the recorder strike the Silver Bible from his records. I believe they are finished with the inventory, except for a hoard of gold coins. They're still counting those. But it's mostly the paintings Queen Christina cares about, and the scientific instruments, all of which are locked in the treasury vault except for the paintings she put in the gallery—some fine Titians—Holbeins too, but she especially likes the Italian artists."

"Those men—the librarian and the one who catalogs the books—you trust them both?"

"The Royal Librarian, Johann Freinsheim, has served since

King Gustav's time and remained here when his daughter, young Queen Christina, took over. The one who catalogs the books came here from the French court. He was Louis's physician and a librarian to Mazarin in France. He likes to be addressed as Monsieur Naudé. Surprisingly, he professes to be an atheist. It's a wonder he admits it openly, but the queen is more tolerant than some." Voullon shrugged. "He may not be here long. It's no secret he wants to return to Paris. You may know he was responsible for Mazarin's massive library—the most impressive in Europe. But of course all that ended when Mazarin fled Paris during the Fronde, those useless skirmishes that harmed both sides." Voullon shook his head. "Worst part is, all those books were sold or given away. It broke Naudé's heart to see the library dispersed. They even burned some of the books, can you imagine? Priceless old manuscripts. Anyway, now Mazarin's back in Paris, and Naudé is being urged to return to France and rebuild Mazarin's *bibliothèque*."

Voullon took a seat on the bench alongside Johan's music score. "I'm uneasy, though, with a murderer running loose in the castle."

"Did you know the victim?"

Voullon scratched his chin. "No one did, except the librarian and Naudé. Freinsheim and Naudé had the task of cataloguing the booty brought back from Rudolph's castle in Prague. They were overwhelmed. Even the royal treasurer, Gabriel Oxenstiern, had been enlisted to help. Then with the queen's permission, Freinsheim hired a goldsmith to assist the treasurer in valuing the coins. Tragically, it was only the goldsmith's second day here, poor man. The body was found slumped over a pile of gold coins he'd been examining. The thief bypassed the gold for the bible." He shook his head. "Doesn't make any sense. But that's not your worry. You're a lucky man, not being here when it happened. So you escape the inquisition."

Johan swallowed. "The queen mother has established an inquisition?"

Voullon chuckled. "Nothing like the Spanish Inquisition, if that's what you're thinking. No. Eleanora—we all call her that, but only among ourselves—has her dwarfs acting as judges, taking notes. They've been ruled out as suspects, because as the queen mother pointed out, any of them would have needed a stool to commit the crime. I tell you it's entertaining, or would be if not so serious. If the dwarfs, or even the queen mother, decide someone is guilty, that person will be at her mercy, and Eleanora's moods can fluctuate like the seasons. I doubt she will get to the truth, though, because she has her favorites. She brought most of the German musicians to court, and now the new queen is replacing them with French, like us, and lately, Italians. It doesn't please the queen mother, but what can she do? To be fair, she'll need to question everyone."

"But what reason would one of her Germans have to steal the bible, and kill a man to get it?"

"Who knows? Most are devout Lutherans, to a man, and may think the young queen's tutor, our secret Calvinist, will win over the queen to his ways. Or they might believe, as many do, that the book has magic powers that can change the world—or a country's religion. For myself, I don't believe that bible is anything but a very old book, worth money to anyone who wants it badly. I was told it is not even complete. Several pages are missing, and have been for years. But I've taken enough of your time." He paused, scratched his graying beard, and gave Johan a friendly smile. "Perhaps we can play a duet sometime." He pointed to his theorboe, an instrument much like Johan's lute except for the longer neck, which to Johan's way of thinking would only make the instrument more difficult to play.

Alexandre had almost reached the door when a quick knock

sounded on the other side. Gunne, the queen mother's dwarf, walked inside, bowing to Voullon as they passed. The practice space in the dormitory seemed to be a gathering place, or a spot where someone went to catch up on gossip. It certainly was not the quiet haven Johan had hoped for.

"Good day, Gunne," Johan said, fitting the lute into its soft leather case, a gift from an old friend, a shoemaker, who had crafted the case from discarded scraps of material. Nevertheless, he had had offers to buy it, and would not sell it now at any price. The shoemaker had been a good friend.

Gunne settled himself on a bench, his chubby legs sticking straight out. "God's teeth but it's storming outside. Haven't looked out, have you?"

"No. It's snowing then?"

"Snowing? It's an ice storm. The snow will come later. A window broke in the queen mother's chamber. She called an end to today's proceedings."

"Have you found the murderer?"

"Eleanora thinks so, but there's no proof. The girl isn't your typical criminal."

"Girl? Who? One of Eleanora's ladies?"

"No. We questioned the young queen's alchemist—you remember her—Zofia, the queen's riding companion. The library cataloguer, Naudé, remembered something Zofia's father said last time he was here, a few weeks back. He's a local bookbinder, the very best. His father, Zofia's grandfather, kept the old king's books in repair as well. Anyway, Naudé recalled Zofia's father spending time looking through the Silver Bible when he was here to repair a book. Seems Naudé showed him another book—the Devil's Bible—but Zofia's father showed no interest in it, only the Silver Bible. The book was here after his visit, but so was Zofia. The question is, would she steal for her father?"

A chill darted down Johan's spine. Was Zofia really a suspect? Surely, as favorite of the queen, she'd be granted anything she wanted. Why steal? He pushed the disturbing thought to the back of his mind. "Maybe Naudé is saying all this to deflect suspicion from himself."

Gunne looked directly at Johan. "I haven't told you the worst. Zofia was seen in the wee hours that Sunday night near the library. One of the guards was making his rounds. As he approached from a side hall, she passed by. Kept her head down and continued on, never spoke. It was dark and he said she probably didn't notice him. She carried a candle and had something in her other hand. It was about the length of a man's upper arm, but he couldn't make out what it was, she went by so fast."

"Did Zofia get a chance to tell the queen mother what she was doing there?"

"She had no chance. We resume tomorrow, and then she gets to speak."

Johan rubbed his lip, deep in thought. It did sound bad for Zofia. "Do you suppose I could be there?"

Gunne shook his head. "Eleanora made that very clear from the beginning. She wanted no one in the room besides the accused and a witness. She said it might give people ideas for their own defense, which is true. But I'll be there and will tell you what Zofia says."

Johan rose and paced the room. For now, he could do nothing. He'd have to wait and hear Gunne's report. For Zofia's sake, he hoped she had an ironclad alibi.

The following afternoon, while Johan practiced in a corner of the dormitory, Gunne arrived, flushed and out of breath. He signaled to Johan and returned to the hall.

Johan put his lute on the shelf and hurried to join Gunne,

who headed for the staircase. Evidently today's hearing for Zofia had ended.

Gunne waited at the bottom step. "I thought it better we talk in private, and my window seat is the best place for that."

Johan nodded and went up the stairs with Gunne following close behind. Predictably, Gunne's secret place was vacant, as was the entire corridor. The dwarf climbed up to the cushioned bench and Johan sat beside him, eager to hear what Zofia had said.

Gunne tucked a pillow under one arm and scratched his chin. "It sure came as a surprise to me, but Zofia told the queen mother what she was doing that night near the library. She said she grows mushrooms near one of the library hearths. She forgot to check them that day, so she rose from bed to go there. She said what the guard saw her carrying was a tool she uses to loosen any compacted dirt."

"You're saying Zofia grows mushrooms in the royal library?"

"Yes. Eleanora asked why there, of all places, and Zofia explained that it was the only place where a fire burned all night. I know that's true. Last winter everyone said there were spirits in there after midnight, breaking precious porcelain pots, but a glassmaker said it was the extreme temperature change. It's hard on delicate porcelain. He said that after the fires burn down, the porcelain cools too quickly. It was the fragile ones near both hearths that shattered. So the queen ordered that the library fires be kept burning."

"Hmm. Well, I'll be. Mushrooms. I thought they grew in the dark. Wouldn't a fire cast too much light?"

"Zofia said she keeps them covered—some kind of box contraption she put together. She also said she wished the goldsmith still lived because he'd swear to what she was saying. He was alive when she passed by. They exchanged a greeting and he returned to his work. They were both involved in a task."

Johan snapped his fingers. "Of course. She told me most of her experiments are searching for ways to relieve pain. She was probably growing her mushrooms for medicinal purposes."

"That's what she claimed, but the queen mother seemed skeptical. She said she'd always heard that mushrooms could give a person the strength of an ox. Then one of her ladies stood and said mushrooms could help find lost objects, and could lead the soul to the realm of gods. Eleanora laughed at that, said it was only superstitious fancies, but said there were real cases where mushrooms had poisoned a man, and before he died he had visions of things that weren't there."

Johan shook his head. "Poor Zofia, having to listen to all that, even an implication she was growing mushrooms as a poison."

Gunne shrugged. "No way of knowing what the queen mother will do. She kept petting her dog and listened to every word Zofia said, but who knows where this goes from here."

They sat silent, each with his own thoughts, until Johan crossed his arms and leaned against the wood panel behind him. "Gunne, do you think Eleanora believed Zofia?"

"I'm not sure. Eleanora seems convinced that the queen's alchemist took the book for her father, the only man who ever publicly professed his desire to own it. And there were witnesses there who swore they have heard her say she'd do anything for her Papa." Gunne leaned forward. "Did you know he once pulled her from their burning house? His arms and legs are scarred, as well as his face. It's a wonder he lived with such terrible burns. So you can understand how a daughter would feel."

Johan spit out the words. "Zofia is no criminal. I hope you made that clear to the queen mother."

"Wait. Don't get testy. I only told you what took place. Zofia has not been arrested. Besides, with the broken window and workmen in Eleanora's room, she may have forgotten all about it by now." Gunne edged forward and began swinging his legs.

It made Johan nervous—or was it the news about Zofia that had unsettled him?

Gunne cleared his throat. "Do I sense a special concern for the yellow-haired alchemist?" He grinned, unnerving Johan even further.

"It's always a concern that an innocent will be falsely accused."

"Especially when it's an attractive innocent, eh, Johan?"

Johan cast him a dark look.

Gunne, evidently knowing he'd made Johan uncomfortable, quickly changed the subject. "Are you in tonight's ballet?"

"Only in the musicians' ensemble. But after the ballet, I understand there will be a dance." He kept to himself the question as to whether Zofia would attend or not.

Gunne nodded. "Oh, yes. Our young queen loves dancing." He lowered his voice to a whisper. "She is not very good, but has a fondness lately for all things French, and so we are all learning new dances, like the minuet. This dance troupe, in fact, was brought here by Count de la Gardie from the Paris court—permanently. There were wagers as to how much he had to pay. The king of France would not easily release his entertainers." He shrugged. "Most courtiers enjoy the mixed dancing after the performance. I rather enjoy dancing myself, although we get pushed around and overlooked, so we stay to one side of the dancing area where people leave us alone."

Johan chuckled at the picture the dwarf painted. "I only know the dances of my homeland, but I can learn, I suppose."

Gunne glanced at the lantern clock on the wall. "I need to get back before someone comes looking for me." He climbed from the bench, waved, and went down the stairs.

Minutes later, Johan sat staring out the window. Today's weather was no better than yesterday's. Trees bent to the ground, whipped by the wind, and balls of ice pelted the shut-

ters. In spite of the sight before him, his thoughts went back to
Zofia. By her own admission she had few friends at court. Would
she mind a visitor?

Johan made his way to Zofia's room, hoping by now she had
forgotten his remark about coming to her for pain relief. Obviously she thought he meant to trivialize her work, and he would
have to weigh his words. To his relief, in response to his knock
she opened the door wide. "I'm not in the mood for treating a
toothache. If that's what you came for, or some other ailment,
go to the physician."

"No, no. It's nothing like that. I came to talk."

She waved him inside. When he passed by, the fresh smell of
lemon sharpened his senses. He searched for the right words to
say. "Um, Zofia. About these court dances, I decided not to go
myself the other night. I needed some practice time, too.
Besides, I'm afraid I know few steps, except for Polish dances,
and German ones."

"Don't worry. No one knows these new French dances the
queen is thrusting on her court. We are all learning. Now, what
did you really come for?" Repressed laughter sparked in her
eyes.

He smiled, acknowledging their shared bit of history, his
blunder she'd evidently chosen to overlook. "I came to see how
you were. Gunne said the queen mother questioned you."

"She is questioning everyone, picking at threads. I think it's
not the murder so much as the stolen book."

"But a valuable one."

"The Devil's Bible is just as valuable—to some even more so.
And Eleanora said it was right next to the Silver Bible."

"Yes," Johan said, "I was told about it." He watched her grind
some beans, pour boiling water on top and add spoonsful of
something dark. "Does everyone at court believe a devil owned

a bible? That makes no sense at all."

She perched on a stool and straightened her skirt. "That's not where the book got its name. They say a monk wrote the Devil's Bible, all by hand, and finished it in one night."

He shifted uneasily. "I find that hard to believe."

"Of course," she said, rising to stir honey into the concoction before pouring it into two cups. "Have you ever tasted chocolate?" She gave him a cup, and he caught a bit of her ever-present scent, the lemon. Combined with the fragrance of chocolate, it stirred his senses in a peculiar way.

"I've heard of it, but never tasted it. A spice from the New World."

"It makes a wonderful drink. The queen gave me some of the beans when I relieved her stomach pains. It was an old remedy I read about, not my discovery at all, and I felt a bit guilty for taking the gift, but she insisted."

He sipped from the cup, the rich, heady aroma filling his nostrils, the taste of the chocolate a treat to his palate. "This is delicious."

"I know, but don't expect to find it in a coffee shop or tavern. It's priceless. Anyway, back to the bible. Some believe the monk had the help of the Devil to complete the book, and so the name has followed the book." She frowned. "Why didn't the thief take it, too, if what he wanted was something valuable?" She picked at her nail. "Someone saw me at the library the night of the murder."

"Gunne told me about that, and the mushrooms."

She looked him squarely in the eye. "A lot of people knew about my mushrooms—most of the servants, and others. I just went there to tend them at a bad time."

He nodded, smiling. "I believe you, Zofia, for what it's worth."

Her gaze softened. "That's worth a lot."

She looked away, and the moment was over. What she said

made sense, and her candor convinced him now, more than ever, that she was innocent. Surely the queen mother would think so, too.

He sipped the warm drink. The exquisite chocolate, and Zofia's friendly demeanor, turned his thoughts to more pleasant things. He decided to take a chance. "Have you decided about the dance tonight?"

She paused, and he wished he had not been so blunt. She was not some tavern maid, but a courtier, with a title of her own. "I see, Johan, you have a lot to learn about court life. Yes, I and everyone else will be there this evening. This is not like the masked ball when we had a choice. The queen has a part in the ballet, so short of being close to death, everyone will be there."

"Then perhaps you will show me some of the dance steps."

"Perhaps," she said, taking his empty cup and putting it in a basin. "Now, I must get to work. Eleanora's inquisition took most of the day, and I am in the middle of an interesting experiment."

He opened his mouth to ask, then closed it again. She chuckled. "You are learning, lutenist. No respectable alchemist shares her work, not until she is finished and has proven her theory."

He gave an exaggerated bow and walked out, wondering if he should wear his best pair of heeled shoes tonight, ones purchased from a visiting Stockholm merchant for just such an occasion.

CHAPTER SEVEN

On Wednesday evening, Johan entered the dance hall and took his place behind a curtain to the left of the stage, a spot less visible to the audience.

After tuning his lute, he waited for a nod from a flautist, and they began. The dancers appeared on cue, dressed in remarkably realistic costumes, complete with fur or feathers, claws and beaks as appropriate. Admittedly, the French ballet troupe surpassed any ballet he had ever seen, but he had only watched traveling groups, mostly Germans, who went from town to town hoping to find a suitable venue. The queen would have the best, of course, because no expense would be spared. Besides, had she not sent de la Gardie himself to practically buy the ballet troupe from under the French king's nose?

As the show proceeded, he kept his mind on the music, only half-watching the ballet with its rising sun, and later the moon. When the queen appeared, wearing a long white robe and carrying a bow, with one of the queen mother's dwarfs holding a quiver of arrows, he remembered what he had heard of the queen, and her fondness for the hunt. Of course, she would have allowed no one else to play that part.

Halfway through the performance, while the scenery was changed and the audience refilled their glasses, he sat listening to the Italian singers, meant to entertain and distract from the workers on stage. During one of the madrigals, one of the flautists missed a note, so minor that Johan knew only a few musicians might have noticed.

When the evening's ballet concluded, the assembled crowd shouted and clapped, the queen smiled at her subjects, and the dance music began, coming from a trio of young university students brought in by de la Gardie. Johan laid his lute aside and scanned the room, looking for Zofia.

Someone clutched his shoulder. He turned in the chair and faced one of the madrigal singers, recognizable by his red cravat and matching cap. "You ruined our singing," the man said. "It proves that madrigals are more properly sung with no instrumental accompaniment."

Johan, taken off guard, collected his thoughts. Wasn't this the same man who had torn the red pennant with his boot that day in the courtyard? He was sure of it. The long wavy hair, the same tone of voice. Musicians remembered voices. Johan wanted to punch him in the face, but decided now was not the time. "I thought your singing went quite well, and—"

"What would you know? I get a chance to sing, and you have to ruin it."

Johan rose from his chair. Repressed anger warmed his face. He balled his fists and was about to speak when the singer walked away, leaving Johan wondering if the man thought it was a lutenist who'd made the musical error, or if he simply wanted to pick a fight. But what did it matter? No one noticed the error, it was simply one tone off, and did not interrupt the rhythm. Johan picked up his lute and was near the door when François, the man who had befriended him that first day and warned him about Henrik's aggressive behavior, fell in step beside him. François still wore his costume, a garish yellow finished off with a wide silver belt. Yellow feathers bloomed from a red helmet. Johan struggled to suppress laughter. Collectively, the dancers made quite an impression on stage, but individually, some were quite remarkable.

François rubbed his bare arms. "I'll walk with you. I need to put on some warm clothes." The dancer removed his headpiece and pushed back his hair. "I see Henrik is after you again. Did he ever apologize for his rudeness that first day you came to the castle?"

"I did not expect an apology. Just now, though, he said I played a wrong note and ruined one of the madrigals."

"Well, if you ask me, that one is a troublemaker. He and one of the queen mother's ladies have been seen together. I wouldn't be surprised if they had something to do with the murder and theft. The queen mother's ladies have privileges other courtiers don't."

Johan made no reply. Henrik might be a suspect, if only for his aggressive attitude, but there was no solid proof. It was not unlawful to be disagreeable.

François headed for the dancers' changing room, and Johan, after storing his lute on a high shelf in his cubicle, returned to the main hall, where festivities were well underway. The queen, he noticed, was now seated in the section reserved for Her Majesty, accepting accolades from those around her. To one side sat Count de la Gardie, and on her other side, looking a bit less enthusiastic than the count, sat someone of obvious military rank. Plump and with a short neck, he nevertheless projected an air of command. His dark eyes were set close together, and his crooked nose carried a long scar. Silver badges were sewn to both his sleeves, and a gold piece hung from a chain around his neck, no doubt signifying reward for his years in service to the court. Johan leaned toward another musician. "Who sits to the right of the queen?"

The musician craned his neck. "Oh, that's the chancellor. He seldom attends a performance. Keeps to himself, but he probably felt obliged tonight, with the queen taking part."

Johan thanked the man, then spotted Zofia, sitting not far

from the queen. He waited for the next dance to begin, and walked directly to where she sat. "Will you dance the *bourrée* with me, Mademoiselle?" He waited for her reply, thinking he sounded like a *beau garçon*, though he was far from actually becoming a ladies' man. In truth, it was not his style, and he had decided long ago to simply be himself, which had worked fine until now. But then he had never met a girl like Zofia before, either.

She extended her hand. *"Mais oui, Monsieur."* She rose and took his arm, and together they joined the dancers gathering on the floor. He concentrated on the quick, skipping steps, and at first he did not notice her evident disinterest in the dance, but as they drew together, she cast a quick glance around the room. Was she wishing for another partner? He decided to be bold. "Do you not enjoy the dance?"

She circled, and met him again. "I am being watched, and need to talk to someone." Once more they drew apart, her soled shoes making clicks on the wood floor. On coming together again she leaned close. "When the next set begins, find your way to the luthier's shop. I'll meet you beneath the staircase."

He nodded, remembering Noël, the lute maker, and his warm little room by the stairwell. The music stopped, and he watched as Zofia made an excuse to one of the queen's attendants before leaving. The dance music began again, this time a stately minuet, and Johan took a cup from a tray held aloft by a passing servant. He needed to look nonchalant, though he felt anything but calm. Zofia seemed overly concerned about something, but women sometimes tended to be frightened over small things. Still, she did not seem typical, this girl who experimented with chemicals and didn't quite fit in with the other courtiers he had met so far.

He found her standing in the shadows, her head tilted to accommodate the low spandrel beneath the staircase. He offered his hand. "I know a better place—more private. Do you trust me?"

She gave him a long, hard look, then a tiny smile broke through the frown. "I don't know why, but yes."

She clasped his hand and together they hurried down the hallway to a set of back stairs leading up to the servants' rooms. After making their way through a storage area they arrived at the small window seat Johan had noticed on his first trip to this part of the castle. Gunne's window seat was larger, but the dwarf seemed to want to keep it private. He would not betray Gunne's trust.

Zofia brushed dust from the thin cushion lining the window seat. While she sat and arranged her skirts, he peeked through the cracks of the shutter. Tonight, a full moon shone on a blanket of snow, a white tapestry that covered the landscape and wrapped up the walls and over the roofs of stables and outbuildings below. He moved to the side of the window and motioned her to take advantage of the view. She looked below, then turned away, pulling her fur-lined cloak close.

"Now," he said, "what makes you think you are being watched?"

"The chancellor came to my workroom late this afternoon— only the second time in the years I have been at court. He asked silly questions, like did I enjoy my position as the court alchemist. Then he asked if my father was well." She turned to face Johan directly. "He said the queen mother wanted the gates to the castle closed—no one comes or goes—until the murderer is found. His mention of Papa made me wonder if they intend to charge him with some crime. Then he asked if I would do anything for my father. From his questions, I know he suspects me of the murder and theft. I'm increasingly worried."

"That's understandable, but right now, everyone is a suspect."

She tapped her foot. "What concerns me most is that they

might want to question my father. I wanted to ask, Johan, if you would go to Papa's house and tell him what has happened. There are ways to leave the castle without being seen, but if I were caught, they would see it as a sign that I'm warning my father, and that lends credence to their theory. Perhaps if Papa knows what to expect, he can be ready to convince them of my—of our—innocence. Will you help? I cannot ask anyone else."

Johan heard the wind blowing against the shutter, and felt icy air seeping between the wood slats. He would be risking arrest. Besides, how could any man find his way through the streets of Stockholm, let alone a stranger who knew nothing of the town? He was only now learning his way around the castle.

"The house is easy to find," she said, evidently sensing his reluctance. "His name is Otto—Otto Lindgren. And you don't have to go tonight. By tomorrow, some of this snow will be melted. Even if you are caught, they know you had nothing to do with the theft because it happened before you arrived."

He could not argue with that. "Very well, I will try."

"I will get word to the stableman. I can trust him, because I know he has visitors in his little shack from time to time— strictly against policy." She grinned. "He will give you a good horse and show you how to avoid the guards at the main castle gates. Come to my shop tomorrow and I'll tell you the way to my father's house. If you leave after dark tomorrow night, no one will see you and you should be back before dawn. Now, we should get back or they will come hunting for me." She rose and hurried away, not waiting for him to follow, which was wise. He would go to the musicians' dormitory and to bed, pleading a toothache, or too much Swedish beer. That would give him time to think about what he had agreed to do. It was a foolish venture, and might put him squarely in the midst of some palace intrigue of which he knew nothing, but he had promised the girl, and there was nothing to do now but go and hope for the best.

The stableman rubbed the horse's neck with his gloved hand. "I put extra blankets on her, but still, take it easy until she warms up."

Johan only nodded, not mentioning he had ridden a horse in cold weather more times than he wanted to remember, but it was plain to see the stableman cared about his animals, and that was reason enough to humor him. After mounting the mare, Johan glanced down the hill. With luck, he could leave the castle unseen. Trouble was, clouds obscured the moon, and he had no idea what hid beneath the layers of snow, or where the path meandered.

"You'll have no trouble at all," the stableman said. "Just head for that tree in the distance. That's the trail to follow. At the fork, stay to the right. The other goes to the main gate." His breath rose in puffy clouds as he spoke, but he seemed unmindful of the cold, and no wonder. He wore a fine fur cloak, evidently a cast-off from some appreciative nobleman. Johan's teeth chattered, but he hated to be rude, so he waited for the man to continue. "The clockmaker's daughter in town makes it up here in worse weather than this, to see her true love." He grinned up at Johan. "I know my secret's safe with you, because you're going against the rules, and if word gets out about my Hilda, I'll say you stole this horse."

Johan, taking in the man's scraggly beard and broken teeth, had trouble picturing a girl who would come to the stable in the dead of winter to visit him, but that was between her and the stableman.

Johan huddled inside his fur-lined coat, pulled the beaver hat over his ears, waved to the stableman, and started down the hill. The snow had turned to a frozen crust, but the sure-footed horse seemed to smell the road beneath. An icy wind blew snow from tree branches and stung his face. What if he missed the turn? What excuse could he offer for being out on such a night?

The horse trod on, sure-footed, ignoring night noises from beyond a copse of trees. A pack of wolves howled from somewhere deep in the woods, and the horse twitched her ears. Far down the embankment, he saw torchlight in the distance and the shape of an enclosure. The horse snorted, then veered to the right. Johan looked back, but could see no indication of a fork in the path. He'd have to trust the horse.

When they were well away from the castle grounds, he turned around, trying to get his bearings, and saw that they had left the torchlight and main gate far behind. He patted the horse's flank. She deserved a treat. The mare reminded him of the one he'd lost—proud, intelligent, patient. He blinked and blotted his eyes with his gloved hand. Must be the blowing snow.

As Johan neared the center of town he saw that the clouds had cleared. In this bright moonlight, the steeple Zofia had mentioned should be easy to find. Still, if it was covered with snow, it might be difficult to tell a steeple from a chimney.

He was about to turn around, thinking he had taken a wrong turn, when he saw the steeple, ice-encrusted and glistening. Beyond that was the row of structures on the right side of the road, as Zofia described.

The bookbinder's shop, wedged between two other shops, was half buried in snow. Smoke curled above the roofline. A little sign above the door swung merrily from its post as if to defy the blasts of winter. Johan tethered the horse beneath a lean-to between the buildings and crossed to a portal covered with snow.

He knocked on the door until it creaked open. "I'm closed for the night."

"Wait. I am Johan Sokolewski, a friend of your daughter's.

May I come in?"

The door swung wide. "Come in. What's happened to her?" The man, garbed in a nightshirt, his sleeping cap askew, grabbed Johan's shoulders.

"Nothing. She's fine." By the light of the candle the bookbinder held, Johan saw that Zofia's father was a big-boned man with a head of white hair. He wore a full beard that gave him the look of an aging scholar. On one side of his face his skin was darkly scarred. Was that from the fire? Whatever the injury was, it had stopped short of his eye. Johan gathered his wits. "Sorry to come so late, but she sent me here to talk to you." He shook snow from his cloak.

Otto motioned toward a narrow flight of steps. "Let's go upstairs where it's warm."

When they reached the upper landing, Johan hung his coat on a peg and followed the bookbinder through an open door. One glance told Johan the room belonged to a serious craftsman. Every surface was covered with evidence of the man's trade: rolls of cording, leather ties, loose sheets of vellum, and stacks of texts waiting for repair. On a side table, in neat piles, were thin planks of wood, stacks of velvet alongside cloth of gold, and gilt-edged vellum lying next to pots of glue. Evidently, Zofia's father had a thriving business going, even in winter. "So," Otto said, donning a warm robe and adding a log to the fire, "what's so important that she sent you here to talk? Is she worried about her old father? I've endured many a Stockholm winter almost this bad." He straightened, and suddenly his jaw dropped. "My God, you're her suitor, correct? You've come to ask my blessing."

Johan swallowed, ignoring the sudden feeling in his chest. "No, nothing like that." He took the cup of beer offered by his host, then sat back. While the fire crackled and burned, Johan related what he knew of the murder, the theft of the Silver

Bible, and the queen mother's investigation. "Right now Zofia is a prime suspect, as she's the only person seen near the library that night."

Otto shook his head. "Terrible thing to have happened, and right in the royal castle. Nowhere is safe now. Everything's changed since Stockholm became a major stop on the trade route. But back to the queen mother's investigation. I know her quite well," Otto said. "She never was meant to be a queen— don't quote me there. Even in her best years she was no help to the king. Did you know, when he went on campaigns, he left behind strict orders for his councillors that Eleanora was not to be involved in any decisions of government? Not many know that, except the old courtiers still around. Who are they questioning, besides Zofia?"

"They are questioning everyone, from the lowest servant to the Privy Councillors, those who were not gone with the queen on her two-day hunt. Others were at the palace in Uppsala, so they could not have committed the crime."

Johan paused, sipped his beer, and continued. "Zofia wanted me to tell you that they questioned her. In addition to being seen near the library, it seems the library cataloguer told the queen mother that you had seen the bible and said, if you had your choice of books, you would choose that one. I understand Eleanora decided that Zofia might have taken the bible for you."

Otto shook his head. "The queen mother has gone mad with grief. She should never be in charge of so serious an undertaking. Did you know she kept the king's corpse in her room for almost two years, refusing to let him be buried, ignoring the complaints about the smell? After all, she was queen, so nothing could be done. I was summoned to the castle once during that time, and made some excuse to bring the work home. The odor permeated that whole wing of the castle. That's not the worst of it. She kept his heart in a box suspended over the bed. Queen

Christina—poor little princess—had to sleep in there, beneath the heart, with her mother. It had to be hard on the child. Eleanora covered the walls with black cloths and kept candles lit, night and day. The councillors managed to send her away for a time, but when the queen came of age, one of the first things she did was to allow Eleanora back. That's why I'm not worried about Zofia. Queen Christina knows all about her mother. She understands her foibles, and tolerates her, out of respect and love. The queen would never allow anything to happen to Zofia."

Johan took a deep breath. This was harder than he'd thought. "All that is true, I'm sure, from what little I've been told, but I assure you, Zofia has cause to worry. She says she's being watched, and I fear, unless we unearth another suspect, the queen mother will become convinced that the one suspect she has is guilty. Zofia asked me to come and tell you what was happening. She believes you may be questioned too, and is earnestly worried."

Otto scratched his chin. "Hmm. That puts it in a different light. Zofia is no ordinary girl, easy to fool, like most others I know. She has always had a good head on her shoulders." He frowned and seemed to be mulling over all that Johan had told him. "I can show them my house—they can search it top to bottom—they will find no Silver Bible."

"That may not satisfy the chancellor or his assistants, who are questioning people on behalf of the guards. They even involved the town burgomaster, but the queen herself seems not interested in the matter, having delegated it to others. And now Eleanora is in charge of the inquisition."

"Inquisition? God's Grace, has it come to that?"

"Not like you would think. Eleanora only questions those who might be suspects. She has her dwarfs sitting in judgment."

"No wonder Zofia is frightened." He pushed some scraps

from the edge of a work table, then picked up a strip of fabric and wound it thoughtfully around his index finger. "I think I should go there at daybreak and talk to Eleanora. She knows me and I can remind her how long my family has served the royal court, and of Zofia's loyalty."

"You know best, I'm sure. I just came because Zofia asked me to. Beyond that, I am ignorant of court procedures."

"You didn't say where you came from. You're not a Swede."

"From Warsaw."

Otto narrowed his gaze. "I won't ask you why you are here. Some things are better left unsaid."

Johan made no reply, except to thank Otto for the beer. He had done what he could for Zofia, and he wanted to get back before he was missed. In spite of these long winter nights, dawn was sure to come.

Riding back, Johan felt drops hitting his hat, and realized he was in the beginning of an ice storm. The horse plodded on, careful and sure-footed. The pale light of dawn shone from the east. As he approached the castle he saw that the torches around the perimeter were lit, flooding the courtyard with light, as if anything but wild beasts would be out in this weather. He arrived at the stable soaking wet, with no feeling in his hands. "Give her extra rations," he said.

"I always do," the stableman mumbled. "Finest horse in the stable, to my mind. But Zofia asked me to let you ride the mare, and Zofia's my friend."

Johan ran his hand down the mare's muzzle, then turned and headed toward a back entrance to the castle, almost slipping on an icy stone path leading from the garden. Now, above the snow, a lone spruce guarded the useless patch of ground, but come spring, the cook would be picking dill to flavor his fish dishes. Johan knocked on the wooden door. Right now, spring seemed years away.

As he stood shivering, a latch slid back. The door opened a crack and from inside came a childish voice. "All the food's gone until tomorrow."

"Let me in. I am Johan Sokolewski, the queen's lute player."

After a long pause, during which Johan was tempted to push his way in, the door opened wide and he stepped inside, coming face to face with a boy of about five. That would be one of the cook's sons. Thank goodness the rest of the kitchen staff was occupied, judging from the smell of burning wood and baking bread. That eliminated any possibility of being questioned. Ignoring the temptation to warm himself by the blazing hearth, he hurried away and headed for the staircase, taking the steps two at a time and hoping the cook would not report a man who looked suspicious, coming in from a ride in weather like this.

CHAPTER EIGHT

After a few hours' sleep, Johan rose to find himself alone in the dormitory. His stomach rumbled, but this late, he'd have to go to the kitchen and hope the cook was in a good mood.

He dressed, taking care not to rub his wool clothes against his aching hands. Even though he had worn gloves for the ride to the bookbinder's house, Johan knew the combination of icy winds and dampness had done serious damage. When the numbness changed to pain, combined with an itchy red rash that covered his hands, he wondered how he would ever play the lute again—certainly not for days. After locating the physician's rooms and learning the man was ill himself and not to be disturbed, he made his way to Zofia's room. He tapped on the door, dreading to ask her what he must, but with the physician unable to see him, he had no choice.

She opened the door. "Johan, come in. Did the stableman give you a good horse? I asked for the mare. Did you talk to my father last night?"

"Yes, and yes. I rode the mare, and I believe your father is coming here. He's convinced he can talk sense to the queen mother and things will be fine."

"He underestimates her will," Zofia said. "She has even questioned the head cook, because he is always grumbling about his small room next to the kitchen, saying with all the wealth the Swedish government has they should give their cook better accommodations." She went back to peering into a glass on her work table. "Amazing," she said, "that something that looks so simple is so complex. Come here. Careful of the glass. It is a priceless lens."

Trying not to think of his aching hands, he joined her, curious as to the source of her excitement. He looked through the glass at the bones of a fish, astounded that the fish bones, viewed through the lens, appeared much larger than they actually were. "An impressive piece of equipment," he said. "What experiment are you conducting?"

"None, not now, only observing. It's interesting to compare skeletons. See here, the vertebral column. The ribs are attached to the spine." She looked up. "Sorry. I forget others may not be interested in a pile of tiny bones." She smiled and pointed to a stool. "Please, sit down. I have a few beans left. Would you like some chocolate?"

He shook his head. "I doubt I could hold a cup in these hands, but thank you."

She leaned forward. "Hmm. A good case of frostbite, but it could be worse. I can give you a salve to relieve the pain, but you have to stay away from extreme cold for a time. Don't play your lute for a while. Give your hands a rest."

He nodded, wondering how he could explain his frostbitten hands should anyone notice, because no man in his right mind would leave shelter in weather like this. "No worry on that account. They hurt too much to play my lute, and I have no intention of riding a slow horse through Stockholm again, not until spring."

She giggled, and he knew, at least for now, the fear for her safety, the feeling of being watched, had begun to ease. She reached to a shelf and took down a jar. When she opened the lid, the pungent smell of goose grease overpowered the light lemon scent he'd come to associate with Zofia.

"Thanks for the salve," he said, rubbing it onto his hands.

"I'll go now and leave you alone with your work." He looked at his greasy hands. "Can we save the chocolate for another time?"

She nodded, engrossed again in examining the fish bones, and he let himself out.

A short way from her door he saw Gunne heading his way, walking as fast as his two legs could propel him. He wore brown breeches, and bright green hose that matched his doublet. A fur-lined cape flowed from his shoulders. He looked the perfect miniature of a well-dressed courtier. "Thank goodness," Gunne said. "I have been looking everywhere for you. The queen mother wants you at once. Her visitor mentioned your name, and they are waiting. Come, I know a short way back." He led Johan into a darkened cubicle and pushed on a panel that opened to reveal a steep set of stairs. "This place used to be a fortress, about three hundred years ago. They built the palace around the fortress, so this part of the castle is like it used to be—with a lot of hiding places." He chuckled. "I, and others like myself, have discovered places no one else knows about because we can squeeze into tight spots too small for people like you." He paused near an opening and pointed. "Like that, for instance. That tunnel leads directly past a dungeon and on to the canal, but we're not going there."

Johan shivered. He had heard tales of prisoners being drowned with a rising tide. It was something he did not want to pursue. "How far to Eleanora's quarters?"

"We're almost there." Gunne opened another door. "Through here, and her rooms are to the right. They are waiting in the antechamber."

Johan followed Gunne through an arched opening and into a room filled with ladies and dwarfs. When the women caught sight of Gunne, they grew quiet, settling themselves near the queen mother like nesting hares, while the dwarfs sat down on stools, strategically placed in two official-looking rows. Johan suppressed a smile. The scene looked like something from a stage play.

It was then he saw Zofia's father, sitting to one side. Otto Lindgren had wasted no time in coming here, but why were uniformed guards standing on either side of the man? Did Eleanora believe the bookbinder capable of harming her person, or was this protocol, since he had come unannounced?

She leaned forward as Johan approached. "Well, you've finally come."

He bowed low. "I'm sorry, Your Highness, I was—"

"Never mind. You are here now. I want the jurors to hear all of this, and you, too, since you are involved." She met Johan's eyes, and he had the feeling the old queen knew more than people gave her credit for—either that, or she had loyal spies. "It is not, however, a formal trial. Now, Otto, tell us again—more slowly, please, so my scribe can make notes. Johan, you may have a seat."

Johan sat on a nearby bench and listened while Zofia's father recounted his story, of how he had been summoned to repair a small tear on the corner of the Devil's Bible. "I spotted the Silver Bible beside it, and inquired about it to the librarian. And yes, I did say I would prefer having the smaller book, but I meant no harm. I swear on all that's holy that I never would ask my daughter to steal. Even if I had, she is not a thief and would have disobeyed me before taking something not her own."

Eleanora tilted her head. "Otto Lindgren, did you know your daughter grows mushrooms?"

"Mushrooms? Why, no. But long ago I ceased wondering about each new project she undertook. She has an inquisitive mind. Why do you ask?"

Eleanora yawned. "No special reason." She drew her brows together, looked down at her hands, and studied her nails. "Explain to me again how you learned of these criminal acts within the castle. You have a home in the city, and the castle grounds have been closed to visitors since the book's disappearance."

Johan swallowed. He had forgotten to tell Otto how to handle that. Now Eleanora would know that the new lute player had directly disobeyed a royal command. In spite of Zofia's assurances to the contrary, he wondered now why he had agreed to the idea so readily.

Otto looked directly at the queen mother. "As I told you before, your court musician came there to tell me. I implore you, do not punish him." He turned to Johan. "I'm sorry—I did not understand that—"

She held up her hand and leaned forward, looking again directly at Johan. "Is all of this true?"

"Yes." Johan shifted his weight on the bench, his mind racing. "I supposed your rule did not apply to someone who came here after the theft." It was a weak excuse, but the only one he could think of, and he had no clear way of knowing it was not actually true.

"Bah. That's an excuse." She narrowed her eyes. "Still, I suppose no harm has been done." She looked at the gallery of dwarfs. "What say you?"

"No harm has been done," they said in unison.

Johan realized he had been holding his breath, and took a deep one. Did Eleanora's jury pronounce a man guilty in unison also?

"Very well," the queen mother said. "Otto Lindgren, because of your long service to the family, I am releasing you now, and I will give this matter of your daughter further thought. You may leave, but the lute player remains." She turned to one of her women. "See that Monsieur Lindgren is given a meal and a room for the night. Dear Gustav, God rest his blessed soul, would never forgive me were I to turn an old friend out on a day like this. I feel another storm coming because my gout is acting up."

As the doors closed behind the bookbinder, the queen leaned to speak to one of her women, then turned back to Johan. "What is your name?"

"Johan Sokolewski, Your Highness."

"That's right, you told me before." She rubbed her forehead, and Johan experienced a moment of pity for the queen mother, who appeared to be a lonely and confused woman.

"I saw you dancing with the queen's alchemist," she said. "To me, they are all charlatans. And I've always feared magic and such. However, I want to be fair in all this. How well do you know the girl?"

"She is only a friend," he said, marveling at the woman's quick recovery from her memory lapse.

Eleanora leaned back and seemed to be considering the matter of the court alchemist. In the growing silence, Johan heard a click followed by a low roar. He turned and saw that the sound had come from a gilt lion clock nearby. He had noticed it earlier when the lion's eyes moved with the seconds, but now, with the lion quiet again, and the lengthening silence, Johan began to sweat. What exactly was going through the queen mother's mind?

She cleared her throat. "As you know, lute player, the girl is the prime suspect. Everything points to her—she was seen near the crime scene, and she has a motive for the theft—to please her father, whom I happen to know raised the girl alone after her mother died. He almost lost his life while saving her from a fire. It is only natural she would want to repay him in some way. But I have a proposition for you, Monsieur Sokolewski. Find the bible and return it to me within twenty days, beginning today. If you do, the girl will not be punished—at least for the theft. If I were you, I would begin looking in her room, where

91

the book is probably hidden until she has a chance to get it to her father. She allows few people in her workroom, not even the chancellor, except under royal command. I saw you two dancing together. I believe you are more than friends, so she will never suspect you. If you find the bible, I believe we also would have the person who murdered the goldsmith." She gave him a meaningful look. "You may want to coordinate with the palace guards. They are more interested in the murder, of course, and might help you in your investigation. You are free to interview anyone. Just don't break any rules."

Johan rose from the bench. "Your Majesty, I must object. I know nothing of coordinating a murder investigation with your royal guards. In all likelihood you would never get the answer you seek. Besides, I can hardly break into a lady's work room and examine her belongings." He had a quick vision of the fragile fish bones and Zofia's carefully arranged books. No, this was too much to ask. He and Zofia were *not* more than friends, but even if they were, she would not take kindly to him going into her laboratory. She would consider him a traitor, and rightly so, but how to explain this to Eleanora?

Eleanora cleared her throat. "If you need help, you can talk to the guards. Begin there. I'll leave it to you how to test the girl's innocence. Now, you are dismissed."

Test her innocence? That was something he would have to work out later. For now, he was being led toward the door and out of the queen's chambers. Perhaps he could sort all this out in a way that made sense. First, he should talk with the palace guards who had actually witnessed the death scene. Could he persuade them to do the investigating?

Johan dressed warmly and headed for the headquarters of the castle guards, a one-story stone building on a section of the grounds that served as barracks for the guardsmen. To avoid looking foolish, he struggled to organize his thoughts. What questions should he ask about the crime?

He tried to remember the questions used by a physician on the battlefield. *When did this happen? Where are you wounded? How much did you bleed?*

Suddenly he was in front of the barracks. He could only try to sound official and hope for the best. Near the entrance, he stomped snow from his boots and walked inside.

A slim guard dressed in full military regalia rose from behind a desk. A shock of black hair fell in waves to just below his ears. He raised one eyebrow. "You have business here?"

Johan gingerly removed his gloves from his sore hands, then took off his fur cap. "I was sent by the queen mother to speak with the commander."

The guard's gaze raked Johan from head to toe, as if judging the validity of what he'd just heard. "Hmm. Yes, well, I'll tell him you're here." He picked up a ledger. "Name, please?"

"Johan Sokolewski, the queen's lutenist." He watched the guard disappear down the hall, surprised at how easily the title slipped from his lips. It had a refined taste about it, but absolutely nothing to do with his reason for coming here today.

The guard returned. "This way. The commander is expecting you. Seems the queen mother got word to him earlier."

Johan followed the guard down a wide hallway. Rooms opened off the corridor, and Johan caught a glimpse of life in the royal barracks. Men at game tables, others lounging in chairs, two playing with a basket of puppies. Who was guarding the castle? Were they purely ceremonial? If so, could they solve a murder?

A door near the end of the hall bore a nameplate: Commander Osterberg. The black-haired guard knocked once and opened the door. When Johan entered the room, a large curly-haired mastiff sniffed his boots. The commander nodded to the guard, who left, closing the door behind him. Johan noted the braid on the man's uniform and paused, taken aback by the vision before him—a Polish *kapral* on horseback, dressed in a dark cape, gold braid on cuffs and shoulders, shouting commands to his scattered army. Johan shook his head, ridding himself of the image. The man behind the desk was a royal guard, not some Polish officer atop a steed.

The commander stood and indicated a chair. "You look like you've seen a ghost." He chuckled and called the dog to his side. "No need being afraid of my dog. Eva only attacks on command." He shoved some papers aside and sat, leaning back, weaving his hands together over his sizeable stomach. A short, neatly trimmed grey beard covered his chin. Wisps of grey-blond hair partially covered a shiny dome. His ruddy face, pockmarked, gave him the look of a battle-scarred veteran. Perhaps that was why he commanded the royal guards.

Johan sat. "I've come about the murder. The queen mother—"

"I know why you're here." He lowered his hand to pet the dog. "How can I help?"

Johan crossed his legs. "I'm not sure. I think she wants us to work together to solve the crime."

Commander Osterberg chuckled. "And she expects a musician to solve a crime that so far has baffled all of us?" He reached for a small silver box, tapped the top, and opened the lid. He withdrew a pinch of sweet-smelling snuff from the box, rolled his fingers together, then sniffed it at each nostril. He shoved the little box toward Johan. "Have some."

Johan shook his head. His nose already ached from the unfamiliar sting of the icy northern winter. Snuff would probably finish off his nose for good. "Did you actually see the murder scene?"

The commander smiled. "Right to business, eh? Very well. I'll tell you what I know, not that it will do anyone any good. The librarian sent a servant to alert us. It was early dawn. My manservant woke me, and after rousing three of my guardsmen, we hurried over there. I always make mental notes. One candle still burned, likely lit by the goldsmith when the others burned low. Wax had hardened on the base of all the candles, so the victim was likely dead a few hours before being discovered. The victim lay slumped over his desk. His glasses had fallen onto the desk and one lens was broken. Poor fellow, his head rested on some of the very same coins he'd been hired to catalogue.

"I had two of the guards remove the body, but it was beginning to stiffen. By then, servants were rising to tend the fires. I stayed with the remaining guard while he cleaned up the place as best he could."

"The victim's clothing? Was it bloodied?"

"Of course. He'd bled profusely where the dagger went in."

"Notice anything unusual? Blood elsewhere?"

"On the edge of the desk, of course, from where he leaned forward."

"His clothing? Do you have that?"

"Yes, but there's nothing unusual. Just the blood, like I said."

"May I see the clothing?"

"Sure, unless it's already been burned with the refuse. Come with me." He rose slowly from the chair, easing his bulk away from the desk. The mastiff rose from its bed of woolen blankets and ambled out behind its master. Johan followed, closing the door behind him.

A storage room at the other end of the barracks held the bloody clothes, wrapped in a burlap bag. Johan pulled the garments out and tried not to breathe in the stench. As the commander had said, blood had dripped from the wound onto the shirt, soaking it through, and onto the gold-colored waistcoat. Johan held the waistcoat aloft, turning it in his hands, examining all the fabric—

for what? He had no idea.

The commander took a step back. "As you see, the killer knew what to do. Straight to the heart."

Johan continued with his examination. Even an illiterate soldier knew where to aim a dagger. He was about to return the soiled clothing to the bag when he noticed, on the left shoulder of the cape, some traces of blood. How would they have gotten there if the victim fell forward? Making a mental note of what he'd seen, he stuffed the clothing into the bag.

The commander laid the bag aside. "As you see, it was definitely a murder. My theory is that whoever stole the bible murdered the goldsmith—either before or after the theft. That's pretty clear."

Johan nodded. "Yes, I suppose, though so far there's no connection. It could be an unusual coincidence. What do you propose we do next?"

The commander arched his brows and blinked. "We? I've done what I could. I identified the victim. He has no living kin, but the queen wants to give him a decent burial. After all, he was one of the town's most respected merchants. As for the bible theft, from what Eleanora said, you're in charge of that. I made my report. While a goldsmith may have plenty of enemies, I think this murder is a theft gone wrong. So you see, my hands are tied. Find the thief and you'll find the murderer. It's all in your hands—yours and Eleanora's." The commander chuckled.

Johan grimaced. He disliked the whole affair. Shouldn't he be garnering clues from all this information? But what did he know about solving murders? Nothing at all.

Before talking to the commander, Johan had hoped he might be assigned as an assistant in the investigation, but it was clear now a musician was solely in charge of finding the murderer. No one else seemed interested that an innocent might be tried for a crime based on the loosest of evidence.

After putting on his hat and coat, Johan slipped his hands into his gloves. In spite of the salve, his skin was still swollen and sore. He could not play the lute with hands like his, not until the skin on his fingers healed. Now was as good a time as any to begin looking for the criminal—or criminals—which would involve learning more about everyone in the palace. He would need help, someone he could trust, and someone who knew his way around.

CHAPTER NINE

Returning from his visit with the commander of the guards, Johan decided there was no time to waste in seeking out the help he needed. He could not very well barge into Eleanora's rooms and demand to speak with Gunne. Still, there was one place he might find the dwarf. Johan took the steps two at a time.

Gunne sat in the window alcove, book in hand. He looked up at Johan's approach. "I'm learning to read," Gunne said. "Eleanora gave me permission, and Sigrid, one of the ladies-in-waiting to the queen mother, is teaching me. She's a weird one, that one is, always telling Eleanora how uncaring people are, and how they should respect the queen mother more, but Sigrid is nice enough to me."

Johan's thoughts went back to that first meeting with the queen mother. Sigrid was the tall girl who had treated him with little respect. Still, some people needed to put others down to elevate their own sense of importance. Besides, she must have a good side. Gunne seemed to like her.

Gunne crossed his ankles and continued. "I have a collection of amber, and Sigrid has her eye on one of the stones, payment for the lessons." He patted the bench. "Sit down. This is a book of essays by Christine de Pisan. She was an astrologer's daughter, brought up in France. The essays aren't difficult to read, but Sigrid wants the first two pages memorized. Want to hear a passage?"

Johan sat and listened politely, and when Gunne was about

to begin another page, Johan spoke up. "I need help, Gunne. The queen mother gave me an impossible assignment. I don't know how to begin looking for a murderer."

Gunne laid a satin ribbon between the pages of the book and closed it. "Better you give up this idea of being a sleuth. Go to Eleanora. Plead. Tell her you are a musician." He stuffed a loose pillow behind his back. "As for the missing bible, with time, some other crisis will arise and all will be forgotten. Let the authorities handle the murder."

Johan shook his head. "I can't. You heard Eleanora. She has it in her head that Zofia stole the bible. Zofia's also a murder suspect, and until that is proven wrong, both she and her father are under suspicion. I have twenty days to free Zofia. The queen mother dumped it squarely in my lap—find the perpetrator, or Zofia will be arrested. Eleanora has no intention of contacting the authorities." He shook his head. "To think I came all this way to escape the endless strife in my own country, and I find the same in a court across the Baltic Sea."

Gunne rubbed the leather binding of his book, looking thoughtful.

Johan tensed. Would Gunne refuse to help? Without the dwarf's knowledge of the court, there was no way Johan could solve this mystery. "I need to ask you something. You've sat through the queen mother's inquisitions. Do you have any idea who the murderer might be?"

Gunne grinned. "And what was the criminal's motive?" He laughed and slapped his knee. "Both good questions with no answers."

Johan considered Gunne's words, given in jest, but truthful, nonetheless. There were more questions than answers, and the list of suspects could include anyone in the palace that night. "I'm thinking, Gunne, that the place to begin is to first decide who was here that particular evening, why they might want the book, and why they might have killed a man who had no obvious connection to the court." He crossed his arms, contemplating the task ahead. "Is there a way of finding out who was away with the queen?"

"I already asked," Gunne said. "I knew you'd need help, unless I could persuade you to back out of this assignment, and you're probably correct. The queen mother would not entertain such a request." He covered his legs with the folds of his cloak. "The Marshall keeps a record of who accompanies the queen, so it was a simple matter of elimination. The other courtiers were here. Most of the servants were with her retinue, as always happens when she goes to the Uppsala palace." He reached inside his vest and pulled out a paper. "Here you are. These people were all at the palace that evening. There are a lot of suspects."

Johan frowned at the list of names, then leaned against the side of the alcove. "This is foolish. You have the queen mother's name here, and Zofia."

Gunne smiled. "Of course Eleanora isn't a real suspect. She's clamoring to find the thief who stole her book."

Johan tapped the paper. "And Zofia? Surely you don't think she's guilty." He swallowed back a new feeling of unease. For that matter, what grounds were there to dismiss either Gunne or Zofia from the list of suspects? Was he being naïve, and simply believing what he wanted to believe?

Gunne shrugged. "I only gave you the names. You can decide who to investigate."

Johan folded the list. "Can you picture Zofia stabbing a man?"

Gunne studied his nails. "Mind you, I'm not accusing anyone, but I feel obliged to tell you what I know, especially since you've involved me in this escapade."

"Of course. Tell me anything that comes to mind."

Gunne pulled his knees to his chest. He puffed his cheeks,

looking uncomfortable with what he had to say. "I know you're fond of the queen's alchemist. She's knowledgeable and clever and has a thirst for learning." He paused and rubbed his legs.

Johan leaned forward. "Go ahead. Say what's on your mind."

"Well, a man's been murdered. We should consider this from every angle."

"So help me, Gunne, out with it."

Gunne drew his brows together. "I was reminded of something this morning by Sigrid, my reading teacher. She rides a horse fairly well, by the way, and took Zofia's place with the queen when she went to Uppsala palace. Zofia said she was coming down with something and begged off. That's why she was here the night of the murder, when ordinarily she would have accompanied the queen."

Johan tensed. Where was this leading? "You were saying, Sigrid reminded you—"

"Oh, yes. She reminded me that Zofia might have knowledge of exactly where to put a dagger in a man's chest. Months back, a renowned expert came to Uppsala to perform a dissection. All medical students were invited to watch and learn, and somehow Zofia found out about the exhibition." Gunne shrugged. "Quite possibly the queen told her, knowing of Zofia's interest in all things scientific. Queen Christina follows her father's generous endowment policies and may in fact have been the one responsible for bringing the man to Uppsala."

Johan gave an audible sigh. "I don't see what this has to do with our problem."

"Let me finish. Very late on the night of the medical exhibition, a servant saw Zofia entering a side door to the palace. Zofia probably thought everyone was asleep. She headed for her room. On the way, she removed the man's hat and cloak that she'd worn, pulled off a wig, and went into her room. Months later she revealed to one of the queen's ladies that she had witnessed the dissection. I guess she figured enough time had passed and no one would care. Soon news flew through the castle that the queen's alchemist had watched the entire presentation disguised as one of the medical students. Women, of course, would not have been admitted."

Johan turned his gaze to the scene below. Rivulets of melting snow furrowed the stable grounds. A farrier sat on a stump, dangerously close to a stallion's powerful leg as he shod the great horse. Gunne was trying to say that Zofia should be considered as a suspect. Trouble was, both Zofia and Gunne might be suspects. Johan grimaced. To be fair, Johan needed proof of their innocence, at least in his own mind. He'd have to devise a test of some kind.

He shifted his weight and continued, feeling disloyal to the dwarf. "I saw the victim's clothing," Johan said. "The guard commander described the scene. The goldsmith's head was on some of the coins. His glasses had come off, and one lens was broken. There was a spot of blood on the left shoulder of his cape. Wouldn't that indicate it came from the killer's hands—or his blade as he withdrew it? So the killer approached from behind, as the commander said."

"Now you're thinking like a first-rate policeman." Gunne chuckled.

Johan gave the dwarf a half-smile. "Knowing how the crime was committed gets us no closer to knowing the killer's name. And that brings us to the next issue. Who might want the bible, and why. We know Eleanora's suspicions about Zofia. What other reasons would someone have to steal the book?"

Gunne straightened his legs and rubbed his knees. "Like any treasure, the bible had two values—one, its age and history, its intrinsic value to a collector who simply wants to own it, and two, what it could be sold or traded for. So it could have been a collector, or a thief looking for a way to get quick money. Thus the conundrum. If not for the murder and Eleanora's obsession with the Silver Bible, the theft would be forgotten by now. Why, at state banquets, silver and even glass goblets go missing, and no one gives it a second thought. Eleanora, I think, somehow connects the bible to her husband's kingship. She insists it was his leadership that finally ended the long war—and she's right, to some extent." Gunne frowned, drawing his brows together, looking for all the world like a thoughtful old man, even a scholar, and continued. "Most of the men who looted the Prague castle and brought the treasures back to Sweden were appointed by King Gustav. Sigrid says all the credit and all the treasure should go to the old queen, since King Gustav was dead by then."

Sigrid again. Johan remembered the tall lady-in-waiting standing beside the queen, the way she listened intently to poor Otto's questioning. But she was gone to the Uppsala palace with the queen the night of the murder.

Gunne climbed down from the bench. "It's late, and time for supper. Let me know what you decide to do and how you want to proceed."

Johan's heart sank. The task before him was better left to other men, but he'd accepted the challenge. There was nothing to do but go forward. Beginning tomorrow, he would approach this one step at a time, nipping away at the list of suspects until there was only one.

Johan sat in the ballet hall, watching the dance master struggle through the afternoon rehearsal, preparing for next week's ballet. Johan's mind, though, was on the problem at hand. He'd enlisted Gunne's help, convinced that the dwarf had no connection to the murder, but what proof did he have? True, the dwarfs had been reported to be sleeping that night, but could one have sneaked out? Why? Gunne had access to books in the royal library, so why steal? Eleanora was right. Gunne could not have committed the murder. Short as the dwarf was, there was no way he could have gotten high enough to pierce the man's heart with a blade—not without a stool, which would have drawn attention to his presence, to say nothing of the pre-planning required for such a venture. That fact, coupled with the guard's statement that no one had left the dwarfs' sleeping area that fateful Sunday night, were solid evidence of Gunne's innocence. Johan crossed his arms, relieved that his friend was above suspicion, and that his trust in the dwarf had finally and firmly been validated.

As if summoned by good thoughts, Gunne approached, wearing a worried frown. "Here you are. I have some news you'll not want to hear, but best you learn it from me. Zofia has been taken from her workshop and is being held in isolation, with visitors only allowed at set times. I checked. If you want to see her, you have a half hour to wait—until three. That's about the time Eleanora will waken, too." He sat beside Johan. "I have other news—none good. Eleanora has dismissed all of us dwarfs from jury duty. She's evidently confident she has the murderer." He patted Johan's arm. "I have to go now. Sorry to be the bearer of bad news."

Johan thanked his friend and returned to his own thoughts. If only there was some way to eliminate Zofia as a suspect. While he pondered and rejected a series of possible tests that would prove her innocence, his thoughts were interrupted by seeing a familiar figure standing in the wings. As the rehearsal progressed, he realized the figure was the same man who had accused him of ruining the madrigal singing by playing a wrong note, the man who had purposely stepped on the pennant that day in the courtyard—Henrik.

Johan leaned to speak with a costumed dancer sitting not far away, evidently part of the second act. "Isn't that the madrigal singer, near the wings?"

The dancer tucked a strand of hair behind one ear. "He does sing, sometimes. Henrik is actually a stagehand, but has a fair enough voice, and fills in when someone is sick. He hangs around the stage a lot, even off duty. Seems to enjoy watching the ballet—or maybe aspires to join the troupe. I have seen him practicing the steps, when he thinks no one is watching."

The dance master shouted, "All right. Take a break." Johan rose, reminded of the hour. It was time to visit Zofia, and she would be hoping for good news, something he could not bring.

He made his way downstairs, dreading what he might find. Would she be in a cell next to murderers and thieves? By the time he reached the corridor leading to the dungeon, he wondered what he could say to comfort her. He was about to enter a dark hall when two guards rose from a table, abandoning their board game for the moment. "What is your business here?"

"I have come to visit the court astrologer," he said, hoping the title might remind them she was no ordinary serving girl but a royal appointee, which might allow him more time with her. "I understand she's being held here, and there were certain hours—"

"They took her away."

Oh no, not yet. Would she be punished without a trial? Were they so uncivilized as to find a prisoner guilty on such slim evidence? He opened his mouth to demand her whereabouts and was interrupted by one of the guards, who had returned to his seat and moved a game piece. "They came earlier and took her to a room in the west wing. I think she's locked up near the queen mother's ladies." The other man took his turn on the board, and Johan knew he was being dismissed.

Once in the west wing, he stopped a chambermaid and asked about Zofia. "She's in the end room," the girl said. "There's a guard outside, but he'll let you in."

A few minutes later, after listening to visitors' rules and writing his name on a list, Johan waited while the guard unlocked the door.

The sight of Zofia standing alone in this sparsely furnished room shocked Johan, even though the room was the size of a small bedchamber. A cot in one corner was covered in linens. A porcelain bowl sat atop a wood chest, next to a small stool. A chamber pot in the far corner was half hidden by a curtain. Zofia greeted him with a wan smile and sat on the bed. "Have a seat," she said, pointing to the stool.

He sat, feeling uncomfortable in so personal a space, alone with her. She, on the other hand, seemed not to notice. He said the first thing that came to mind. "Gunne got word to me. I went to the cell, but you were gone. Tell me what happened."

"They came early this morning to my workshop and took me to that horrid cell. I was later brought here. One of the guards said Queen Christina had intervened, else I would still be in the dungeon. I saw a rat larger than Pepe, the queen's favorite dog." She shivered.

It crossed his mind to console her, to hold her in his arms. Then he remembered where he was and who she was. His daring slipped away, as if he had lost it somewhere in the Baltic. To make a brazen move would never do. He would only drive her away. "I'm sorry about all this, Zofia."

She shrugged. "So far, they feed me well and see to my needs, but it's maddening, sitting here, when I could be doing something productive." She leaned forward. "Thank goodness Gunne saw what was happening and got word to you. Now, I have a favor to ask."

Not another journey in the snow. "Yes, Zofia. How can I help?"

"Go to my workshop. You won't need keys. The lock does not work properly and I have asked about getting it fixed, but the queen's workmen are kept very busy. I was told they were even enlisted to help build some stage machinery. You'll have no trouble getting in if you just push hard on the door. Once inside, go past my workbench and in the far back of the room, on the second shelf, you'll find some papers. Don't let anyone see you. I don't want people getting the idea they can go in when I'm not there. I'd be so obliged if you bring the papers here, along with a quill. That way I can work on something and the time will go faster."

He swallowed. Why would someone facing punishment want the time to go faster? Did she even know that Eleanora had put an amateur in charge of proving her innocence? He decided she deserved to know that. "Did anyone tell you that the queen mother put me in charge of the murder investigation?"

Her jaw dropped. "You? Why?"

"I have no idea, except she said you and I were friends. Perhaps she thought an outsider—a newcomer like me—might be more fair."

"Fair? There's nothing fair about this."

"I know," he said, trying to calm her. She was getting more agitated by the minute.

She rose from the bed. "Her reasoning is crazy. And now she has half the court believing I am a murderer." Her eyes glistened with tears.

"Hardly that, Zofia. Besides, you said that Queen Christina knows you are innocent."

She passed in front of him, and the scent of lemon wafted through the air. "I said the queen trusts me. That is different, and besides, she is not interested in all this. She is only interested in her hunts, the next ballet, and studying ancient languages. Queen Christina knows that her mother's mind is not what it should be, but out of respect for Eleanora, the queen will not interfere in all this. So you see, I'm no better off than the lowliest cook's helper." She sat back down.

Johan licked his lips. Did he dare make a suggestion? "Then if I were you, I would open the laboratory for inspection. Give the chancellor a chance to see for himself—you have nothing to hide."

She pushed both fists into the linen bedcovers. "Never. I will never allow anyone to poke and prod through my workshop. No alchemist shares his work, and I am not about to be the first." She leaned forward, her eyes large, focused on his. "Do you think I have the bible hidden somewhere? Do you think I'm a murderer?"

"No, Zofia. I only thought that would put an end to the conjecture."

She sighed and shook her head. "You do not understand. Eleanora will never quit until the bible is returned to its rightful place."

Johan considered her words. She was right, of course. From the little he knew of Eleanora, one thing was clear: she did not intend to let the issue be forgotten. And by arresting Zofia, Eleanora had made it impossible for Johan to avoid the task she had assigned him.

Unable to think of words to comfort Zofia, and knowing she waited for an answer to her request, Johan rose from the stool. "I'll do as you wish, though they won't let me back to see you until tomorrow, so I'll bring the papers then."

She gave him a wide smile and he left the room, feeling helpless and hopeless and racking his brain for what to do next, but the harder he tried, the bigger the void got—and she was depending on him.

Having decided to get the papers now and keep them in the pocket of his breeches until his visit with her the next day, he made his way to Zofia's workroom. Nightfall had darkened the hallway, as the season of Advent was approaching, with shorter days and colder nights than ever Warsaw had seen. He reached the door to the laboratory, glanced over his shoulder to make sure no one was around, and twisted the latch. He gave a push, as she had instructed, and the door opened. A candlestick stood near the glass contraption where she had studied the fish skeleton, and after closing the door, he groped his way to the candle, pulled the small tin from the pouch at his waist, and cursed. The char-cloth felt damp. After struggling several minutes, a spark caught and he lit the candle. Holding the light aloft, he made his way to the back shelves. Was that a rustle in the shadows? He froze in place, then decided he had imagined the sound. He retrieved the papers, turned, and retraced his steps. A few paces later he heard it again, sure this time he was not alone. *Best to keep walking.* He passed a work table, his eyes on the door.

Someone jumped him from behind. He struggled, wrestling with his attacker, and felt a sharp blow to his head. The candle dropped to the floor. A campfire's glow and the moans of wounded comrades drifted through his mind before he sank into darkness.

CHAPTER TEN

Johan dreamed he was in the hold of a ship, on the open, quiet sea. Where were the deckhands? Was he floating? He rubbed his fingers on linen. This was a bed, not a wood deck. He opened his eyes. Angels drifted overhead, moving among the rafters. He clutched the sides of the bed to steady himself and realized he was in an unfamiliar room.

When he turned his head to the side, Gunne's face swam into view. Johan closed his eyes and images rushed past. Stockholm. The palace. The queen mother. The blond-haired girl—what was her name? Zania. No, Zofia. She'd sent him to her workshop for papers. "Gunne, is that you?"

"Yes. I'm here. You took quite a blow to your head. What were you doing in Zofia's workroom anyway? Never mind. Just lie still. The doctor said you would be fine if you ever woke up, and you're awake."

Johan opened his eyes again. The room had stopped moving and the angels had obediently taken their places against the plaster. He tried to think . . . remembered leaving Zofia's little cell, walking in to get the papers . . . "Gunne," he called, listening to his own strained voice.

"You should rest."

"The papers. I had Zofia's papers."

"You're lucky the papers caught fire. That's how we found you. A guard passed by, saw the open door and smelled something burning. He went inside and sounded the alarm.

110

How did you fall?"

"I didn't. Someone else was in the room. I lit a candle and found the papers. I struggled with someone. Probably dropped the candle in the scuffle."

"And your attacker ran before the papers caught fire. When they found you, no one else was in the room."

Johan turned his head at the sound of footsteps crossing the threshold. Someone had come. The footfalls stopped at the bedside. "So, my patient has wakened. I am the court physician."

With effort, Johan focused his eyes. Gunne sat on an upholstered bench. The doctor set his case in Gunne's lap, then straightened, looming tall over the bed. He leaned close to examine Johan's eyes. "I see you have a friend to keep you company." He straightened, still peering down at Johan. "What happened to your hands?"

"Frostbite, but they're better now. Almost healed."

"Yes, I can see that. While the new skin grows, stay away from wet and cold." He rummaged in his case, while a startled Gunne looked on. The doctor retrieved a blue bottle and handed it to Gunne. "If he complains of pain in his head, have him drink this." He turned back to Johan. "In a few days the lump will be gone and you will be as good as new." The doctor closed his case and took it from Gunne's lap. "Come and find me if he goes to sleep and you cannot waken him."

When the physician was out the door, Gunne leaned forward. "No bedside manner, but Eleanora swears he's the best doctor in Sweden. When I told her I had a sick friend, she sent for him. I figured if you went to the infirmary, the whole castle would know how this happened, though word may get around anyway."

The room had quit spinning. Even Gunne appeared normal, not hazy like before. Johan cleared his throat. "Can you put some pillows behind my head?"

Gunne arranged the pillows and climbed back into the chair. "Did you see the person who attacked you?"

"Not at all. He hit me from behind. I suspect it was someone up to no good. Zofia is touchy about who comes into her work space."

Gunne swung his legs. "Someone may have followed you inside, thinking you were stealing something of Zofia's. She told me she had sent you there, and she feels terrible about all this—blames herself."

"If someone thought I was stealing, wouldn't they report me? Why knock me out?" The angels were moving again and Johan closed his eyes. "I wonder . . ."

"If this has something to do with the crimes?" Gunne asked. "I think it does, but what?"

Shortly after dawn the following day, Johan woke with a bitter taste in his mouth. He sat up slowly and looked around the room. Judging from the table at the end of the bed where his feet had been resting, and the child-sized clothes hanging from a hook on the wall, this was Gunne's room. Johan struggled to his feet, shuffled to a corner basin and sat down on a low stool. After a few minutes he rose, determined to wash his face and rinse the taste from his mouth. Even this cold, the water felt good, bringing him back to the present. Had his attacker meant to kill him, or was it only a warning? Considering what could have happened, he decided the lump on his head and dull pain from the blow were not so bad. As he reached for a towel, Gunne walked in. "Oh my, the physician wants you to keep abed until tomorrow."

Johan patted his face with a linen. "I need something to eat and I'll be fine."

"Then wait here." Gunne walked into the hall, returning a

few minutes later. "My serving boy is bringing something from the cook. That way we can talk."

Johan shot him a grateful glance.

"You can sit there," Gunne said, indicating a regular-sized chair. Narrow, highly polished legs and a rush seat made it look like one of those chairs used by ladies to sit in front of a fire.

Gunne chuckled. "It's sturdier than it looks. I reserve it for guests, but I prefer furniture my size. I get tired of carrying my steps around, but don't tell the carpenter. He is quite proud of himself—gave the steps to me on my name day, but they are heavy—solid oak."

Johan sat. He needed to find out exactly what happened last night. "Are Zofia's papers completely burned?"

"Totally, but she said most of it was in her head anyway. She's as puzzled as I am about why someone would want to harm you, and furious that someone went in her laboratory without permission, but she agrees it may have something to do with the investigation. Whoever it was evidently knew her circumstances and that she would not return. They did not count on you coming in."

A server entered and set a heaping tray on a low table next to where Johan sat. "Ah, good," Gunne said. "There's enough for two." He pulled his own small chair close and tucked a linen into the high collar of his doublet.

While Johan sipped hot coffee, he felt a slow anger rise. Whoever had come into Zofia's workroom had not followed him there, he was sure of that. More likely the scoundrel had already been inside doing mischief, otherwise Johan would have heard the latch click. A musician has keen hearing.

"While you were sleeping," Gunne said, interrupting Johan's musings, "I went to check the latest gossip." Gunne licked jam from his fingers and took another pastry from the tray. "John Matthiae, the old king's chaplain, stopped by Eleanora's apartments this morning. I heard some of what they said, until Eleanora started crying. Sigrid saw me standing near the door and shooed me away. You haven't met Matthiae yet, have you?"

"No. This Matthiae, what did he say that made her cry?"

"I don't know exactly, but from what I heard of the conversation, he was asking her to forgo the questioning. He told her the entire court was on edge, that everyone had enemies, and accusations were flying. He wanted her to forget the whole affair and let the palace authorities handle it."

Palace authorities? Johan had a quick mental picture of the Commander of the Guards, who had dumped the investigation squarely into Johan's lap. "They won't help, and have washed their hands of the whole matter." And why would this Matthiae want to let the thief go unidentified—either that or let a possible innocent take the blame? "So," he said, almost to himself, "that makes two who want an end put to the investigation. I'm thinking of my attacker, and this Matthiae."

"Two? You can strike Matthiae off your list of suspects. He has been here for years, was well paid, and after the old king died, he tutored Christina. He owns several farms, all given to him by the king and Christina. He could probably have asked for the bible and it would be his. He has no motive to steal, let alone murder."

Johan rubbed his temple. A headache was coming on. He took a cake from the tray. "I'm not saying Matthiae had anything to do with all this, only it seems that a cleric would want to see justice done. Also, I think any theologian would want that bible."

Gunne crossed his short legs. "What you say makes sense. Matthiae leans toward Calvinism, but supports the Lutheran cause, of course, because he supports the queen. He would consider the bible to be popish."

Johan's brows shot up. "How do you know all this? Lutherans use the bible."

Gunne grinned. "You forget. I have ears to hear. Eleanora never tires of talking about her book. It meant a lot to her—she probably connects it somehow to her dead husband, because it was his army that brought it here. Of all the booty, she chose that as her favorite. The Silver Bible is a translation of the Gospels into the Gothic language, probably for Theodoric the Great, a supporter of the pope." Gunne scratched his chin. "But forget the bible for now. I suppose it could have been Matthiae in Zofia's workshop."

Johan grimaced. "The murderer, whoever it is, may have made a quick calculation that they would be better off with me gone. They wanted to end my investigation before it started. So it had to be someone who knew I was investigating the murder."

Gunne smiled. "By now, most of the castle knows that." He tugged at his doublet. "You said it happened fast, so what makes you think your attacker knew you?"

"I had the candle in my left hand, near my face. My attacker saw me plainly."

"But you said you were grabbed from behind."

Johan nodded. "I was. Whoever was there had to be hiding near the wall, behind some boxes, otherwise I'd have seen them. When my attacker lunged at my back I dropped the candle. We struggled. That's the last I remember."

"How tall do you think this person was?"

"I'm not sure. Maybe a little taller than I. Well-muscled arms, I remember that, from trying to loosen his grip on my waist. And agile on his feet."

"That could describe Matthiae, along with several others, except old Bureus."

"I haven't met him either."

"He keeps to himself. Must be past seventy by now, but in good health. He was librarian for the queen's father, and tutored the king too. He is a mystic, or claims to be. Studied the Rosicrucian Manifestos—you know, truths of the ancient past—all that sort of thing. But back to your attacker. If this was our bible thief, that person may be a murderer, too. That would make you a lucky man."

Johan swallowed. He hadn't thought of that. "I suppose so." He considered the long list of suspects. "I think we should talk with Matthiae, see what he says about all this. Besides, I might find some way to put him in Zofia's laboratory the night I got hit." He chuckled. "The day I came to Uppsala seeking a scholarship, little did I think I would get involved in such as this. Now, it seems, I'm on the hunt for a scoundrel I know nothing about."

Gunne removed the napkin from his neck and pushed back his chair. "I know where Matthiae spends his time when he's here, which is most all winter. He hates the weather and says it makes more sense to stay here instead of traipsing back and forth to one of his houses. If you want, we can go find him now. Are you feeling up to it?"

Johan nodded and rose from the chair. "How many homes does this man own?"

Gunne shrugged. "Several. Those loyal to the royal Vasa family are rewarded with large tracts of land. A palace, too, sometimes, or a farm. Matthiae has served the Vasa family well, so he received payment from Eleanora as well as from Queen Christina."

They left the room together, making their way to another wing of the castle. Gunne led Johan down a marble hallway where spacious windows leaked cold drafts. The windows now were covered with heavy drapes that would be opened by a page when the sun struck this side of the castle, allowing any random rays of sunshine to warm the cold walls.

Matthiae sat alone on a bench across from a small chapel reading a book. Nearby, a shaft of sunlight brightened the floor near his feet, bringing to life a bold floral pattern of red and blue tiles. Matthiae's modest boots looked out of place on the costly mosaics. His breeches, comfortably wide, were made of fine dark grey wool. A heavy black cloak fell from his shoulders and spilled onto the bench. Long grey curls flowed from his head to below his shoulders. On his upper lip he wore a neatly trimmed moustache. The long beard on his chin matched his hair—full and grey. A large man with broad shoulders, Matthiae's high arched brows gave him a permanent look of surprise. As Johan approached with Gunne, Matthiae looked up from his reading. "Gunne. What brings you so far from the queen mother's rooms?" He patted the bench. "Shall I guess why you're here?"

Johan smiled, hoping this would go well. He had no idea how to question a stranger without seeming presumptuous.

Gunne broke the ice. "Meet the new lutenist at court."

Matthiae removed his spectacles and laid them on the bench beside his book. "Johan, from Warsaw. Is that right?" He smiled. "We don't have that many newcomers—just visitors who come on business, ambassadors and such—so a new court appointee is of interest."

Johan flinched. What else did the man know about him? "Yes, I'm Johan. I hate to disturb your solitude, but if you don't mind, could we ask you some questions?"

Matthiae chuckled. "Of course. It's about the murder, correct? Eleanora questioned me but I'm willing to answer your questions. Strange, though, that anyone would suspect a fifty-eight-year-old cleric of committing a murder. Ask away."

Johan cleared his throat, feeling a bit foolish beneath the stare of this wizened courtier. "You know of the Silver Bible?"

Matthiae nodded. "Everyone does, I suppose, or anyone familiar with the library. Christina never made any effort to hide the treasures from her advisors or anyone else she trusted."

117

"I see. And did you know the murdered man?"

"Not well, but I've had a few dealings with him. He was the best goldsmith in Stockholm, at least to my mind. I've been to his home. In summer, the smell of roses permeates the air nearby. I smelled it when alighting from my carriage." He chuckled. "It's said he can identify each rose while blindfolded. He's considered an expert, and his roses are in great demand by perfume factories. But that's not why you came. You want to know about his murder." Matthiae shrugged. "I don't know much, but I'll tell you what I do know. It was his first day working here. Far as I know, no one besides Freinsheim, the librarian, and Monsieur Naudé, the man who catalogs everything going in and out, even knew that the goldsmith would be working that night. I'm sure they're the ones who hired him. They had catalogued everything else and left the coins for last, because some were ancient and neither man knew the value. I'm sure the queen advised them to get an expert's advice."

Johan rubbed his chin, trying to sort his thoughts. He wanted to further pursue something Matthiae said, but that would have to wait. They were getting off track, and Matthiae was guiding the conversation. "One more question," Johan said, "and you can get back to your reading. What were you doing that night—the night of the murder and theft?"

Matthiae grinned, showing yellowed, straight teeth. "I wondered why no one asked that before. I was with Bureus. We stayed up late talking, and drinking his good German wine. That from the Rhine valley is good for the stomach, but that night I drank too much. I fell asleep in a chair with a cat in my lap, and I normally fear cats—the way they watch and suddenly jump. As luck would have it, the maid who cleans Bureus's room—only once a week, mind you—found us both asleep the next morning. Bureus called her Lida. I'm sure she'd remember because she went right to work, complaining about the mess his rooms were always in."

Johan extended his hand. "Thank you, and I'm sorry to have bothered you."

"No bother. I've nothing much to do these days. I hope you catch the murderer. It's a fine thing when townspeople can't be safe in their own monarch's castle." He waved good-bye and picked up his book.

With Gunne at his side, Johan hurried away, his mind whirling. Near the end of the hall he turned left, heading back to the other wing of the castle, the place he knew best. "Any ideas where to go from here? If not, I'd like to talk to the librarian, Freinsheim."

Gunne nodded. "And while we're there, maybe we can talk to Naudé too. He's the Frenchman who does the book cataloguing."

"Along with recording all of the booty from Rudolph's castle in Prague?"

"Yes, with the help of the Royal Treasurer. I'll tell you about him later."

They approached the office adjacent the palace library. Gunne knocked on the door.

From behind them came a deep male voice. "Looking for someone?"

Johan spun around.

The man extended his hand. "I'm Johan Freinsheim, the royal librarian." He bent to greet Gunne, then straightened. In spite of his imposing height, it was his eyes Johan thought notable, deep brown with specks of light. Brown hair peeked from beneath the edges of the librarian's wig, a finely wrought hairpiece with two rows of neat curls that came to just below his ears. His moustache was neatly trimmed, extending only to the corners of his mouth, softening his sharp features. Johan guessed Freinsheim was not much past his fortieth year.

Gunne stepped up. "We'd like a few words with you, if it's convenient."

"Of course." Freinsheim ushered them into a cubicle that held a desk, two chairs, and stacks of paper. Johan suspected such a place would go up in flames in a moment should a spark land anywhere near. Did the guards, assigned to keep the castle safe, know of such a firetrap?

Johan sat in one of the chairs and waited for Freinsheim to take his place behind the desk. Once he was seated, Johan leaned forward. "I've been assigned the task of doing an investigation."

Freinsheim frowned. "Yes, I know. The murder. A ghastly affair, and right here in my library." He leaned back and crossed his arms over his chest. "I hope you can get to the truth of the matter. Until then, no one is really safe." He shook his head. "To think, a murderer walks among us."

Johan steered the conversation his way. "Tell me what happened."

Freinsheim rubbed his beard thoughtfully. "I'm an early riser. I open the drapes on that side of the room every morning, the east, where the sun can help warm the room. There are only two hearths in there, and as you may know, the library is huge. At the desk I saw what I thought was Gabriel Oxenstiern, slumped over. Thinking he'd fallen asleep at his work, I went over. From the back, it looked like the treasurer, but when I got close and saw the face I recognized the goldsmith. If I'd been fully awake, I'd have remembered our newly hired goldsmith had worked that night. He said the library was too noisy during the day." Freinsheim turned his mouth down in distaste. "It was an awful sight—blood on the desk and on his hands. I called his name, but I already knew he was dead. I ran out and sent for the guards and a physician. The guards and their commander got here first, then the doctor, who said the poor man had been dead for hours. Since his hands were bloody, I asked about suicide, but the doctor said that came from grasping at his chest for the few moments he lived. According to the physician, whoever did it knew where to strike. The blade punctured the heart and lung." He drew his brows together and frowned, eyeing Johan. "I don't understand why they would involve a newcomer in a murder investigation."

Gunne spoke up. "That was the queen mother's decision. She may have thought a stranger would be more fair-minded, knowing nothing of court politics and such."

Freinsheim leaned to his desk. "That's possible." He shook his head. "I hope the killer is found. That poor man had no family, and no enemies anyone knew of. It's as though someone just wanted to kill. Do you have any suspects so far?"

Johan adjusted the scarf at his neck. It was getting cold in here. "Right now everyone's a suspect. Which reminds me—your assistant, Monsieur Naudé. Can we speak with him?"

"Yes, but he knows nothing. He only works sporadically, and very little lately. He works best when he's alone, and asked for a few days off until the others finished assessing the value of those last unrecorded treasures. His work was limited to recording the manuscripts and books. He made that clear when he came here."

Johan nodded. "Still, we'd like a word with him."

Freinsheim hesitated. "Very well, but don't expect cooperation. Just between us, I'll be frank. The man is unhappy here. I suspect he'll be gone before long. He never made friends, and comes only grudgingly to the queen's social events." He leaned forward. "I learned recently that Mazarin, since returning to Paris, is intent on reconstructing his library. I suppose you know, during the Frond and after, those French fools distributed the books to anyone who wanted them. They even burned some. Can you imagine that? A collection it took Naudé years to accumulate. But now that Mazarin is back and safely established in Paris again, he wrote Naudé, vowing to make the public library what it was before." Freinsheim's features softened. "I can't blame the man. He wanted to establish a library for the citizens of Paris. High ideals. And Naudé, being the man he is, will probably take Mazarin up on the offer to return to Paris. I don't think he could be persuaded by anything from the queen's treasury to remain here once the weather is fit for travel." He sighed aloud. "I'd like to get away myself, but recording and finding a place to keep all these treasures has required long days of work. I promised my family I would relinquish my position here, once the queen finds a suitable replacement. I'm looking forward to living on one of my estates in the countryside. This murder has made me even more eager to leave."

Johan smiled, pretending interest, but his head spun. If Naudé had in mind to rebuild Mazarin's library in Paris, what better book than the Silver Bible with which to start it?

Johan rubbed his temples. The brief encounter with the grumpy Naudé had been a waste of time. He had crossed his arms and stared belligerently at both his questioners, something that made Gunne, seated on an uncomfortably high chair, swing his legs in disdain. To make things worse, Naudé had laughed at the notion that the Silver Bible was a worthy addition to a library. "You can't be serious. The book is not even complete. No librarian I know of would give it a glance, not when the great classics are out there, bound in leather, with gilt-edged leaves . . ." Naudé's eyes had glazed over and Johan exchanged glances with Gunne. The dwarf slowly shook his head.

Now, sitting in the rear of the great hall late in the afternoon, Johan shared a cold pastry with Gunne. After he finished, Johan withdrew a linen from the waist of his breeches and wiped his hands. "So far, after speaking with three men, we've learned little. Matthiae has an alibi. Freinsheim, should he want a book, has time and chance to take it without murdering a man. This Monsieur Naudé certainly would have a motive—though he declares otherwise."

Gunne licked his fingers, swallowing the last of his own tart. "Like the character in a London play I saw, methinks Naudé protests too much."

"That's possible. It may be a deliberate ruse to send us elsewhere. Still, I'm inclined to believe he was in earnest with his protests about the bible. He seems more taken by bound classics. For now, let's move ahead. Who's next?"

"Well, there's Gabriel Oxenstiern. He was here that evening, taking a night off and letting the goldsmith work at sorting through all those coins and writing down their value."

"Is Gabriel any relation to Axel Oxenstiern, the Lord High Chancellor? I understand he's the most powerful person in Sweden, after the queen."

Gunne nodded. "You're right about Axel. As chancellor, he's also the most senior member of the queen's privy council. Gabriel is his cousin."

Johan raised one eyebrow. "Do we dare inquire of Gabriel?"

"I think we should talk to him. He was heavily involved with recording all these treasures. Besides, there's something you should know. Mind you, I hate gossip, but this might give you something to think about. A few months back, way before you came, word went through the castle that there was a shortage in the treasury, discovered by a court clerk. An auditor was called in, and sure enough, twelve-thousand *daler* copper coins were missing. The treasurer himself was called before the court and after Axel spoke on behalf of his cousin, we heard nothing more." Gunne shrugged. "Perhaps it was a mathematical error."

Johan clasped his hands behind his head and looked up at

the ornate ceiling. "Or perhaps not. We could assume the treasurer wanted the Silver Bible to sell in order to replace any new funds which may turn up missing. I've been thinking. This goldsmith took the place of the treasurer that night. Whoever killed him may have assumed that he was killing Gabriel Oxenstiern."

Gunne nodded, a smile crossing his face. "Ah, hadn't thought of that. So that would eliminate Gabriel as a suspect. That leaves only a few more names on our list. Voullon, a French musician, and Marin de Courlas, but he's an unlikely suspect. He's a professor who lives in the city, but has been staying here in the palace to instruct the queen in charcoal sketching."

Johan raised an eyebrow again. "Sketching?"

"He's an expert, and his family is French. The queen, as you have surely learned by now, is interested in all things French. Marin is a newcomer to the palace so likely has nothing to do with the theft or murder. He may not even have known about the Silver Bible."

"A newcomer? We need to talk to him—and then to the treasurer as well. Perhaps Gabriel Oxenstiern, with so important a position, will have an idea about all this—or about who may have wanted him dead."

The following afternoon, as Johan rose from the bench in the dining hall, Gunne gave him a nudge. "Look there," he whispered. "The fellow with the limp. That's Marin de Courlas, the queen's sketching instructor. Are you prepared to question him?"

Johan smiled down at his friend. "Of course. Come along." He approached the drawing teacher with a cheerful greeting. "Good day. I'm Johan, the queen's lutenist. Is there somewhere we could talk?"

Marin frowned. "Talk? About what? I hoped to take a nap. I'm due to give the queen a drawing lesson shortly."

"This won't take long."

An annoyed sigh escaped Marin's lips. "Very well. Come to my room." His voice barely rose above a whisper, and Johan wondered if he were timid or had a bad throat.

Marin took them down a little-used corridor, past the kitchen, to a room not far from the storage area. "The queen kindly gave me a place of my own in the castle so I can sleep here in bad weather rather than returning home." He opened a door and indicated a couch. He hesitated only a moment, then took his own seat behind a desk. A cot took up one side of the room, and the couch and desk left little space, but it was cozy, with a framed drawing on the desk along with an inkpot and drawing materials. Marin drew his brows together and leaned forward, gazing at Johan with blue-grey, haunted eyes. They were so deep-set in his face that his expression was unreadable, but his guarded mannerisms evidenced his discomfort. He rubbed the edge of the desk, and Johan noticed the man's fingers—long and slender. Marin de Courlas looked down, and Johan could see tiny veins in the man's eyelids. They gave him a look of fragility. He glanced up, once again exposing those sad eyes. "And now, what did you two want to speak with me about?"

Johan straightened. "As I'm sure you know, there is an unsolved crime in the castle. I'd like to ask you a few questions."

"Yes, I know. Some poor man dead, and a theft. Supposed to be a valuable book."

Gunne leaned forward. "And the murder victim would say his life was valuable."

Marin lifted a quill from the desk and rolled it between his fingers. "I'm afraid I can't help you at all. I was asleep. I sleep soundly. Didn't hear or see a thing."

Johan rubbed the back of one hand. This Marin could be a bit abrupt. "Can anyone vouch for your whereabouts that night—anyone who might be willing to swear you were here in your room?"

"Of course not," Marin said. "I sleep alone. So you see, you men are wasting your time."

Johan leaned forward for a closer look at the framed drawing on the desk. "An example of your work?"

"No. It's only a sketch. Not important."

"A sketch of what?"

Marin scratched his nose. "Really, it's nothing. A simple drawing."

Johan strained to read something in tiny letters—a name, perhaps, but the sketch appeared to be of a building. The castle? The image was too far away.

Marin turned the sketch face down. "Now, if you don't mind, I'd really like a few moments to myself before meeting with Queen Christina."

Johan rose, thanked the drawing instructor for his time, and followed Gunne out the door. Once out of earshot, Gunne shook his head. "He's a strange one, but still, it seems unlikely the man has any interest here in the palace. He probably knew nothing of court politics before coming here."

"Perhaps you're right. Still, I'd have liked a better look at that drawing on his desk. Did you see him turn it face down? Do you think it might have been a layout of the palace?"

Gunne grinned. "Perhaps we'll have to figure a way to look at it more closely without him around. If it's what you suggest, why would he keep it there? He knows his way around by now."

"Yes. It may be nothing, but we should follow every clue, especially since he isn't a palace regular." Johan sighed. "For now, though, let's finish the list and eliminate the suspects one by one. And we still have the French ballet group."

"Not all of them. Some went to the Uppsala palace that night."

Johan grinned. "Thanks, but that still leaves a sizeable list."

"I'll be in Eleanora's rooms most of tomorrow," Gunne said. "The dwarf in charge of our shows wants to teach us a new routine. He said the queen mother is getting bored with repeats."

Johan nodded. "Fine. I need a break myself." He waved as Gunne headed to his room. Besides, he wanted to think things through. What Matthiae had said about the murder victim's fondness for roses and his sensitivity to smell might be important, especially for Zofia's defense. How could a man with a keen sense of smell miss the ever-present fragrance of lemon soap? He'd have known someone was close behind and turned around. Johan's spirit soared. This might not be enough to convince a royal jurist, but, together with the husky attacker that night in her workshop, it had convinced Johan. Zofia was innocent, and he had to find the killer before the twenty days were up. He'd already used five, with little to show for it.

Chapter Eleven

Following a day filled with interviewing ballet dancers, Johan went to his cubicle, changed to warm sleepwear, and climbed into bed, reviewing what he'd learned. All those he questioned had alibis, sworn to by the court physician, who had treated injuries from a brawl and kept them in the infirmary for the night. The others, the ballet director grudgingly admitted, had been allowed to stay at a Stockholm inn known for all-night gambling.

Johan turned in bed, listening to pellets of ice pounding the shutters while wind blew through the rafters. Only a few dancers remained to be questioned. He pulled his fur-lined nightcap over his ears and tucked the covers closer, an assortment of quilts, woolen blankets, and furs of dubious origin.

The following morning, waking to the sound of servants stoking the fire pits in the dormitory, Johan reached for his warmest clothes. Nothing could chase the cold from the walls of this ancient fortress. The hallways held a kind of permanent chill. He slipped on two pairs of socks and tossed a fur cape over his layered woolen shirts. His hands had healed fast, thanks to Zofia's soothing concoction, but he'd keep them in the pockets of his cape just the same.

Lured by the smell of baking bread, he made his way to the dining hall to break his fast. François, the ballet dancer who had befriended him his first day here, waved him to a table. "Sit," he called out, his voice carrying above the din of conversation in the room. "There's space on this bench. Quite an ice storm that went through the city. Woke me from a sound sleep, and it's still blowing. Makes for dreary weather."

Johan smiled. "I hardly recognized you without your yellow costume."

François laughed good-naturedly and poured his cup full from one of the pitchers on the table. Johan sat across from him, broke a piece from one of the long loaves, and dabbed jam on one side.

François leaned across the table. "I hear you are investigating the theft and murder. How is that going?"

Johan chewed slowly, wondering how he should answer so blunt a question. He weighed his words, remembering that both he and Gunne had agreed the less said to others about the investigation the better. "It's going about as expected." He reached for a pitcher and poured his cup full. He'd learned to like the colorless, heady *brännvin* that smelled of ginger. It burned his throat with every sip but left a warm feeling behind.

François, evidently used to the drink, drained his cup in one gulp. "What say we go to the game room later? A few sets of *brädspel* will dispel the gloom. I have to be back for a later rehearsal, but I have a few hours."

Johan nodded, finished his meal, and followed the dancer to a room set aside for card playing and board games. They chose a table near the blazing fire, and François set up the board. After a throw of the dice, Johan moved one of his pieces. In all his life, he had never met a ballet dancer. What to talk about, except life in the palace? He said the first thing that came to his mind. "Did you learn ballet as a child?"

François moved a piece from his corner. His expression darkened. "Yes, when I was quite young, so I have had years of practice. My parents were determined that I should excel in ballet, as my brother did. They saw that I had the best teachers in Paris."

"Your brother—is he in the troupe?"

"No. He died in a fire—a crowded tavern, and after that everything changed. It was as if my parents wanted me to turn into my brother."

Johan took his move, uncomfortable under François's bitter revelation. "But you must have talent, to be included in the royal ballet troupe."

"Perhaps, but what good is that if your heart is elsewhere? I have no interest in anything but—"

"What, François? What is more important to you?" He thought of himself, of the young boy whose collection of wooden cannons and wagons were the envy of his friends, and of how he wanted to be a soldier and ride a real horse, until he discovered his love of music.

François broke into Johan's thoughts. "I love science."

"That's a broad field. What part exactly?"

"All of it, but it makes no difference now what is important to me."

"You could always take up another profession, François, young as you are."

"You don't understand. They gave me the best teachers, who made me practice for hours. I was quite good, and my instructors began giving me solo parts, pushing me, saying it would please my mother. Like every young boy, I wanted to please my parents. Then an outbreak of plague came to Paris. My father was gone on business, and I was in boarding school. I was called home the day before Mother died. Our last night together, she made me promise to pursue the ballet. So, you see, that's what I must do. Other men take ballet to be better at fencing, or to excel in handling a horse. For me, ballet must be a profession."

Johan, feeling a surge of pity, allowed François to take the game. "How well do you know Henrik, the stagehand?"

"Not well, but I have always been curious as to what he has against you."

"Who knows? Everyone was out of sorts the day I arrived here. We got off to a bad start."

"But there was the incident with the missed note."

Johan straightened the game board. "He was simply mistaken, that's all—or he may resent me, a newcomer, being given authority to investigate a murder, but I couldn't refuse a royal order."

François paused, and Johan noticed he had tightened his fingers on the wooden game board. The dancer leaned close, his voice almost a whisper. "I was told the queen mother believes she has the perpetrator. Why are you still investigating? Is there a question that the thief and murderer may be different people?"

"There's a question as to the suspect's guilt on either count, François. It would be terrible if the accused is punished and the real criminal goes free."

François straightened. "Rest assured, the queen mother is thorough. Mind you, I've nothing against women. In fact, I'm quite fond of them, but the queen's alchemist is a strange one." He moved a game piece, sat back, and crossed his arms. "Whoever heard of a woman in science? I mean, as an assistant, perhaps, but no girl can do scientific work. Think. There's Aristotle, and Copernicus, and Kepler—a long list of names, and not a woman in the bunch. I used to think Henrik was guilty, but I've changed my mind. If you ask me, the queen mother has the guilty one, but it's none of my affair." He shrugged and rose from his chair. "I have to go now."

"Yes, well, perhaps we can play again." But François was gone, leaving Johan to put the game board and pieces away. François had forgotten to collect his winnings.

★ ★ ★ ★ ★

A short while later, Johan entered Gunne's room after a quick knock. The dwarf indicated the only regular-sized chair in the room. Johan sat, anxious to share what he'd learned. "It is beginning to look hopeless, my friend. All the dancers have an alibi. However, all it takes is one trickster, clever enough to time things right—maybe leave the infirmary and return undetected. Or should I trust them and move on?"

"You have free access to their dormitory—you can do a bit of investigating yourself, and say you were just walking through, on your way to the musicians' section. If you find no evidence, then we can cross off their names."

Johan shook his head. Inspecting the dancers' dormitory was out of the question. Did Gunne really think, if a man caught someone looking through his belongings, that person would believe the intruder was just passing by? "Impossible, Gunne. You want me to rummage through each dancer's belongings— sweaty costumes, rehearsal records—for what?" Johan sipped the last of the mulled wine Gunne had given him.

"Anything that might connect the owner with the theft. You may even find the bible itself. It was bitter cold when the book went missing, and winter set in shortly after. No one has left the grounds, save the queen and some of her council."

Johan said, "You forget Hilda, the stableman's lady love, who seems to come and go at will."

Gunne shook his head. "She'd never get past the cook, and the stableman stays in his shack, or sleeps in the stable. No, the bible has to be somewhere in the castle."

Johan grimaced. "I suppose I should learn more about each dancer. I'll ask the dance master himself, who knows them better than anyone."

Gunne nodded. "He may not like being questioned by a

newcomer, though. If I were you I'd take him something he'd appreciate—like a warm drink."

Johan paced the anteroom outside the queen mother's chambers, thinking Gunne's idea the most daring yet. The dwarf had convinced him that by using a clever contraption inserted in Eleanora's tiled stove, he could produce hot coffee in minutes. As he watched Gunne maneuver the burner, Johan realized the dwarf had used it several times before, in bitterly cold weather like this, when he knew the queen mother would not return for hours. Still, what harm had been done, and why let a good invention go to waste? When the brew was finished, Gunne adjusted the burner and poured the coffee into two cups. Johan took the cups and left the room, hoping the hot drink would not cool before he reached the dance master.

He found Antoine de Beaulieu seated alone, watching the afternoon rehearsal, his face contorted. The man looked distressed, and probably was. Count de la Gardie, Johan now knew, was one of the queen's favorites, and had brought in a court full of new musicians, all French, except for men like himself, who had been rewarded not with a scholarship but with a significant position at court, like his own appointment as royal lutenist.

Beaulieu was different, having been brought here by the queen mother to work with her German entertainers. Easy to understand why the new recruits tried his patience. He was no young man, and while his talent was undisputed, he had relegated much of the work to two trained assistants. Johan felt a moment of pity for the dance master. No doubt he knew his place at court was tenuous at best; he could be replaced at any moment by another young Frenchman.

Johan handed Beaulieu one of the cups, an offer never refused in a castle where the occupants were always visibly cold, shaking like branches in a winter storm and bundled from head to foot unless doing manual labor. "Am I interrupting?"

"No. Sit. Thanks for the hot drink."

Johan sat beside the dance master. "How is the rehearsal going?"

Beaulieu wrapped both hands around the cup and sipped. Like everything else, the brew would soon turn cold. He wiped his mouth. "Well enough. It is next week I'm worried about, but it's out of my hands. I am too old for this, training all these new recruits de la Gardie thrusts on me."

"None of them meet your standards?"

Beaulieu turn to Johan. "I noticed your hands earlier. Are they ruined for lute playing?"

Johan considered his hands, almost healed, the blisters gone. "They are not ruined. In fact, I'll join the ensemble next week."

Beaulieu's attention had returned to the stage. "See the tall one to the left? An excellent dancer, one of the few. Then there's Louis—moving to the front just now. He's talented and a good boy. See the one with the yellow hair, wearing the green wings? If he'd keep his mind from the girl he would be trainable, I suppose, but I had rather he remain as a stagehand."

Johan recognized the light-haired dancer. It was Henrik. He seemed to be everywhere at once. "You mention a girl. Is he married?"

"No. In his off time he hangs around the queen mother's chambers, hoping to see one of her women when they come out. I can't blame de la Gardie for him. Henrik came here earlier, brought from an orphanage by the queen mother. I suspect one of her ladies put in a word for him and that's all it took, but why could he not be satisfied with helping on the set? He has no talent for the dance." He shook his head. "They expect miracles—all of them—but I owe the queen mother. She hired me when the king was alive, and I will serve her as long as I'm able." He put down his empty cup. "Say, you are the one who got knocked on the head. I heard a rumor you were trespassing."

"That's untrue. I had been sent to the alchemist's laboratory to pick up some papers. My assailant was the trespasser."

"Did they find out who that was?"

"No. It's a dead issue. No one cares, and I suppose it is not important."

"I understand they are holding the alchemist—accused of theft and murder."

"That's who I was trying to help." Johan wondered how much to tell Beaulieu, but he sensed the man had troubles of his own, knew almost everyone in the palace, and cared for nothing much but his ballets. Johan decided to find out what he could. "I have no idea who hit me, but either they were looking for something, or they wanted to discourage me from helping the alchemist."

"The castle hums with secrets, my friend, but likely the thief just decided to barter something valuable for money. I think he was interrupted by the goldsmith and had to kill him. Isn't that logical? Did they question the servants?"

"I understand they did that first. All of those not with the queen were accounted for. Besides, the queen's library is not far from her sleeping chambers. Only trusted courtiers are allowed there, but the queen scoffs at security for her person. That's part of the problem. The library was accessible to most anyone that evening, save the servants sleeping downstairs."

Beaulieu shouted something to one of his helpers and turned back to Johan. "Then there are people loyal to the pope to think about. They're always around."

"Do you mean your own dance troupe?"

"It's possible. There are others, like the other lutenist—the one who plays that long-necked lute—Alexandre Voullon. He's a secret Catholic, although the queen knows. She protects some of her courtiers, daring the chancellor to oust them."

"I have met Voullon, the theorboe player. Seems a nice fellow, one of the first musicians I met. He came to the practice room my second day here. They questioned him about the theft. He told me all about the queen mother's jury. He suggested we play some duets, but we've never found the time—not yet."

"You should. But back to Eleanora. Most of the gossip you hear about her is lies. She almost died of grief when the king died, and many think she lost her mind, but I don't. She is simply a lonely, bored widow. She and the king only had the one child—Queen Christina, whose reign began when the king died. Eleanora misses her life as queen, as you can imagine."

Johan crossed his legs and finished the last of his coffee, now as cold as the room in which he sat. "One of the dwarfs said Eleanora loved the bible for its beauty, and because it represented the end of the long war. She connects it somehow with the king—I can understand that."

Beaulieu chuckled. "What amazes me is, when something like this happens, they never look to question those at the top. What about someone like General Horn? He spent seven years in a Catholic prison. Do you imagine he's happy to have the Silver Bible in the queen's library, let alone the book being practically considered a sacred relic by the queen mother? He hates the Catholics, and for good reason. He was a commander in the war. The queen lavished him with honors when he returned from prison. A learned man, too, and he has access to the queen's library. I imagine, from what I know of the man, if he saw his chance, he would burn the Silver Bible and anything connected with the pope. He's bitter, and not without cause."

Johan rubbed the rim of his cup. General Horn was on the list of suspects yet to be interviewed. "General Horn may be bitter, but he and others like him, the ones who brought home the booty, had ample time to take what they wanted—and probably did."

Beaulieu shrugged. "Think what you like. For myself, I'd think it difficult to steal anything in the field without being seen by comrades."

Johan was about to respond when a commotion on the stage brought Beaulieu to his feet, agile for a man half his age, making Johan wonder if he should take up dancing instead of the sedentary art of lute playing. "Enough for today," Beaulieu shouted, and the troupe poured from the stage.

Johan rose and headed for the door, but the dancers, anxious to leave, blocked his exit. He stood to the side to wait and noticed Henrik, this time minus the green wing costume. A lady slipped her arm through Henrik's and together they disappeared through one of the side doors. Johan started to follow, to get a glimpse of the girl's face, in case he needed that information later, but Henrik was out of sight. Besides, what did it matter? Right now, he had other worries. He was getting no closer to finding the murderer, and it felt like clues were slipping from his hands. Already seven days of his allotted time had passed, and each day brought Zofia, who counted on him to free her, closer to whatever punishment was meted out in Sweden to a thief who would steal from the queen's own possessions and murder while carrying out that theft. The thought made him more determined than ever to follow the smallest lead. What if Beaulieu was right about General Horn? There was only one way to find out. He'd begin with a search of the man's room. That would have to be arranged, some time when the general was nowhere around.

The following evening, as Johan sat inside his cubicle playing his lute, grateful he'd not lost his technique while unable to practice, he heard a quick rap on the door to the musicians' area. Before he could answer, Gunne pulled back the curtain of his cubicle and stepped inside. "You'll be pleased to know, I've learned where General Horn stays in the Castle of Three Crowns."

Johan laid the lute aside.

Gunne put his hands on his hips. "We should go, right now. The queen called an evening meeting of her advisors— something about the New World settlement. I heard one of our ships ran aground before reaching New Sweden. It may be a short meeting, but they usually spend about an hour, so General Horn will be gone awhile. I know a back way to his room. No one will see us going or coming."

Johan nodded, donned warmer clothes, and followed Gunne down long, quiet corridors. The thick cold walls reminded him of a tomb or underground cavern. He hoped the queen's meeting lasted long enough for a decent inspection of the general's chambers. Johan wanted to take no chances. Already he was getting a reputation for being in the wrong place at the wrong time. It was only the vision of Zofia, a noose slipping around her white neck, that drove him further.

Tonight's search, he hoped, would turn up something. As Gunne turned a corner, the lantern went out. He tripped in the dark and cursed, first the lamp maker, then the floor mason who had left a piece of rock sticking up, and the general and others like him who chose to stay so far from the main section of the castle.

Johan swallowed a chuckle. "Did you bring flint?" he asked.

"Yes, but we should go on. By the time I find it and light the lantern, we could be there. Once inside, the general will have lamps. Besides, I don't like this area. It's too close to the dungeon." His voice echoed, bouncing off the walls of the corridor.

Johan paused. "How close?"

"We pass by on the way to the next tower. The dungeon is no longer used, but some say the screams of the dead can be heard on the eve of All Saints."

Johan shivered. That hallowed eve would soon be upon them. Carefully feeling his way, a few paces behind Gunne, he almost fell when Gunne stopped abruptly. "Ouch. Hit my toe. Watch the steps. Careful now."

Johan followed Gunne up the narrow stairwell, hoping the queen would keep her advisors longer than usual, because they had used precious time with the slow going in the dark. They reached a landing and Gunne paused, waiting for Johan. "We go left here, and keep to the wall." Johan felt a blast of cold air and heard a rush of water. "Only a creek," Gunne said, "that feeds a duck pond."

As they crossed a wooden footbridge, the boards of which felt slick beneath Johan's feet, he heard a girl's laughter. "Someone else is nearby," he hissed, trying to catch up to Gunne. In spite of the dwarf's short legs, he was making good time, but he had an advantage—he knew his way through here, whereas Johan had lost his bearings.

"Lovers, probably," Gunne said. "There are benches below, and bushes overhang the pond. Courtiers who were here when the king reigned used the spot below us as a place to meet— away from the eyes of their husbands or wives."

Johan paused, listening.

Gunne moved closer and whispered, "It was a popular hideaway, even in weather like this. Now I guess some of the newcomers have discovered it too, although this area is sup- posed to be off limits except to those like the general who live in the tower." Gunne nudged Johan. "Let's go."

They ducked beneath a low arch and entered another cor- ridor. "This leads to the west tower," Gunne said.

Just then, Johan heard the flap of wings and something flew

by his face, coming near enough that he felt the breeze from its passage. "What's in here, besides us?" he asked, not expecting an answer.

"Pigeons and bats."

Johan caught his breath, remembering his grandmother's warning that a bat flying past meant someone was trying to deceive you. His grandmother remembered every proverb and superstition she had ever heard, and while Johan placed no trust in the supernatural, considering it a result of years of empty speculation, still, his grandmother had been one of the wisest people he had ever known. He trusted Gunne, whose size alone had ruled him out as a suspect, but the bat incident was just one more obstacle to be surmounted in what was becoming a long chain of coincidences. To convince the queen mother of someone's guilt, he needed something besides circumstantial evidence. Without that, the blonde-haired alchemist would likely swing from a rope, or suffer whatever punishment was meted out in Sweden for a violent crime.

By now even Gunne was breathing hard. After taking another turn, well away from the sounds of the waterfall, they came to an opening in the wall, and Johan remembered the castle had once been a fortress. He glanced down and saw that from here, an archer would have full command over the land below. Leaving behind the welcome shaft of moonlight illuminating the stone wall, he hurried on.

Gunne paused at the foot of a staircase. "Not far now. These are the tower steps. Once up there, the general's room is the third on the right. Mostly storage up there. I guess that's why he chose this place. From what little I was able to learn, he's sort of a recluse. They said he changed during his imprisonment."

They climbed the steps and after crossing the landing, Gunne stopped at the third door. "Here we are. Now we'll see if these keys work. I had to bribe Eleanora's secretary to get them. He wanted one of my amber stones. Luckily, he knows nothing about amber and selected an inferior piece. According to him, one of these keys will open the general's room." He stood on tiptoe to reach the keyhole, then fitted one key after the other, with no luck, until at last the latch clicked.

Once inside, Gunne set his lantern down and reached for the flint and tinder in his waistcoat. He struck flint and the lantern came to life.

Johan closed the door behind them, shocked at what he saw in the general's room. It looked much like a cell, except for tapestries that covered the walls, the images so faded that Johan suspected they were leftovers from when this part of the castle was a fortress. A cot, the candle stand, and a cabinet for clothes lined the perimeter of the room, and a large gleaming desk sat in the middle. Inkpots and various quills lay near the pots, and stacks of parchment were arranged in an orderly manner to one side of the desk. Evidently the general had been writing before he left; a paper, tilted to one side, lay prominently in the middle of the desk. Johan stepped closer. The general had a distinctive script, clean and easy to read, and Johan found himself studying the general's words instead of looking for the bible.

Dear Brother, Johan read. He was about to look away when he saw mention of the Silver Bible. His heart raced. Leaning closer, he saw that the general had made a list of suspected spies, and below that, the letter continued. *They are all Catholics, to the last man. I shall not rest until the palace is rid of the papists. The young queen is enamored of their music, though she seems now to be turning toward the Italians, mostly because of the impression the paintings from Prague have made on her. If I were younger, I would take things into my own hands. As it is, I must bide my time until an opportunity presents itself to speak to the queen about these matters. If left alone, the French will take over our government.*

Johan caught his breath. Had the general's imprisonment driven him mad? He continued reading the letter:

I had almost persuaded the chancellor to sell off the bibles—they have no place in a Lutheran library—but before he took action, I had a better idea. I suspect it was no different than that of the queen's Catholic dance troupe—a stranger bunch of men you will never see.

A large drop of ink, where the quill had been laid in evident haste, ended the letter. What more would the general have added if he had finished? Apparently, the time had gotten away from him, and to be late to the queen's meeting would be no small matter.

Johan called to Gunne, who had been searching the room on his own. "Read this, Gunne. The general writes his brother, and it looks like he intended to remove books from the queen's library—ones he considered offensive. It's not clear whether he actually carried out the theft himself. I think someone got there first. And he mentions the dance troupe, but I—"

A whirring sound interrupted his thoughts. It came from a clock on a nearby table. Two little doors on the clock opened and a mannequin came out, only to turn and go back in. "That came from his travels, evidently," Gunne said. "He probably paid a fortune." The doors on the clock clicked shut and Johan, reminded of the hour, said, "Our time is up. Let's go." He extinguished the lamp and had shut the door behind them when footsteps approached. Johan froze. Out here in the corridor there was nowhere to hide, and now there were two sets of footsteps coming their way. Either the general had company, or someone else lived in one of these tower rooms.

He pulled Gunne into the shadows. Johan's heart pounded as he pressed his back to the wall and waited. Gunne muffled a cough with his cloak, and Johan held his breath, hoping the sound would not give them both away.

When the newcomers reached the general's door, one of them

spoke. "While I am glad to see the bible gone, one wonders if that will end the papist propaganda. Paris is swarming with it, and no telling how many secret Catholics are in this very court."

"I wanted it burned."

"And it still may be, Hans. Well, goodnight, my friend."

"God bless."

The door closed, and the general's companion continued down the corridor, passing so close to Johan he feared the man would sense their presence. Every muscle in Johan's body tensed while the stooped, shuffling figure of General Horn's confidant passed by and disappeared down the corridor. Johan straightened. One less murder suspect. The shuffling would have alerted the goldsmith in time to save his life.

However, there was still Horn to consider. If he was involved in the theft and murder, then there was another mystery, because according to Gunne, the general was approaching sixty. Johan rubbed the back of his neck. The man who attacked him in Zofia's workroom had been young and strong, certainly no aging general. Still, this evidence tonight certainly gave General Horn a strong motive to steal the book. The man had killed in battle. Why would he hesitate to kill again?

Gunne nudged Johan's leg, a signal it was time to go. Not daring to light the lantern until they were well away from the general's tower room, they made their way back across the footbridge, through the corridors, and as they approached Zofia's vacated laboratory, Johan heard the door to her workroom close.

A figure dashed past, clutching something to his chest. Johan spun around and gave chase. The trespasser leapt over a banister and ran noiselessly up the stairs. With Johan in pursuit, the intruder bolted into a corridor that opened to a labyrinthine set of tunnels. Johan paused to catch his breath. The culprit had outwitted him, and evidently was familiar with this older part of the castle and its maze. By now the intruder could be far from here, having taken any of the passageways. He blew air through puffed lips. Finding the trespasser now was hopeless. He turned back, heading for the main corridor.

Why would anyone want to be in Zofia's workshop? Was someone stealing from her? Was this elusive figure the same man who had been there the night Johan was assaulted? He scratched his head and ducked under an archway. How had he missed that before? He hadn't. Somehow he'd taken a wrong turn, and here, the walls all looked alike. He continued on, and when the hall ended at a stone wall, he grew desperate, trying every corridor, until at last he found himself back in the main area of the palace. Gunne waited, arms crossed. Johan straightened. For sure, he had one very good friend in the palace.

"I lost him," Johan said. "Whoever was in her workroom is familiar with the castle."

Gunne shrugged. "With time to explore, the tunnels and secret openings are manageable." He adjusted his cloak over his shoulders. "I was about to leave. I've been given an additional duty. I'm the new guard outside Zofia's room in the ladies' wing."

Johan had a quick thought. "Indeed. And I was just thinking I wanted to talk with her about these new suspects."

"Then come along. We can talk on the way."

Johan straightened his cap. "I guess, after seeing Horn's friend, the shuffling way he walks, we can cross him off the list. Hans something. Do we have more than one Hans?"

"I don't believe so. That must have been Hans von Königsmarck. I've heard of him. He has the reputation of being a great commander. It was his flying column that made it possible to bring back the treasures of the palace in Prague."

Johan wrinkled his brow. "Two generals, both devoted to the queen, both of whom had reason to want a Catholic bible removed from the palace library. The letter General Horn wrote casts suspicion on him." Johan frowned. "However, I'm fairly sure this person who is sneaking into Zofia's lab is neither General Horn nor the queen's sketching teacher, Marin. Marin limps, the man I pursued does not. Also, if General Horn is nearing sixty, as you said, I doubt he could flee that fast." He grimaced. "General Horn's letter has muddled the clues. As for this last incident, the person leaving Zofia's workshop in a rush, who better than Zofia to tell us why someone might be there? Also, she may know something of interest about General Horn."

CHAPTER TWELVE

As Johan followed Gunne to Zofia's room, he leaned down to speak with the dwarf. "How did you get assigned as Zofia's guard?"

Gunne buttoned his waistcoat. "Eleanora wants to know who comes and goes on this wing. I guess she's uneasy since the theft of her book. Her royal guards are posted outside her quarters, so she asked for volunteers to escort anyone coming to this wing, unless they're on royal business with her. I volunteered. I have to report back to her, name, time, and purpose."

Johan frowned. The queen mother was making sure no one helped Zofia escape. "Has Eleanora mentioned anything more about Zofia?"

"Not about Zofia, but she has not forgotten your assignment. She asked how you were proceeding with your investigation. I was non-committal." He looked down. "I didn't want to tell Eleanora we had met with nothing but false leads so far. She might decide to speed up the process."

Johan drew his cloak close against a sudden chill. "Surely not now, not when things are beginning to happen. That's why I wanted to see Zofia again. If anyone knows what she may have in her workroom that someone would want, it would be her."

As they reached the room where Zofia was being held, Gunne paused by the door and looked down at his feet. "Sorry, but I have orders not to leave the two of you alone."

"Don't feel bad. That's your job. I suppose they believe we might plot together. That's absurd, of course, but you are welcome to stay. Zofia won't mind, and besides, you may be able to help. I am at a disadvantage, not knowing anything about the courtiers, so I can't guess at motives."

Gunne looked up. "Thanks for understanding." He gave a quick knock. "Is it too late? I brought Johan to see you."

"No," she called through the closed door. "Please, come in."

He unlocked the door and Johan came face to face with Zofia. He thought her face lit up when she saw him, but she quickly stooped to embrace Gunne.

"We have to leave the door open," Gunne said, "but there's no one outside."

"I have nothing to hide." Zofia sat down. "Johan, there's coffee in that pot. Both of you, have some. They treat me very well—in fact, one of the queen's women seems to have taken a liking to me, bringing me books and pastries and such. Sigrid never lets me go hungry."

Sigrid, Johan remembered, was the young lady-in-waiting who helped Gunne learn to read, and curiously, she had been the only one who treated Johan poorly the morning of his hearing before the queen mother. No matter. The girl might have problems of her own. His thoughts returned to the subject at hand, and what he wanted to ask Zofia. He poured himself a cup of the rich, dark brew and sat on a stool. Zofia indicated a pile of cushions on the floor. "You can sit there, Gunne, if you like."

Gunne arranged them squarely and sat. "Sigrid gave me a book of French essays. Did she show you those?"

Zofia shook her head.

Johan spoke up. "We can talk about books later, perhaps. Right now there's something more important."

Zofia gave him a startled look, her large green eyes reflecting surprise.

Johan rubbed the edge of his cup. She and Gunne were only making conversation, but did she not realize what danger she was in? Had she accepted her fate? He decided instead that she was trying to make the best of a difficult situation—and so was Gunne. Johan cleared his throat.

After explaining the dark figure fleeing from her laboratory, and how he had pursued and lost the chase, Johan said, "I wanted to ask you, Zofia, to search your memory. Do you know of anyone who might be interested in what's in your workroom?"

"Like I said, there's no one I can think of. That's why I was puzzled when you were attacked before. The queen is the only one at court who even knows anything about my experiments, and she only understands that I am trying to find a permanent relief for her headaches. I do other experiments, too, but I share those with no one."

"Yes," Johan said. "I recall that." They exchanged a smile. He sipped his coffee. "What about your notes? Anything someone might be interested in reading?"

She shook her head. "Those are mostly formulas. I doubt anyone but another scientist, or someone with knowledge in my field, could understand them, and I am the only alchemist in the queen's service."

Johan remembered his other question. "How well do you know General Horn?"

"Not well. He has the queen's trust, of course." She sat straighter. "Surely he's not one of your suspects." The corner of her mouth twitched. Was she laughing at him?

"He has a motive for taking the bible, and he's killed before. But he doesn't fit in other ways."

She raised one eyebrow, waiting, until he explained about the letter.

"Hmm," she said. "From what you say, he seems to have strong feelings. You don't believe he was the man in my workshop, do you? I can't imagine him outrunning you."

Johan smiled. "I agree, so nothing quite fits together."

Gunne rose from the pile of cushions. "Ah, that always makes a good challenge." He rearranged the pile, the way she had them before. "I hate to interrupt, but visitors are given ten minutes."

Johan set his empty cup aside and rose from the chair. Zofia stood up, too, thanking them both. Her gaze lingered on Johan.

Gunne tucked his thumbs into his breeches and walked to the outer hall. "I'll wait out here, but don't be long."

Once Gunne was out of earshot, she looked up at Johan. "Gunne is very perceptive. I wanted to speak with you alone, to thank you for trying to help me." She sighed. "I am afraid my days at court are numbered. Sigrid advised me to admit my guilt and said if I did, the queen mother's punishment might only be expulsion from court, not something more serious. She hinted that Eleanora would likely plead clemency for the murder. Can you imagine, me, a murderer? Anyway, I can't be sure of all that. I'd have Queen Christina's protection too, but even that's not certain, not if she believes I murdered a man." She lowered her lashes. "I suppose it could be worse. Thankfully, I have a home to go to, if I am allowed to live—and am banished from the palace—but I won't be able to do my work. The chemicals cost money, to say nothing of the equipment. Papa, though, will give me a job with the bookbinding."

"We still have time, Zofia. Don't give up, and don't listen to Sigrid or to anyone who wants you to make a false confession. We still might find the real culprit."

"It has to be soon, Johan. Ooh, if only I could get out of here, do some snooping around, I might help. Time is short."

"Gunne is helping, as you are too. This is perhaps the safest place for you to be right now."

"Safe? I don't want safe. I want to catch the person who goes into my laboratory." She balled her fists. "Don't you see? I feel helpless in here, and I can't do a thing about it." She crossed her arms. "I know you and Gunne are trying, it's just—so tiresome, sitting here, while minutes tick by."

Johan felt a surge of pity. For a girl like Zofia to sit back, helpless, depending on others, must be hard, but neither of them had a choice in the matter.

She waited, rigid, by the door. Was she holding back tears? "Go now, Johan, and thanks for coming."

He walked past her and into the hall, leaving behind the fragrance of lemon and the concern in her worried eyes. Sadly, Zofia could be right. The real culprit might never be known.

He walked partway with Gunne, then turned from the corridor and headed to the dormitory, more determined than ever to follow every possible lead. His thoughts returned to the girl Sigrid. Strange, he thought, that the queen's lady would advise Zofia to confess to something she did not do. Still, Sigrid seemed to have befriended Zofia and was making life easier for her. Also, Sigrid had taught Gunne to read. Kind as she was, Johan could not shake the idea that he should talk to Sigrid. There was Henrik to think about, too—and his girl, whoever that might be. Johan rubbed both hands through his hair. There were too many suspects to keep track of. A man was murdered, working his first night on a new job. Perhaps the royal treasurer Gabriel Oxenstiern, saved from death by the circumstance of the goldsmith's presence instead of his that night, needed to be questioned.

The following morning, seated alongside Gunne, Johan broke his fast with his customary hot drink and fresh, warm bread spread with jam. As Gunne finished eating, Johan leaned close.

"Want to come with me to the royal treasurer's?"

Gunne nodded, dabbed his mouth with a linen, and climbed from the bench. Together they went to the treasurer's office, situated not far from the queen's quarters. After a quick knock, the door opened. They were met by a young, bespectacled man with ink stains on his waistcoat and fingers and papers in his hand. His broad shoulders blocked their view. "Yes?"

Johan stepped forward. "We'd like to speak with the treasurer."

The young man stood to the side and looked behind him, as if waiting for directions.

Gabriel Oxenstiern rose from behind his workspace, dismissed his scribe, and reached behind his ears to undo red silk loops attached to the frame of his glasses. He offered two chairs near the ornate, highly polished desk. "You're the new lutenist. I suspect you're here to learn what I know of the murder, and sadly, I know nothing. So you're wasting your time and mine as well."

The treasurer turned his gaze to Gunne as the dwarf climbed up to sit. "I've seen you before. You're one of the queen mother's entertainers, correct?" Without giving time for an answer, he looked back at Johan and tapped his fingers on the desk.

Johan shifted uneasily. Were they being dismissed, just like that? If so, maybe the treasurer had something to hide. The thought spurred Johan on. "Oh, we have no questions about the murder itself. In fact, I believe I can help you."

The treasurer's face registered surprise. "Ha. An ordinary lute player? How could you possibly help me with anything? And I'm not at all interested in anything musical, unlike some of these other courtiers who make fools of themselves, dancing and carrying on for the entertainment of the queen." He looked away, as if regretting his outburst. After all, it did smack of disrespect for the monarch's royal pursuits.

Johan pressed on. "I believe someone may have wanted you dead. Do you have any enemies?"

Gabriel frowned, and Johan detected a slight twitch at his jawline. The treasurer quickly regained his composure. He crossed his arms on the desktop and leaned forward. "That's what worries me, that someone was trying to kill me instead. The goldsmith was in my usual place, sitting at my desk, doing the work I'd been doing for weeks. Perhaps someone killed the wrong man."

Johan looked down at his boots, feeling almost sorry for the man in charge of the royal treasury, in spite of his lofty position. He was probably very lucky to be alive. "That could be. But I need to know if you have any ideas about who might want you dead."

Gabriel rubbed his eyes. "Of course I have enemies. Who in my position would not? As to who would be willing to kill to settle some past grievance, I have no idea. A duel, perhaps, but killing an unarmed man?" He shook his head. "I'm afraid I can be of no help. A family like ours has a multitude of friends, but also many enemies. As for anyone who's capable of killing, no. I can't help you with that."

Johan gathered his courage. There was something he needed to know. "I understand you were accused when there was a shortage in funds, a few years ago."

Gabriel's face colored. "My God, they told even you, a newcomer?"

"I'm only asking because I wondered if they caught the real thief. Once someone steals, it's easier next time."

Gabriel rose from the desk, balling his fists. His face turned the color of the rosy florals in the tapestry behind him. "How dare you insinuate I'm a thief? The case was tried fairly and they found no evidence of theft. The auditors were mistaken. Now leave, before I turn you over to the guards for insulting a member of the queen's Privy Council."

Gunne slid down from his stool and went to wait near the door.

Johan rose and extended his hand to the treasurer. "If you think of anything that might help, get in touch with me. I believe you're in danger until we catch the real murderer."

Gabriel exhaled a little puff and licked his lips. "Yes, I suppose you're right. If I think of anything I'll let you know."

Outside the treasurer's rooms, Johan looked down at Gunne. "We're right where we started, with no new clues as to the murderer."

Gunne smiled. "No, but we gave the treasurer something to think about. I'm betting he looks over his shoulder until we find the killer. Which reminds me. Did you ever search the dancers' dormitory?"

Johan shook his head. He had hoped that wouldn't be necessary. Now, though, he was desperate for anything that might lead to the killer's identity. What better place to start than the dancers' dormitory? He locked his hands together, deep in thought. Best would be to ask Eleanora for permission, but she might turn down his request. She had told him not to break any rules. Would she consider this rule-breaking? He could not afford to risk asking her. He'd just have to take his chances and hope for the best.

CHAPTER THIRTEEN

The dormitory allotted to entertainers was a vast, comfortable space along a back corridor of the original fortress. A wall separated the sleeping area of the dance troupe from that of the musicians, but did little to eliminate curses from the musicians when the dancers rose early, exercising before dawn to the shouts of an appointed leader.

Johan yawned. No sense trying to sleep now. He rose and dressed, wondering how best to carry out the task before him—searching the dancers' storage area for clues. The layout, from the few times he'd been inside, was similar to the musicians' quarters. A short hallway leading between the two dormitories had been converted to storage, with doors on either end, and one in the middle separating the two storage areas.

Johan's thoughts raced ahead. That middle door had likely not been opened for months. Once past that, he'd be fumbling in the dark, rummaging through costumes and such, in an unfamiliar storage area.

He sighed. No sense postponing the task. With the Winter Masque going on, this was the perfect time. Both dormitories should be empty. Besides, his hands had healed and Beaulieu, the dance instructor, had asked him to join the ensemble for tomorrow's performance. This was probably his only chance to search without interruption.

He hurried to the dining hall, broke his fast, and returned to the musicians' dormitory. Begin with the obvious: look for the bible and hope the thief had hidden it in his belongings. Short of that, any clue would be welcome.

After making his way past cubicles, through the arched opening and into the instrument storage area, he neared the closed door separating the two sections of storage. The door opened with the turn of a knob, and an odd smell wafted from the room. Of course. Sweaty costumes and practice shoes. What did he expect? Ignoring the unpleasant odor, he considered his dilemma. A drape divided the storage space from the dancers' dormitory. It blocked the light from a window, but at least offered a bit of protection should someone return unexpectedly. Best to leave it alone.

He paused, peering up at the shelves in the half-light. No names on them, or on any of the stacked boxes. Without knowing whose items were where, even if he found the bible, how to determine who put it there? He took down the first box and removed the contents. Only personal items.

He moved to a lower shelf. Nothing unusual here, only a pair of well-worn slippers, some feathers and ribbons, and a fur hat. He replaced the items and was about to return the box to its place on the shelf when he heard voices. He froze in place. *Pray God they need nothing from the storage room.*

The voices faded and he returned to the task at hand. One by one, working as quickly as he could, he looked through each box, finding nothing but keepsakes, medals from past dance awards, shaving items, and ordinary personal belongings. The final box was one of the smaller ones. He removed the contents and a paper fluttered to the floor. He was about to return the scrap of paper to its rightful space, thinking it a drawing of a dance step, or a love note, when he noticed the paper contained an emblem of some kind. He walked nearer the door, the only source of light, and examined the pattern from every angle. It was a rough drawing of a rose and an unfamiliar landscape. He turned it to one side. Intricate lines flowed from the center. Was there a secret meaning? Likely it had nothing to do with the stolen bible, but he could not shake the feeling that Zofia's interest in alchemy and the unknown had permeated every corner of the castle.

When he heard a commotion near the main door to the dancers' dormitory, he thrust the paper in the pocket of his breeches and replaced the other items in the box. If this drawing proved to be a clue, he would have to figure a way to find out whose belongings these were.

To his horror, he realized the entire troupe was returning from morning practice. He slipped through the middle dividing door and barely managed to close it when he heard voices behind him in the dancers' storage room. They would be tossing costumes and such onto the shelves. He blotted his face with his sleeve. In spite of the winter blizzard outside, he was sweating. These close calls were wearing on his nerves.

That afternoon, having persuaded Gunne to unlock Zofia's door, Johan sat in her tiny room, explaining his morning search of the dancers' belongings. "I found nothing of importance, except maybe this." He handed her the paper.

She studied it, frowning, then handed it back. "I have no idea what this is. What makes you think it has anything to do with the theft or murder?"

"I thought it an odd drawing to be in a dancer's belongings. And it's peculiar that someone sneaks into your laboratory when you have never had any trouble before." He glanced at the sketch. "I was hoping you could tie it to one of your experiments."

She shook her head. "It's nothing I recognize. As for the intruder and his timing, someone wanted something I had, and took advantage of my absence. It's that simple."

Johan shoved the note in the pocket of his waistcoat, wondering why he had even kept it at all. She was probably right, which left him further behind than ever.

Later that day, mulling over the recent events which had turned up nothing, Johan went to the ballet hall to watch rehearsals for the evening's performance. Perhaps a change of scenery would help clear his mind.

The dance, a particularly difficult one, choreographed by a visiting Englishman, had made Beaulieu, the dance master, threaten to leave Sweden forever, but the queen had calmed him down with a promise of even more pay, and now he sat in the fourth row making notes. Johan took a seat nearby. "How are things going?"

Beaulieu smiled grudgingly. "As well as possible, given that we only had a few days to practice. Tell me, any luck with your investigation?"

"Not much," Johan said, surprised that Beaulieu would remember their earlier conversation. After all, the dance master had a lot going on, with the queen demanding new ballets every few days. Just then, a man seated two rows in front glanced over his shoulder. Had he overheard? "Who is that?" Johan asked.

Beaulieu leaned in and whispered, "Svante Oxenstiern. He's the chancellor's bastard son. Comes here every day, just to watch the set construction. His father, of course, would rather his son be tending to state affairs, but Svante seems not inclined. He is especially interested in the machinery and how things work. Sooner or later, as one of the chancellor's sons, he will be expected to take his father's place in government, but the son has an obvious interest in the theater." Beaulieu went back to his notes, leaving Johan with his own thoughts. Svante Oxenstiern and François, the friendly ballet dancer who'd left the game room without his winnings, had something in common; neither man was happy with his career, and both, it appeared, had a duty to fulfill. Svante, as a member of the Oxenstiern family, was expected to become a political player, in spite of his interest in machinery, and François had promised his mother to pursue a career in which he had no interest. Johan wondered fleetingly what his life would have been had his father not given his children free rein to choose their livelihood. Would he have joined the king's army without his brother's coaxing? Would he be here now, playing in court for the Swedish monarch, caught up in a hopeless hunt for an elusive thief?

Svante Oxenstiern had gone to the stage and was talking to one of the stagehands. Johan rose and made his way to the alcove, the spot where he did his best thinking. Perhaps there he could clear his mind and decide what to do next.

That evening, determined to put aside all thoughts of the bible theft, Johan took his place in the ensemble. The musicians, dressed as various forest animals, were sharing the stage with the actors for tonight's performance. Johan flexed his fingers and wrists to warm his hands. His wolf costume, which he expected would be fur, was instead made with canvas and horsehair, not likely to keep him warm, except for the fur cap, a poor representation of a wolf's head. The musicians' costumes, while not clearly visible from the audience, were intended only to add to the scenery. Thank goodness, the torches lining the perimeter of the stage would help heat the room until they burned out, which he hoped was hours away. The musicians had a full schedule ahead, having to play before the masque, during a break in the middle, and again at the end. Then there was the dance after the elaborate production. It would be a long night.

The masque, favored entertainment of the queen, was to be the highlight of the winter season. The earlier masked ball had been merely a preliminary, building excitement up to this evening's production. What took the most preparation had been the set design, a clever assortment of a rolling sea, a flying machine, and other imaginative creations, all wrought by the queen's imported set designer, an Italian. It was whispered the designer had been lured from the French king's palace by Christina's offer. While no one knew the exact figure, it was common knowledge the queen and her councillors had argued about the expense, their words overheard by one of her women and quickly repeated through the castle.

Gunne, recounting to Johan what he had learned about the gossiping incident, gave a chuckle. "The queen was never fond of her ladies, preferring the company of men, and when she learned that one of the women had overheard her spat with the councillors and carried it back to the others, who in turn had whispered the news to the rest of the court, she vowed to rid herself of the ladies, once and for all. Of course it won't happen. She has threatened this before. She is in bad humor, with Zofia, her favorite lady companion for the hunt, confined to that little room. Still, the queen rides out from time to time, weather permitting."

Johan's attention returned to the music before him, a new composition by an English composer the queen had taken a liking to. With no time to practice, both Johan and the lutenist to his left had refused to play without a wooden music stand on which to prop the score.

Horns sounded, a signal the masque was about to get underway. A few moments later, a man appeared on stage, dressed as a Greek soldier. One glance at the costume and Johan knew no expense had been spared for the main characters. This garment was made of leather and metal, put together with gold studs. The leather appeared to be of the finest quality, even down to the greaves on the soldier's legs. With all vulnerable parts protected, the actor looked ready for battle, but it was the helmet that interested Johan the most, an elaborate design meant to show power while protecting the head of the wearer. It covered most of the face and looked as though it could deflect a spear. The plume, made of horsehair, would distract an attacker and help prevent an accurate aim. Johan's thoughts went quickly back to the deadly battlefield, where sometimes it was impossible to detect the enemy. With helmets like these, changes in the design would allow men to distinguish friend from foe.

As the allegory unfolded, Johan studied the set, admiring the skill of the designer. Contraptions in the rafters would pull the flying machine across the stage, but from where the audience sat, clouds would cover the working parts, leaving only the flying machine visible. Johan looked overhead, studying the system of weights, one of which hung directly above him. He would have worried, except that the set designer's reputation left no reason to doubt his experience and considerable skills.

A battle cry went up, and Johan watched with amusement as the helmeted soldier led his men to fight an army of dragons. The dragons, breathing fire, poured from the ship, outnumbering the king's soldiers. The battle was well underway when wood nymphs appeared on stage. At the same moment, the first set of flat wings glided silently from the stage and revealed a forest scene. This was the signal for the lutenists to begin playing. As the music flowed from the section of stringed instruments, the lutenist to Johan's left turned the page and the next sheet fluttered to the floor. Johan, hoping his onstage companion remembered the music well enough to cover for them both, lunged from his chair to retrieve the errant page. A loud crash sounded behind him. The music stopped. He looked back and saw that the weight from the stage machinery had shattered his chair. Bits and pieces of wood lay scattered across the floor.

CHAPTER FOURTEEN

The dance master shouted from the wings and the masque resumed with only a slight pause in the music. A stagehand brought Johan a stool and he sat, thoroughly shaken by the narrow escape. While the performance continued, workers dismantled the weight and carried it from the stage.

Johan tried to concentrate on the music before him, and during the second act, his thoughts took a different turn. If he had not leaned forward to pick up the page of music, he would no doubt be dead now. Who could withstand a chunk of iron weighing close to a *lispund* striking his skull? That was more than a cook's bag of wheat weighed. Landing squarely on one's head, that would break a man's neck if nothing else.

Suddenly he was sweating beneath the flimsy costume, and by the time the masque ended, he realized he had no idea who won the mock battle. Thank goodness, other musicians would play the dance music. Already the queen had risen from her chair, the best spot in the hall from which to see the stage. For once she had chosen not to perform, but now, as actors left the stage, still wearing their masks, she took her place in the opening dance, a signal that the others could join in.

Johan was about to return to the dormitory to change from his costume, having lost all thought of taking part in the dance, when he saw Svante Oxenstiern standing in a circle of men. Suddenly Johan remembered Beaulieu's telling him that Svante watched the building of the machinery, day after day.

Did Svante have something to do with the mechanical failure? Not likely. What motive would the chancellor's son have? He could likely command anything he wanted. Was tonight's mishap simply an accident, or was it deliberate? Could Svante be involved with the book theft or the murder? Not likely, but how did he know that for sure? What was certain, though, was that Johan had become involved in a dangerous scheme. First, there was the attack in Zofia's workshop, then a frantic chase through the castle after a shadowy figure who could have been anyone—and now this, a possible attempt on his life.

Johan headed for the closest exit and made his way around a group of couples who waited for the dance to begin. "Wait," a male voice called. Johan turned around to see a man removing his mask. This was the famed set designer, the man Gunne had pointed out earlier, the Italian who was rumored to have been paid with gold from the Swedish treasury, compliments of the queen. "I forget your name," the man said, "but I know you're a lutenist. I am Giacomo Torelli."

"Johan Sokolewski." Johan extended his free hand to the Italian, hoping the man was not given to long conversations. The wolf costume was itching, and he wanted a cup of wine. He hated wearing costumes, but Beaulieu was insistent—the musicians, even though they sat to the side, away from the performers, were nevertheless part of the scenery. Dressed in ordinary attire, they would ruin the effect and take the audience from the imaginary world. Johan scratched his shoulder. "I'm pleased to meet such a lauded set designer."

"Please, my apologies. Thank God you were not injured tonight. Nothing like that has ever happened before. My reputation will be ruined if word gets out that—"

"Rest assured, I will not speak about it to anyone."

The craftsman had fallen in step with Johan and seemed in no hurry to leave. "Is there somewhere we can talk privately?"

A wee inner voice cautioned Johan to listen. This sounded serious. Maybe he should hear the man out. "I was going to the musicians' dormitory. I'd like to change."

"Of course, yes, that's fine."

While Torelli waited on a bench near the storage area, Johan went to his cubicle and exchanged the itchy canvas for his own clothes. When he returned, he saw that Torelli had helped himself to a cup of wine. Where he'd gotten it, and whose it was, Johan had no idea, but he preferred his own. He returned to his cubicle, retrieved a hidden bottle, poured a generous amount into his own pewter cup, and returned to sit next to Torelli. "What did you want to talk with me about?"

"The machinery failure, of course." Torelli frowned, rubbing one finger around the rim of his cup. He drew his bushy brows together. "It makes no sense at all. I personally check the pulleys and weights before each performance. If you had not moved—and had the Fates, or an angel, not been with you—doubtless the queen would have charged me with murder." He wiped his brow, as if the thought of what could have happened made him sick. "There are great rewards for serving the highest in the land, but much is expected."

"Of course," Johan said. "Was this what you had to tell me?"

Torelli shook his head. "I'm convinced someone tampered with my set. Right after the performance, while you and the other musicians prepared to leave, I inspected the equipment. The hemp used to secure the weights looked as though it had been cut partway through with a sharp instrument, probably a knife. Given time, and considering the size of the weight, the hemp was sure to break with stress. I have yet to hear the queen's opinion about the mishap, but then she may not have seen where it landed. The dancers may have blocked her view. Beaulieu was wise to continue with the music. He's a master at performance, better than most. Do you know anyone who may have wanted to hurt you?"

Johan felt a cold chill. Was he being naïve? Was he a target for some crazed madman? Or was this, like everything else seemed to be, somehow tied up with the disappearance of the Silver Bible, the library murder, and whatever someone wanted from Zofia's laboratory? "I have no enemies at court." He drank from his cup of wine. "If it was a deliberate act, the perpetrator would have to know something about the system you devised for the flying machine and the moving ship. Am I correct?"

"Ha. No one understands my system, not completely, though others have tried to copy it, with disastrous results. Oh, I consult with others in my craft, if the money is right, but here at court, I can't think of anyone, except . . ." He bit his lip, then swiftly drained the last of his wine from the cup.

"Yes?" Johan leaned forward. "Who here at court would know enough about stage design to make the weight drop during a performance?"

"Possibly Axel Oxenstiern's son, but of course he is above reproach. Svante Oxenstiern enjoys seeing how the sets are put together—even helps with set construction. He's talented, but his skill will be wasted. He will be a commander and go to battle like his father. Too bad, to waste a talent like that. You should speak with him. He asked about you, and knew you had lately come to court, then he asked about the musicians and where they sat during a performance. He was puzzled that musicians would be allowed on stage with the actors instead of in the galleries as is usual. I told him what the queen told me, that she liked to watch the instrumentalists, and wanted them closer to the performers."

While Torelli drained his cup, Johan pondered what he'd just learned. So, Svante Oxenstiern had asked about the seating for the masque performance. Johan ran his hands through his hair, flattened from the wolf headpiece. Svante Oxenstiern's father practically ran Sweden by himself, and it was common knowledge he had as much power as the queen. His son, even a bastard, would be destined for great things—far beyond set design. Johan tried to recall what Béaulieu had told him about Svante Oxenstiern. Not much, but Gunne might know something more. "Anyone else who may have spent time around the set, long enough to figure how to do such a thing?"

Torelli set his empty cup aside, as if he had lost interest in the conversation now that he had made his apology. "There was one man—one of the dance troupe. He and a few others came early to practice their steps. The mask he wore covered his face, and I did not watch him long enough to recognize his movements as belonging to any one dancer. He did wander over and talk to my assistant. I called my man to help me because the dancer was in the way and we were running out of time."

"His name? I don't suppose your attendant would recall—"

"Heavens, no. I didn't see them talking much anyway. It was mostly just looking. I guess he was curious as to how the machinery worked."

Johan nodded. Voices outside reminded him that the dance might be breaking up. It had been a long night. Besides, Torelli had probably told him everything he knew. It seemed evident that someone had deliberately damaged the equipment. Torelli was sure of it. Was it the masked dancer? Was it the same man who had attacked him in Zofia's workshop? Or could it have been Svante Oxenstiern, the Lord High Chancellor's son? What concerned Johan most was who would want to harm him, and why, and how soon he would strike again.

Torelli had wiped the cup and stashed it on a shelf. After wishing Johan well, the set designer left the room. Johan rubbed his arms, suddenly chilled. No doubt about it. Someone was trying to send him a warning. This business with Svante merited a closer look. Perhaps Gunne could add something more to what Johan had learned from both Beaulieu and Torelli.

CHAPTER FIFTEEN

Johan laid his lute aside and rubbed the back of his neck. Even in the quiet of the practice area, he was unable to concentrate, his mind on yesterday's unnerving experience. Maybe Torelli, the set designer, was correct. Fate, or a watchful angel, had made Johan retrieve a sheet of music, the only thing that had kept him from being the victim of either an accident or a deliberate act.

If it was planned, Svante was a prime suspect. He had the knowledge and opportunity to sabotage Torelli's stage equipment, but what motive could a chancellor's bastard son have to harm a lute player? Unless he wanted the investigation ended, but why?

Johan rose from the bench, stored his lute, and set out to find Gunne. The dwarf sat in a shaft of sunlight beneath one of two windows in the hall leading to the queen mother's quarters.

Johan sat beside him. "I want to ask you some questions—about Svante Oxenstiern."

"Let's go somewhere private," Gunne said. "The upstairs alcove?"

Minutes later they sat at the window as the light of day dwindled to darkness. A single torch illuminated the hallway, and smoke rose from the fires that blazed in every hearth, filling the rooms in the castle with the smell of charred timber, a dark and heavy odor like burnt woodland. Johan opened the shutters a crack, inhaling a clean breath of air, and glanced at the scene before him. Snow had fallen for days and a blanket of white covered the grounds below. With short days, six hours of light at best, he found the sight depressing.

"Leave it cracked open, Johan, so we can breathe. With fires burning night and day, my eyes sting. I can't help but think all the smoke is unhealthy. Now, tell me what Torelli had to say."

Johan put his hands on his knees. "He wanted to apologize, and insisted he had checked the rigging just before the show. Now, what do you know about Svante Oxenstiern? Torelli said Svante took an interest in the machinery and in set design. What is even more interesting is that he inquired as to where the musicians would be sitting onstage."

"Axel's bastard son? He's a quiet sort, and no wonder. His father casts a long shadow. Still, it's strange that he would take an interest in you, or in where the musicians would sit. But it's hard for me to see what motive he would have for hurting you."

"Perhaps he knows I'm investigating the crimes. I believe the man who attacked me in Zofia's workshop also knew, though God knows how."

"Everyone knows by now. Word travels fast here at court. In winter there's nothing to do but play board games and gossip." Gunne laughed, then grew serious. "Did you ask Torelli what could have happened?"

"He insists someone tampered with his set—said a load-bearing cord had been partially cut, part of his system of weights and pulleys. He takes pride in his work, said he inspected the machinery after the last rehearsal, as was his habit. Oh, yes, he said a masked dancer had been there earlier, going through his routine, but he had no idea who that could have been."

Gunne, after a fit of coughing, which he insisted was brought on by taking too many baths, blew his nose and took a sip of a medicinal brew he said would cure anything short of a death blow. He tucked the tiny flask into an inner pocket of his breeches. "Hmm. Svante Oxenstiern usually has a knife at his waist. Of course if he works on set designs his knife would be useful. I've seen Torelli's helpers use a sharp instrument to scrape paint."

Johan drew his brows together. "I wish I had thought of this earlier. If Oxenstiern's son used his knife to cut a hemp rope, we might have found threads on the knife. By now, though, any rope particles would be gone."

Gunne's face brightened. "Not so. We may be in luck. The queen rode out not long ago with her Privy Council. Oxenstiern and his son would have gone along. They love the hunt as much as the queen does. Svante would take a crossbow or a musket, and likely a longer blade. Maybe he left his knife behind."

"Are you saying we should take a chance and look around in his chambers? A son of the most powerful man in Sweden?"

Gunne looked thoughtful. "There will never be a better time. They'll be gone probably two days."

One of the shutters banged open and Johan rose to hook them closed. Something moved below, and he saw, by the light of the moon, a dark figure standing beside a horse, silhouetted against the snow. From here it looked like Alexandre Voullon, the theorboe player. No one else wore a broad yellow hat, pointed in the back. He had seen it with Voullon's belongings, even commented once on its color. "Strange," Johan said, "for anyone to be saddling a horse on a night like this. Wonder where he's heading in this weather."

Gunne scrambled up to look out, blocking Johan's view. "Hmm," Gunne said, "I just saw him slip something into his saddlebag. It looked like a book. You don't suppose . . ." He turned to face Johan, who was already leaving the alcove.

"We'll need warm clothes," Johan said, "and there's no time to spare."

★ ★ ★ ★ ★

Minutes later, while the stableman lay passed out on a pile of hay surrounded by empty jugs, Johan hurried to saddle a horse, while Gunne kept an eye on the disappearing rider. They had wasted precious minutes getting warmer clothes, but Johan had learned his lesson about frostbite, and now wore thick gloves and a fur hat that covered his ears. Gunne's hooded cape, hooked closed in front, covered all but his boots and face, half of which was hidden behind a wool scarf. Johan lifted the dwarf to the horse's back, then jumped into the saddle.

Following new hoof marks in the snow, they trailed behind the rider, each agreeing that curiosity, rather than common sense, had brought them out on a night like this. "I can't be sure it was Voullon," Johan said, "but if one wanted to rid himself of a stolen bible, tonight would be the perfect opportunity. Perhaps it is all prearranged and he has a buyer waiting."

A gust of icy wind blew across the open path and Johan nudged the horse toward the tree line. Two darkly clad figures on a dark horse would be easy to spot on open terrain. At least the trees, snow-laden as they were, offered a bit of cover. Johan brushed new snow from the side of his face and peered ahead. No matter what, he had to keep sight of their quarry.

Gunne tugged at Johan's arm. "No telling how far he's going. What about turning back? We could wait until he returns and ask him questions. I'm freezing."

Johan, tempted by thoughts of a warm fire, and knowing the ride back might turn out to be a long one, considered Gunne's request. Still, they had come this far. No man would go visiting on a night like this. Something was up.

He was about to speak when he saw the rider had come to a wooden building and reined in his horse. Johan crossed the snow-covered field and brought his own horse up an embankment. A shed not far from the building's front entrance afforded some protection from the weather and gave a clear view of the larger structure. Fires blazed and torches burned inside, a welcome sight at another time, but right now, it looked foreboding. Gunne relaxed his hold on Johan's waist. "Looks like this was definitely an arranged meeting."

Johan blinked. That was Voullon's profile, clearly silhouetted in the torchlight. A rush of regret gave him pause. He liked the theorboe player, but clearly the man had left the castle under cover of darkness to avoid detection. Voullon dismounted, then reached into the saddlebag and pulled out a book. "The right size for the bible," Gunne whispered.

Johan swallowed. What now? Should he go back and alert the palace guards? That was too risky, and a waste of precious time. It would take an hour to ride back. The queen mother would want proof of Voullon's deceit, along with the bible itself—if, indeed, that was what Voullon had. By then, that proof might have vanished. What was to keep the buyer here, once the exchange was made, if that was what this meeting was about? "I have to go in, Gunne."

"You can't. You might be killed. No telling who else is in there, and you are not armed. We should get the guards and let them handle Voullon."

"I have a knife, and I can use it."

"Suit yourself. I'll wait out here to give your body proper burial."

Johan dismounted, trying to ignore Gunne's attempt at humor. He handed the reins to Gunne with a confidence he did not feel. Going inside a building where he had no idea what might greet him seemed like a foolish move, but what else could he do? Besides, he'd been trained to use a blade in close contact. "Don't worry," Johan said, "and stay close by. I may have to leave in a hurry."

Keeping to the shadows, shivering from the cold and wondering if his hand was steady enough to use a knife should it come to that, Johan crept toward the front entrance, the same door Voullon had gone through moments before. He strained to hear voices, but no sound came from inside. Was money being exchanged even now?

Having decided there was nothing to do but go blindly in and catch the thief making the exchange, he lifted the latch, opened the door, and stepped inside.

Chapter Sixteen

Johan's heart pounded. He was alone in an empty room. Where had Voullon disappeared to? What was going on here? A smoldering fire and empty ale cups told him the room had been recently abandoned. He crept across the floor, hoping a loose board would not give away his presence should anyone be close by, and entered a darkened hallway. Several paces later he saw light streaming from beneath a door. He pressed his ear to the opening. Silence. He lifted the latch and went in.

An oil lamp illuminated the room, but it was the two stacked floorboards that caught his eye. He walked over and peered down into a black hole, barely large enough for a man to go through. His heart quickened as he heard the sound of human voices. When his eyes adjusted to the dim light, he saw a ladder extended into the space below. Did he dare go down? How else could he learn exactly what Voullon was up to?

After a quick prayer, he descended the ladder. He reached the bottom rung and realized the voices came from behind a set of wooden doors across the room. He crossed to the doors and put his ear against the tiny crack between the two panels. Footsteps came near the doors. Johan drew back. One of the doors opened and a bearded man stared at him. "Who are you, and why are you here?"

Johan took a deep breath before speaking. "That's what I wanted to ask you."

The man glanced over his shoulder, as if wondering what to

do next, then closed the door softly behind him and looked warily at Johan. "Now, why have you come?"

"I need to speak with Monsieur Voullon."

"I see. He did not mention he invited a visitor."

"So, may I step inside?"

"Not now, but I'll get Voullon."

While Johan waited, he rehearsed what he would say to the theorboe player. First, he would demand the bible. If Voullon gave it peacefully, there would be no trouble. If he refused, Johan would have to take it by force, which would be no easy task with the others around. How many were there? If the plan was to split the money among them, he would have to fight them all, and would lose. Perhaps he should have listened to Gunne and not come in at all, but it was too late now.

The door opened again and Johan stood face to face with Alexandre Voullon. "Johan. What brings you here? I had no idea you—"

"Give me the bible and I'll be gone. Otherwise, you'll be taking responsibility for what happens."

"Bible? Do you mean my—"

"The Silver Bible, the one you carried in here."

Voullon's expression changed from frustration to disbelief. "You think I have the Silver Bible?"

"You're a suspect, yes. I have a witness outside. We both saw you pull a small book from your saddlebag."

Voullon's mouth opened to reply, but gradually, as if a fog had lifted, his lips widened into an amused smile. "Oh, Johan, I see it all now. You must have followed me here. Wait, I'll get the book I brought in. Stay here. I don't want to disturb the others." He opened the door and walked inside. The room, Johan could see now, had been transformed into a chapel. Most of the occupants mumbled a prayer, while Voullon went to one of the benches, picked up a book, and returned to Johan, closing the door behind him. "My prayer book, and now you know my secret. Yes, I am Catholic. We meet here weekly—it's as often as we dare. I pray you, do not make this public. It would embarrass the queen, who looks the other way. Her subjects will say she coddles Catholics."

Johan handed him back the book, feeling foolish, but more than that, sorry for Voullon, forced to worship in secret. While he had no patience with men who waged wars in the name of God, a man should be free to worship in peace. "Go back to your prayers, Alexandre. You'll hear no more from me, and no one else but Gunne, the queen mother's dwarf, will ever know. His lips are sealed, as are mine."

Voullon extended his hand. "Then we are friends, and all is forgiven." They shook hands, and as Johan climbed the ladder and hurried to meet Gunne, he knew his little friend would remind Johan that they should have turned back.

While riding back to the castle, Johan recounted what had taken place. "So there you have it. I feel a bit foolish."

"Well," Gunne said, "we have eliminated Voullon as a suspect. Look at it that way."

"Yes, but our time would have been better spent examining Svante Oxenstiern's room, the way we planned."

"Then we should go there tonight, while he is still away."

"I'm tired and it's late." Johan rubbed his eyes. "Still, we may not have another chance, so I suppose you're right."

A half hour later found them making their way to a stairwell in the newer part of the castle. "We can wait in the shadows near the landing," Gunne whispered. "It's the only place that is safe. Several elite guards patrol all these corridors because rooms up here are occupied by the queen's most important advisors."

"But why so many in one area? Have they reason to be afraid?"

"Axel's life has been threatened before. It prompted a request from the Oxenstiern family for increased security."

They reached the top landing and hurried to take cover far from the torchlight at the far end of the corridor. Now, waiting in the dark, Johan wanted to ask Gunne who the Oxenstierns' enemies were. The queen, he knew from dormitory gossip, frequently disagreed with the chancellor, but she was known to fiercely defend him at other times, reminding the challenger of the moment that Axel had been her tutor for years, that she had learned about governing from his lectures.

Brought back to the present by a nudge on his calf from Gunne, Johan judged it was time to make his way through the half-opened door, a sign of Svante Oxenstiern's trust in his guards to protect his chambers from prying eyes. Gunne whispered. "I'll wait here. When I see them making their third round I'll let you know. Then get out quick."

Johan nodded and stepped inside the room. After lighting a candle, he cast a quick glance, hoping to see a knife. With luck, it might still have hemp fibers on the cutting edge. Seeing no knife, he decided to begin with the chest nearby, an ornately carved oak one with brass trim. The lid opened easily, revealing an assortment of clothes, all handsomely tailored of fine materials. *Nothing here.* He moved to a desk, where stacks of papers were placed in an orderly fashion.

His gaze rested on a letter lying near the front of the desk. The script, finely drawn, had flourishes scattered throughout. Whoever wrote the letter had taken time in the writing. He read the opening line: *My dear and beloved Svante: The hours since we parted have turned day into night. I long to be with you again, and if we cannot . . .*

Johan turned away. Svante Oxenstiern's personal life was

none of his affair. Besides, time was limited. He crossed from the sitting area into Svante's sleeping chamber.

The bed, an elegant design with four posts, was piled high with furs, most likely from animals that once lived on the royal hunting grounds. For a moment he remembered Zofia's distaste for the hunt, her refusal to participate in the killing. Would she sleep under furs, or opt for woolen blankets?

Remembering he had little time left, he surveyed the room with a quick glance. Other than a straight-backed chair, there was only a small dark corner table next to the bed. He stepped closer. There, on the table in clear sight, lay a knife and sheath. His heart raced. To be left here, near the bedside, the knife must have been lately carried. Carefully lifting it from its resting place, he slid it into the sheath and tucked it inside his boot. As he straightened, he saw the yellow glow of a lantern reflecting on the white walls of Svante Oxenstiern's outer room. He whirled around and faced a member of the queen's uniformed guards.

CHAPTER SEVENTEEN

Propelled along between two of Her Majesty's guardsmen, Johan knew something had gone terribly wrong. He had only a moment to think, while the guards took his purse and his only two coins. They searched his pockets and both sleeves, then returned his empty purse.

Why hadn't Gunne alerted him? He was to have warned Johan before the patrolling guards made their third pass. Was the dwarf safe, or had they taken him earlier? Surely Gunne could talk his way out of this, claiming an errand for the queen mother. If the worst happened, Johan vowed to take the blame. He would explain that the dwarf had only been trying to help, and knew nothing of Johan's intent.

As they proceeded down the first set of steps, he saw Gunne below, doubled over in a fit of coughing. So that was it. Gunne had left his post to avoid being discovered by his incessant coughing, thereby missing the chance to give the warning.

The guards passed hastily by Gunne, and Johan dared not look at his friend, which might arouse suspicion. Instead, he opted to distract the guards from Gunne's presence, so far from the queen mother's quarters. "Where are you taking me?" Johan asked.

The guards walked straight ahead, their silence raising alarm in Johan's mind. Would he simply be thrown in prison without a trial? After all, he had been caught red-handed, and while no blood had been spilled to justify any colorful accusation, the breach of trust that came from entering the private chambers of one of the most important families in Sweden without permission might be considered tantamount to murder in this country.

After descending two more sets of stairs, he realized he was being taken far below ground level. He broke into a sweat, remembering tales from his childhood of what rulers did to traitors. Thank God they had not searched his boots. By the time they paused at a cell, enclosed by iron bars, he knew he had just done the dumbest thing in his life, and what for? In search of a thief he knew nothing about, who had stolen a book he had never seen, for the sake of a blonde-haired alchemist who, for all he knew, had reasons of her own for taking the bible, as the queen mother believed.

The guards shoved him into the cell, and when their footsteps retreated, he stood listening, a quiet desperation creeping over him. What now? Would Gunne have any influence with the authorities? Likely not. He was simply another entertainer. As the helplessness of his situation became more obvious, Johan found himself pacing, and at last, fatigued from all that had happened, he leaned against one wall and peered up at the only source of light, a small window near the ceiling. Through it he could see the beginnings of dawn. Was the window his way out? He walked the few paces to the wall below the window and rubbed one hand across. Smooth brick, with no stones to gain a toehold. Of course. Dungeon builders would know better than that. He heard a quick, low-pitched squeak from the window area. Looking up, he saw two rats on the ledge, tails swishing. Blessed Mother. Rats in here, and vermin likely crawling on the dirt floor. How did they live in this freezing weather with no heat? For that matter, how could he? A new wave of desperation made him cross to the iron rods enclosing the cell. He shook with all his might, but they remained firm from floor to rafter.

How long before someone returned, or did guards even come

here? Would they feed him, or leave him to starve? The only person who might suspect he was down here was Gunne, and if the dwarf's part in the scheme had been discovered, he would end up in the same place.

Unable to stand any longer, he slid down the wall to the floor. Minutes later he heard footsteps in the corridor heading his way. He looked between the bars. One man carried a tray of food, the other a slop bucket and a blanket. His hopes of reprieve plummeted. This was no temporary holding cell. It looked like he would be here for days, rotting away in the dark.

As the door clanged open, Johan gathered his courage. "How long am I to be held?"

The guards exchanged glances, situated the bucket in one corner, handed him the blanket and tray, and left, locking the iron door behind them. Johan gritted his teeth. His stomach rumbled, but the food smelled like warmed goose grease. He set the tray aside, wrapped the blanket around his shivering body, and pondered his fate. Soon the cook would be serving sausages and hot bread in the dining hall. Would he even be missed?

As the sun rose in the sky, he dozed. Later, wakened by the sound of footsteps in the corridor outside his cell, he straightened and rubbed his neck. What now?

The footsteps paused and Johan heard a key inserted in the lock. The door swung open and a guard stepped in carrying a bundle of clothes. "Here, put these on. The queen mother demands your presence. Make yourself presentable. Guards will be back shortly to take you there." He flung the clothes at Johan and walked out, securing the door behind him.

Johan removed his boots, his breeches and shirt, and put on the clean clothes, fitting the knife back into his boot. What did this mean? Would he be tried by the dwarfs? Would Eleanora even remember he was the queen's lutenist? He wished now he'd found out more about the state of the queen mother's mind. Was she delusional, as some said? Would he be tried for trespassing? She could confine him, as she had Zofia. If so, what about the murder investigation? Would she push to convict Zofia, having lost patience with the unscrupulous foreigner?

By the time the earlier guards returned, Johan knew his future lay solidly in the hands of an elderly queen. All he could do was tell the truth and hope his punishment was not too severe. He went with the guards to the upper floor, then was taken to another section of the castle, a newer part he and Gunne had never explored. Soon they were in the corridor leading to the queen mother's rooms. Johan's head swam, partly from hunger, but mostly from confusion over the myriad twists and turns that had brought them here. He doubted even Gunne was aware of the passages these guards had taken.

They paused by a door opposite the royal portraits, several paces before the queen mother's rooms. One of Johan's guards knocked and the door was opened by an armed guard in uniform. Johan's own guards released their hold on his arm. "Wait in here. They'll call when it's your turn." As they left, the armed guard pointed to the benches lining the perimeter. "Sit anywhere," he said. Johan barely took notice of the other prisoners in the room.

He sat and crossed his arms. Across the way one of the cook's helpers waited, mumbling to himself. A man sitting nearby scooted next to Johan. "Your first time here?"

Johan nodded, hoping the man would move away. His sour breath made Johan nauseous, but the speaker was determined. "Nothing to worry about. Be glad you didn't go before the court tribunal, which could have sent you to the town judges—a meaner pack you've never encountered. The old queen is more lenient. Last time I was brought here they had caught me stealing imported wine from the cellar. I had to scrub the kitchen floor for a month, but that's nothing compared to what regular criminals get. They go easy on palace insiders, thank goodness." He winked at Johan and commenced picking his teeth with a splinter of wood. "I clean the latrines. How about you?"

Johan was wondering how much to say when a voice called out, "Johan Sokolewski." Johan jumped from the bench, forgetting the other man's question in his haste to learn what punishment the queen mother would mete out. He felt the knife sheath move in his boot, the leather ties rubbing against his bare skin. With any luck, he would soon find time to inspect both the knife and sheath for evidence, an impossible task inside his dark cell. He recalled the lens in Zofia's laboratory, and the fish bones, but his thoughts were interrupted by the guard's raspy voice. "You're next. Too bad. She's in a foul mood."

He entered an antechamber, different from the one he had seen on his first visit to the queen mother's presence. The dwarfs were nowhere around, eliminating the possibility of slipping the knife and its protective sheath to Gunne for safekeeping. Here, the room and its occupants were somber, a reminder this was no caper. He had committed a grievous offense, and against an important personage.

The queen mother sat on a dais, her long brocaded skirts spread in a whirl at her feet. Below her sat six men, all strangers. From their ceremonial dress, he wondered if these were judges from outside the castle. If so, that meant Eleanora considered this case too important to be tried by her dwarfs.

He bowed and suddenly straightened. The sheath had shifted again inside his boot. Come what may, he would have to inspect the knife for clues, and soon Svante Oxenstiern would return from the hunt, if he had not already. Time mattered. If he didn't return the knife before the owner found it missing, Johan's crime would be theft on top of trespassing.

One of the robed men stood to read the charges. "Breaking

into a private bedchamber with the intent of harming the occupant." He turned to his colleague. "Was anything missing?"

"Nothing reported. The guards checked this man's purse. He had only a few coins. They found him before he had a chance to steal."

"Wait. I know this man." The queen mother leaned forward and Johan thought he detected a look of impatience from the judges. "Aren't you the lutenist?" she asked.

"I am, Your Majesty. In my zeal to carry out your wishes, to discover the thief—"

She held up her hand, silencing him mid-sentence. "Gentlemen, you are dismissed. I will handle this personally. Take those other prisoners back to their cells until tomorrow." She leaned back, and the judges gathered their papers and left the room.

"Move closer. I can hardly see you."

Johan stepped toward the row of chairs, empty now of his judges, a sight that gave him reason to hope. Eleanora rang a bell and her women appeared from behind a wing, taking their seats beside the queen mother. When they were settled, she said, "Johan Sokolewski, I gave you permission to find a thief, not to be one. By all that's holy, what were you doing in Svante Oxenstiern's bedchamber?"

Johan shifted uneasily. Anything the women heard would be common knowledge an hour from now. "May we speak in private, Your Majesty?"

She shook her head. "I trust my ladies. You may speak freely."

Johan could feel Sigrid's eyes on him, waiting. He dared not lie to Eleanora, a crime most likely punishable by death, but how to clear his name? His thoughts raced. "I learned that Svante and I had a common interest. I am an entertainer, and he expressed curiosity about the unusual seating for the masque. I would like to speak with him, to clear all this up." He swallowed. This was mostly true. He would like to clear this up,

183

and they did have a common interest in theater.

"The Oxenstierns are all in the queen's hunting party. That's why all this has fallen to me. Even her councillors went along." She pinched her lips together, clearly annoyed. "But we are getting nowhere, and from what you say, this is a frivolous charge, brought on by overzealous guards. You are free to go."

Johan, startled by the queen mother's words, opened his mouth to thank her and saw that Sigrid had risen and was whispering in Eleanora's ear. Johan made a quick bow, not waiting for the queen mother to change her mind, and backed from the room.

He hurried to the kitchen, grabbed a bite to eat, and proceeded to the dormitory where he shed the too-tight garments and washed at a basin. He pulled on a clean wool shirt and breeches, put on a warm cloak, and set out to find Gunne. As he approached the dwarf's room, he saw his friend lying asleep on a bench in the corridor. "Gunne." He touched Gunne's shoulder. "We need to talk."

Gunne blinked, then sat upright. The book he had been reading earlier fell to the floor. He slipped down from the bench and picked it up. "Let's go to my room. You can tell me all about your hearing."

"There's not much to tell. Eleanora dismissed the judges and let me go."

"You're a lucky man, Johan."

Johan nodded and followed Gunne inside his room. Once there, he knew why Gunne had chosen the corridor for his afternoon nap. "What's that odor?"

"It smelled worse in here before," Gunne said, "but I managed to put the fire out before much was damaged."

Johan glanced down at a small table. Ashes and soot covered the top. "What caused the fire?"

Gunne tucked his thumbs in the waist of his breeches, barely covered by the newly fashionable shorter doublet. "I tried to heat coffee in the incense burner. The device would have worked had I used something a little wider to better support the bowl."

Johan choked back laughter, then produced the leather sheath from inside his boot.

"Sorry I let you down," Gunne said, "but I knew my coughing would bring the guards running. The palace physician told me to drink licorice root tea but I don't like the taste. At any rate, I'm relieved the queen mother let you go." He took the knife from Johan and slipped it from the sheath. "Nothing would stick to this metal, except perhaps here." He rubbed his thumb over a nick in the blade. "The bone handle is worn smooth. Probably a gift from his father or uncle."

Johan said, "If we find any hemp, it will be in the sheath, left there when the knife was slipped in, but I was thinking, something that fine—"

Gunne looked up, smiling. "Zofia's looking glass."

"Exactly."

The dwarf handed the knife to Johan. "Let's go. I want her permission. After all, it's her equipment."

Zofia, Johan saw, had a sizeable pile of books on the floor near her chair. She laid the current one aside and greeted Johan and Gunne. "Good news, Johan?"

"I'm afraid not—nothing yet, but we may be getting closer."

She leaned forward excitedly. "Who do you suspect?"

Gunne broke in. "We're not sure yet. It could be any of a number of people, but we need to ask a favor."

"Yes?" She glanced at Gunne, waiting, and Johan noticed her lashes, long and blonde like her hair that curled to her shoulders, a few strands touching the lace at the edge of her bodice. Johan swallowed. Like all magicians, she would know how to charm.

"We would like to use your glass, the one for the bones," Johan said.

She laughed. "*Mais oui, Monsieur.* You may use my bone machine, as you call it. You need to inspect some bones? How can this help—"

"No. We need it to inspect evidence," Gunne said. "If our suspicions prove to be correct, it may lead to the thief—in a roundabout way."

She crossed her arms. "What do you mean? Either it's evidence or it's not."

Johan spoke up. "We both believe that someone wants me to abandon my search for the thief and murderer. We have an item to inspect."

"Very well. Careful you don't break my lens, and please don't touch my specimens. The bones are fragile."

Johan chuckled. "I won't touch your specimens. You have my word on that."

CHAPTER EIGHTEEN

Late that afternoon, in the confines of the musicians' dormitory, Johan reviewed what he'd learned so far. The first interview, with Matthiae, the Calvinist, had gone nowhere. He had an alibi and witnesses. And was the theft of the bible necessarily tied to the murder? Would any learned man believe a book would give power to its owners?

He'd hardly framed the thought before he knew the answer. *Of course.* Superstition was rampant, and peasants were not the only believers. In some places, witches were still burned at the stake, and charlatans were on every street corner, even in the larger cities.

Then there was Freinsheim, an unlikely suspect. He'd served in the king's court and seemed interested in nothing but a quiet retirement in one of his numerous homes. His assistant Naudé, though, had a motive. Bringing the Silver Bible to France would be a coup. Once in France, he'd be safe from prosecution. Then there was General Horn, who suspected anyone French, or so it seemed. His letter, though, might have a deeper meaning. Marin, the queen's sketching teacher, had a secret, and it had something to do with the framed drawing, though not necessarily with the theft or murder. And now, Chancellor Oxenstiern's own son, Svante, might be connected to the crime.

Johan glanced up at one of the high dormitory windows. Darkness had descended. The hallways would be empty, with dinner underway in the royal dining room. There was no better time than now to take advantage of Zofia's laboratory and her amazing lens in order to inspect the leather sheath for shreds of hemp. With luck, they would be closer to finding the thief after tonight. He walked to the appointed meeting place, where Gunne waited in the shadows.

Johan paused. "Did you drink the licorice tea for your cough?"

"I did. I wouldn't let you down twice." He grinned. "Now, it's all clear. Go ahead."

Johan made his way down the corridor toward Zofia's laboratory. Once inside, he closed the door behind him and lit the largest lamp he could find. Using a blade from Zofia's supplies, he cut the leather stitching of the sheath, exposing the darker leather inside, where he hoped to find the evidence. Zofia's fish bones lay to one side in a dish, as if waiting to be served to unsuspecting diners, a thought that amused him—or were his nerves playing tricks?

He looked through the lens, twisted the flattened leather to a better position, and leaned close. Unless he was mistaken, these were hemp fibers, up near the opening of the sheath. So the rough spot on Svante's knife had probably left those behind. This sample was coarse, the quality that made hemp the favored rope of mariners, whose lives depended on weather-resistant rigging.

Johan returned Zofia's blade to her neat row of tools next to the lens. He selected some brass tweezers from her collection and put Svante's knife under the lens. There, lodged in small nicks along the blade's edge, were several tiny fibers. He placed them in a jar, corked the top, then put the jar and sheath in the pocket of his breeches. The knife went into the leather purse at his waist. He extinguished the lamp and left the room, hurrying to where Gunne waited. At last, he had something that might tie a suspect to the murder and the Silver Bible theft. True, it might only be evidence of who had cut the rope that held up the stage weight, but knowing that might lead him to the villain.

The corridor loomed empty and dark, but Johan felt as though a thousand eyes were watching. When they reached Gunne's room, Johan emptied the cream-colored fibers onto a black waistcoat. Gunne lifted one of the fibers, studied it carefully, and put it in the jar. "I have no doubt this is hemp. Let's keep all this together. It will be needed later."

Johan nodded. Svante Oxenstiern had some explaining to do, but that would have to wait. Right now, he needed to hide the evidence from prying eyes.

He hurried to the dormitory, hoping no one had returned from the night's entertainment. The jar weighed heavy in his pocket, but he wanted to keep it close until he could confront Svante Oxenstiern with the evidence.

Standing next to the row of shelves, he reached for his bundle and froze. The leather drawstring had been loosened. It was his habit to draw it snug, protecting the contents from crawling insects. Why would anyone want to look at his belongings? He grimaced. Gunne would see the hypocrisy in that question, he thought, after the exploring they had done in others' possessions.

He emptied the contents of his bundle onto his cot: a bag of seeds, his mother's rosary, some bright-colored hose, a wool blanket, a hat, and the red pennant.

Footsteps passed by the door, a reminder to Johan that he should make an appearance in the dining hall. He counted the items. Nothing was missing, so it had not been greed that moved someone to ransack his satchel, but curiosity. Someone wanted to know more about the lutenist from Warsaw.

To assure himself his lute had not been tampered with, he took it from the shelf, then stared in disbelief. The strings, all but one, had been cut. A paper, wedged beneath the only taut string, made his heart pound. This was proof; someone wanted to do him harm. Henrik? Svante? How many enemies did he have at court?

He unrolled the paper, dreading what he would find, and saw a note penned in an unfamiliar hand: *They have the murderer. Stop the investigation or next time it will be your neck.*

He gripped the lute, fighting back a wave of anger. The culprit had waited until such time as the room would be empty, so no one would report his deed. Johan wadded the note and stuck it in his bundle. He would have to get new strings and tune the lute. He left the dormitory, hoping the luthier was still in his shop.

He gave a quick knock and the door opened. "I was just heading out," Noël said.

Johan backed away. "I'll come tomorrow."

The luthier eyed the lute. "Only broken strings? Give it here. That won't take long. Come back in a few minutes."

While Noël replaced the strings, Johan went to the kitchen, where the cook grudgingly gave him a plate of what was left of dinner. As Johan ate, his mind raced ahead. By now, Torelli would be installing his revolving stage, a costly device that had taken days to build. According to Gunne, the invention was the main reason the queen had brought the Italian set designer to court in the first place. The stage was meant to impress the visiting dignitary, Rebolledo, a Spaniard poet/soldier sent as ambassador to Denmark, but his real assignment was to keep an eye on Sweden and to try to convert Queen Christina to Catholicism. The queen, over her councillors' objections, had welcomed him before, and rumor had it that the queen knew full well his true purpose, but was entertained by his poetry, his gallantry, and most of all, amused by his duplicity. What puzzled Johan was that Rebolledo apparently had no idea the Swedish queen knew his intentions.

Still, the stage construction had come at a good time. Svante

Oxenstiern might be nearby, a perfect opportunity to question him. For the chancellor's son to have gone to the musicians' dormitory unseen and stayed long enough to locate Johan's belongings, rifle through a knapsack, and cut the lute strings, seemed implausible—but this whole affair was implausible. Could the lute damage be the work of Henrik? Possibly. Henrik was the only man he knew who had a permanent grudge against him—at least, the only man he knew of for sure.

After reclaiming his lute and thanking the luthier, Johan returned to the dormitory. Whoever had damaged the lute evidently had no idea who Johan Sokolewski really was, or how determined he was to see this thing through. No amount of petty mischief would make him turn back, not as long as he had breath to spare. Zofia needed him. Imbued with a new sense of urgency, and of burgeoning pride, he laid plans for the following day. There was nothing to do but confront Svante Oxenstiern with the evidence.

CHAPTER NINETEEN

As Johan hoped, he found Svante Oxenstiern sitting alone, not far from Torelli, watching preparations for a new ballet. The chancellor's bastard son resembled his father, Axel Oxenstiern, only so far as the thick, short beard and stern, fixed expression of his dark eyes. While his father's hair was grey, Svante's was blonde and wavy, worn to his shoulders. He must have inherited his mother's features—a soft round face with rosy cheeks. Johan set the man's image in his mind. Svante appeared engrossed in what was taking place near the stage. A complicated system of ropes was being installed, an invention that would move an elevated section of the deck, thereby changing scenery quicker. It was clever, Johan thought. No wonder Torelli commanded huge sums of money for his services.

Johan took a deep breath, reviewing what he would say to Svante. Johan would remind him of the humiliation for the Oxenstiern family should everyone at court learn the truth. Svante might look at the hemp fibers and admit the crime, seeing the futility of denying his involvement. He would appear before the queen mother, and Zofia would be freed. If, on the other hand, he denied cutting the rope, who would Eleanora believe? A man from one of the oldest and most respected families in Sweden, or a foreign musician? What bothered Johan most was that even if Svante admitted cutting the rope, could that be directly tied to the theft and murder? Johan would argue that it must, that the only plausible reason for Svante to harm him was to end the investigation.

Feeling less bold than before, but resolved to get this behind him, Johan sat next to the chancellor's son. "Svante, I am Johan, the lutenist from Warsaw."

Svante turned to him. "I know who you are. Nothing is secret here. The walls have ears. What do you think of Torelli's new design?"

"Perhaps it will be safer than overhead weights," Johan said, hoping for a reaction from Svante.

"Oh, they'll be keeping those, too. Say, weren't you the one the falling weight just missed?"

"That's what I wanted to speak with you about." Johan pulled the jar from his pocket. "First, I should warn you, the queen mother knows I was in your room, and she understands why. In fact, she's the one who put me in charge of the investigation." He opened the lid and withdrew a thin strand. "Hemp," he said. "The rope was cut with a sharp instrument. Torelli is convinced it was done on purpose. This came from the sheath of a knife found in your room. Why would you want to harm me?"

Svante raised his brows, and his eyes widened. "You have the wrong man, my friend. I wish you no harm. In fact, I knew you had been in my room uninvited. I asked around when I noticed my knife was missing. It's an ordinary knife, of no real significance. I figured you simply needed one." He shook his head and frowned, then met Johan's eyes. "I'd no idea you thought me an enemy. I decided the queen had enough on her mind without my reporting some minor theft."

Johan hid his surprise and plunged ahead. "Can you explain the hemp fibers on the inside of the sheath, the very night a hemp rope was cut deep enough to cause it to break?"

"Hemp fibers, you say? You should stick to music, my friend. Hemp is a common material. It has many purposes—clothes, horse bedding, paper—"

"True, but courtiers mostly wear silks and fine weaves—nothing as common as hemp. Your writing papers, if I am not mistaken, are imported from France. And you are not a stable-man."

"You seem to know more about me than I do about you."

"I don't know enough. And someone went through my belongings yesterday, even damaging my lute."

Svante Oxenstiern shook his head. "Perhaps you'd do well to give up this search of yours. Yes, I know about the investigation. Like I said, I'm privy to most of what happens at court. Evidently someone wants you to forget about the crimes, but it's not me. I attended a meeting in Uppsala and was gone all yesterday. I can furnish names of those who were in attendance. They'll vouch for my presence. So you see, it was impossible for me to rummage in your belongings. I can explain the hemp fibers, too. I helped Torelli the afternoon of the production. He had me cutting canvases to fit the frames. The painters worked in a frenzy to complete the set designs in time. You can ask Torelli if you like. He's right over there."

Johan nodded, rose from the bench, put the jar into his pocket, and approached Torelli, feeling a bit foolish. Still, Svante could have been bluffing, hoping Johan would believe his story.

After exchanging greetings with the acclaimed set designer, Johan decided the best way was to get this over with. He repeated his conversation with Svante, and when he finished, Torelli crossed his arms and frowned. "I remember little of that night. I'm always upset when anything goes wrong, but that weight falling . . ." He shook his head. "That was the worst. But now that you ask, yes, I do recall his helping me cut canvas that afternoon. We were running behind. Without him, I doubt we'd have gotten everything completed. Some of the stagehands are useless, but they're what I have to work with, so I was grateful for some real assistance. And yes, I asked him to hang around yesterday in case I needed help again, but he said he had a meeting—something about university funding. Svante seems like a pretty trustworthy fellow."

Johan felt as though someone had punched him in the stomach. While he had been garnering false evidence against the chancellor's son, the real culprit, the man he should be watching, had been free to do his evil. Wait until Gunne heard this—he would laugh until tears came.

Returning to where Svante sat, Johan extended his hand. "I owe you an apology."

"Not at all. Just return my sheath and knife."

Johan nodded. Before he could do that, he would need to repair the sheath. Instead of being closer to solving the murder, he had to start at the beginning and take a fresh look, and there was no time to spare. Seven days from now, unless he had something to show for his efforts, Zofia would be punished, and he had never been further from a resolution than he was at this moment.

That night, lying on his cot, Johan found himself going back to his first days at court, how he had come here as an unknown lutenist, and what had followed. Whether by his attraction to the alchemist, or owing to his talent, or the queen's fondness for lute playing, or the sum of all three, he was now a participant in solving a mystery. What madness had propelled him to think he could discover who had committed a murder? The mixed unknown of politics and religion at the Swedish court, instead of helping, had driven him into a maze of unanswered questions—and into harm's way. When first coming here to Sweden, he'd envisioned an idyllic life as a university student, with only another new song to challenge him. Instead, he had been lured by a sweet-faced alchemist and a queen mother who thought a musician could solve a crime.

He turned his head from the moonlight, hoping for sleep, but his mind raced, going back over every significant event since his coming to court. Somewhere he had taken a wrong turn, led by his suspicions and the words of others, to believe that the bible had been taken because of religious or political beliefs. And what if the theft had nothing to do with the murder? What had he missed?

It had begun with the queen mother's hysteria. To her, the bible was another way to connect with the dead king, the same as the heart suspended above her bed in the months following his death.

Johan pulled the coverlet to his chin, warding off the chill that settled in once the fires died down. His thoughts returned to that first morning, the queen mother's sudden courtyard appearance and frantic shouts about a stolen book. If not for her status and the current queen's charity, Eleanora would still be locked in a distant castle. Instead, she was surrounded by her dwarfs and ladies-in-waiting, one of whom had taken a particular interest in Zofia and her predicament. Gunne, too, had benefited from Sigrid's favors, even learning to read. There was something about Sigrid—something indefinable, like a strange taste in a cup of good wine.

However, it was no woman who attacked him in Zofia's workshop—definitely not Sigrid. Tall and willowy as she was, she could never have passed for the muscled person with whom he had briefly wrestled. Puzzled, he wadded his pillow and stuffed it beneath one arm. And what appeal would Zofia's laboratory have to anyone but an alchemist? He needed to backtrack. Somehow, he had overlooked the very thing he needed.

A few hours before daybreak he fell into a fitful sleep, dreaming again of his mother's death and the village sorceress. He lifted his mother from the flames and a lady came to stand at his side. She smelled of lemon and pointed to a table where the sorceress stood. The sorceress gathered some jars from the table and disappeared into the writhing flames. As she ascended, he saw that one of the jars she held was filled with sheep hairs. The flames disappeared and he looked at the girl beside him. She wore a lace cap and pushed back a strand of reddish-gold hair.

He woke in the icy cold of the dormitory, but paid no mind to the discomfort, reliving, instead, the pleasant ending to a nightmare that had plagued him so long.

Still pondering the meaning of his dream, Johan followed Gunne to a table in one corner of the dining hall, out of the way of passers-by. As Gunne reached to fill both their cups, Johan noticed the dining hall, usually full with hungry courtiers, was near empty. "Where is everybody?"

Gunne sipped from his mug. "They've already broken their fast," he said, reaching for the butter. "Most came here before dawn to eat. They need to help prepare for the queen's reception."

Johan's brows shot up. "Another ambassador?"

Gunne shook his head. "No. This is in honor of delegates from the New World. The sailing ship they were in was to have landed months back. With no word, everyone believed the worst—that the ship sank in the Atlantic. A few days ago, the queen mother told us Queen Christina received a message. The vessel was blown off course but the captain managed to bring the ship safely to port. There was a special service in the queen's chapel—only for family and advisors—but it was to give thanks. The ship was supposed to land at the Stockholm port in two days. Right after that, the queen mother went into a frenzy, wondering what gown she'd wear."

Johan chuckled and reached for another piece of a small loaf they had shared. He was about to speak when he heard a commotion in the outer hall and looked across the room. Workers scurried by the open doors.

Gunne drained his cup. "It's only the servants, carrying gowns outside to be aired. Foolish, in weather like this, but the women insist their clothes smell like a fire pit. The guardsmen must weather the cold as well, and are complaining. No matter the icy conditions, they've been told they must fly banners everywhere—the corner towers, the gatehouse, even the windows if they can figure a way to do that." He leaned forward. "I understand Torelli's craftsmen were ordered to leave the warmth of the rehearsal hall and help with the effort. I heard them talking. The queen's generous offer of extra coins seems not to matter, because the workers grumbled loudly when passing me by. For myself, I've no intention of going out in this weather. Besides, what help would I be? I can't even see over the wall."

Johan recalled the pain of his frostbitten hands, and nodded. With luck, they could both avoid going outside. "I've been thinking, Gunne, about how our investigation is going so far."

"Not well," Gunne murmured, taking another piece of the loaf.

Johan ignored his friend's comment and continued. "This last misstep—searching Svante Oxenstiern's room and taking his knife—could have been a serious one, but luckily, the chancellor's son wanted to make no fuss."

"I suppose, with a father like his, he is resigned to notoriety," Gunne said.

Johan reached for a pot of jam. "Tell me more about Sigrid. Were her parents royal?"

"No. In fact her father was lowborn. He joined the army and served the old king—rose quickly in rank, distinguished for his bravery. He was killed on the Prussian border, fighting for Sweden."

"And the widow—Sigrid's mother?"

"She died during the plague. Sigrid was taken to the orphanage at Riddarholmen. That's an island not far from here. The orphanage used to be an old abbey. Story has it that Eleanora went there one Advent to disperse cakes to the orphans. She was entertained by a choir of young voices, and when she learned one of the children was the daughter of a general, she whisked her away from the orphanage, along with Henrik."

Johan tensed. Henrik and Sigrid. So quite possibly they knew each other before coming here.

Gunne continued with his story. "Eleanora had Sigrid fitted with clothes appropriate to court, and she's remained here ever since, eventually taking her place as one of Eleanora's ladies. Why do you ask about Sigrid?"

"No reason, I suppose." He remembered the last time he had seen Sigrid, when she leaned to whisper in Eleanora's ear. "I get the feeling Sigrid harbors some dislike for me, though why, I've no idea."

Gunne seemed to be considering Johan's words. "You could confront her directly, I suppose, but the queen mother would not take kindly to that. Unlike Queen Christina, Eleanora is fond of her ladies."

"No. I'd not ask Sigrid outright. I doubt I would get a straight answer." He paused, weighing his options. What was the best way to learn about a person? Was that why someone had rummaged through his knapsack? Was the intruder looking for something in particular? No matter, he traveled light, so there was little to see. Still, the items one cherished could tell a whole story. Had Henrik not learned that Johan was from Poland, just from a pennant? Johan's angered reaction probably revealed to Henrik that the pennant was more than just a battlefield memento. What someone treasured, and the books they read, told more about the owner than any chronicler could ever write. "Is it possible to visit with Sigrid in her room?"

"In God's good grace, you don't expect to find the Silver Bible there." Gunne's eyes, blue as a Warsaw sky in summer, rested on Johan's.

"No, not the bible—mementos, perhaps. There's not much time left, and Zofia is counting on me. Will you help?"

"You know I will, but this will not be easy to arrange. The queen mother frowns on her ladies having male visitors."

That afternoon, Johan learned that the queen mother's backgammon tournament, set to coincide with the weeklong visit of the New World delegation, would take place in a large room off the main hall. Eleanora's ladies, in charge of making the wreaths that would decorate each table in an elaborate design of candles and spruce, were busy sorting and winding the branches. Sigrid, insisting Gunne would owe her a choice piece of amber, agreed to a short visit. "Besides," she said, "I hate making wreaths. The needles scratch my hands and the smell makes me sneeze."

As promised, when they arrived, she answered Johan's knock and brought them quickly inside. "You may sit there," she said, pointing Johan to a dainty armchair.

"I'll stand," he said. "We won't be long." He ran his hand down the shining blade of a saber. "Your father's?"

She nodded, then patted the bed. "Gunne, you may sit here, but not too close lest someone, God forbid, come inside." She straightened her skirts and eyed Johan. "Just what is so important that you needed to meet with me?"

Johan paused near a shelf of books. "I thought perhaps you could help me with the investigation. You hold an important post and are involved with court activities like no one else."

He scanned the book titles—mostly poetry, until he came to one titled *Woodblock Printing on Silk*. And another, *The Use of Colored Blocks for Printing*.

She rose from her seat on the bed, smiled, and adjusted her sleeves, obviously enjoying the flattery. "Well, yes, I am quite involved in court affairs. What did you want to know?"

He strolled toward her dressing table. Jars and pots of all sizes sat to one side, along with powder boxes, perfume, and an oil bottle. A silver brush and hand mirror were shoved to the back to make room for a pamphlet: *Plays for the Puppet Theater*. Beside the book lay a tiny wax girl doll. An arrow lay next to the doll. He shivered and turned to face Sigrid, who was occupied at the mirror, smoothing her hair. Johan crossed his arms. "I wondered if you had any ideas about who may have taken Eleanora's book." He glanced into an open wood cabinet—nothing but ladies' clothes and a row of slippers.

She shook her head. "Not exactly. I only know that Eleanora is miserable. She believes she has the guilty party. Perhaps Zofia will confess soon and save everyone a lot of trouble."

Gunne climbed from the bed. "I hear the ladies coming."

Sigrid's hand flew to her mouth. "Out, both of you, and hurry. Oh, I knew this was risky." She pushed them out the door and into the hallway.

Gunne grabbed Johan's arm. "Quick. This way. The women are close behind us." The dwarf darted ahead. At the end of the corridor Johan saw Gunne's bright-colored cloak disappearing into another hallway. A flight of stairs led downward, and once more Johan was reminded of how much Gunne knew about the workings of the castle and the building's history. Finally, when they came to a secluded section of the castle, Gunne slowed to a walk. "The ladies must have become skilled at wreath-making. I thought we had plenty of time."

Johan looked down at his friend. "I found something interesting in there. Sigrid has an interest in printing methods—and puppetry. I saw books on both subjects."

"What does that have to do with the murder or the stolen bible?"

"I'm not sure. And I saw a wax doll. It could have been a small puppet. You don't suppose she practices more sinister hobbies, like sorcery?"

Gunne laughed. "Don't go imagining things. After all, Sigrid knows how to read, and she just might want to learn something new, like printing. An inquisitive nature does not make one a thief. As for the doll . . . some girls never stop playing with dolls."

Johan shrugged. Gunne was probably right. There was nothing odd about Sigrid having a doll. But why the arrow?

CHAPTER TWENTY

The day after his visit with Sigrid, Johan rose from the midday meal and hurried to retrieve his lute for rehearsal. He was already late, having remained after the other diners to speak with Beaulieu about a new musical score. As Johan entered the dormitory he came face to face with Henrik. What was he doing in the musicians' section? As Johan walked past, heading for the shelf that held his lute, a slow anger rose. This man had dirtied the red pennant with his boot, but beyond that, might be guilty of other things. The dropped weight? The murder? Rummaging in Zofia's workshop? What if these acts were all done by the same man? He retrieved his lute and made a quick decision. Why not confront Henrik, or try to make friends? His mother would say you could catch more bees with honey.

"I see I'm not the only one late for rehearsal," Johan said. He braced one foot on a bench and plucked a string. The instrument held its tune remarkably well.

"I'm not on until the second half. We should talk, lutenist."

"That's what I was thinking. You go first." Johan plucked another string. Evidently Henrik was serious.

"I see you are keeping the pennant with your things. You should be more careful with something like that."

The hairs on the back of Johan's neck bristled. Friendship with Henrik was out of the question. He removed his foot and crossed to where the stagehand sat. "What interest do you have in a pennant you almost ruined?"

Henrik narrowed his eyes. "A returning soldier, one of the few who came back alive from my father's regiment, brought one like it with him when he came home. He took it from a dead Polski and gave it to me, the same night he told me how my father died. He explained it all, how the Polish army took over the towns, ordered the best food in the tavern, then bedded the prettiest girls . . ." Henrik's nostrils flared. "A Pole killed my father." He stepped closer. "The man may have been a relative of yours—or a friend." Anger hardened his features and he clenched his fists.

Johan stepped back. Henrik was mad with grief. Johan remembered that feeling. For both their sakes, Johan had to remain calm. "That's all behind us, Henrik." He bit his lip. Part of what Henrik said was true. The garrison had taken over the town while preparing for the battle—their last battle, but it had helped them forget what they'd done, helped wipe out the memories of burning homes and fleeing women and children. "Our garrison isn't blameless, but as for the taverns—that's where people eat," Johan said, hoping to end the conversation.

Henrik smirked. "You cannot dismiss the facts so easily. And about that pennant: It was foolish to bring it here. The emblem, the twisting serpent—to many of us it is a reminder of lives lost."

Johan stepped closer. "We lost loved ones too." He wanted to strike Henrik's jaw, then remembered that would settle nothing. Perhaps plain talk would. "Why were you looking through my things?"

"You can't prove that I did." Henrik's smirk had changed to cold contempt. "Besides, I had a feeling, the way you came into the courtyard—you arrived here on the last boat before winter, with worn boots. You had a look about you."

Did it show? Did he wear the pain of his loss and guilt like other men wore cloaks? He tightened his grip on the lute, trying to control his rising anger. "So what's your point?"

"You're a deserter. The returning soldier told me of a battle in the Ukraine—a slaughter, where most of the men died that day, except for the ones on both sides who deserted."

Johan winced at the recollection. He had seen the hopelessness of it all, how outnumbered they were, and as a fresh wave of the enemy approached, his brother shouted at Johan with his last breath. *Ride, Johan. Ride for your life.* Johan had wheeled his horse and ridden full speed, not looking back until he reached the tree line.

He blinked back tears, hearing the words again, as real as ever, the words that had saved him. As darkness settled over the field of battle, the full moon shining on the corpses of dead soldiers, he had crept from his hiding place in the woods to retrieve his brother's body. Both armies had retreated, bringing the wounded to their camps and leaving the mortally injured for burial the following morning.

While Johan built a coffin with boards from an abandoned wagon, he'd kept one eye on the blanket that kept flies from his brother's body. By morning he had dug the hole, maneuvered the coffin into place, and covered it with dirt. When the sun came up, he said his last good-bye to his older brother. Below, buzzards circled the field, but they would never come close to Domonik Sokolewski.

Johan blinked, recalling the lonely, galloping ride back to the empty barracks, where he'd snatched up his lute and fled into the night. Henrik was pressing forward with more questions, more insults. Johan, strengthened by the memory of who he was, of where he had come from, put down his lute and closed in on Henrik. "How dare you question my intentions? And I warn you, if I find you again, rummaging through my things—"

"Oh, there won't be another time. I've found out all I needed, but considering that, you should hear me out."

Johan turned to go. He was already late, an imposition on the others in the ensemble. Besides, if he stayed here longer, he would give Henrik what he deserved, and what would that solve? "We've talked enough."

"Not about your investigation."

Johan froze. Was his adversary about to admit to being the thief? Was it this easy? He felt suddenly baffled, as if a great wind battered him to and fro. "What about it?"

"Unless you want the whole court to know you are not the courtier you appear to be, but only a common deserter, you will drop your investigation. The queen mother already has the guilty one." He smirked. "Or I could raise the possibility that you're not actually a deserter, as the facts would claim, but a spy sent by the Russians. They'd do anything to gain control of trade routes in the Baltic, and right now Sweden holds the power there." He shrugged. "Seems reasonable enough that the Russian government would send someone to snoop in the palace, listen to conversations . . ."

"Why would you suggest such a thing? Is there no end to what you'd do to make me quit the investigation?"

"Like I said, they have the guilty one. She was seen at the library. She's a witch, too, or didn't you know? She has no place in the queen's court. Why, who knows what goes on in that laboratory of hers? She pretends to be a scientist, to save herself from the stake, but they'll learn before long. She can cast spells and make an army lose a battle. She has even watched a human torso being cut up. What kind of woman would watch that?"

Johan backed away. The man was half crazed, accusing Zofia of being a witch. Did Zofia know this man at all? After rehearsal, he should go to her and warn her about Henrik and his wrath, and what it might mean for her.

The unease Johan felt in Henrik's presence stayed with him, and after ensemble practice he returned to the storage area, replaced his lute, and glanced at his knapsack. What had possessed Henrik to look there to begin with? Was he simply hoping to find something more, as if being a deserter was not enough?

Now he had a new worry. Would the Swedish government, intent on retaining control of the Baltic trade routes, believe Henrik's wild assertion? A foreigner, convicted of spying, would face serious punishment. And here, in a country that valued its army above all else, how would a deserter be treated? Did Henrik know there was a reward for any deserter's return? Would that mean a return to Poland to face punishment? He was not ready to die, and a life in prison, away from his music, would be hell on earth. Still, the truth would out, eventually, and he wanted to tell it his way.

Henrik's threat had changed everything. Solving the mystery of the theft and murder now held a new importance. Success would prove to himself and others he was a man worthy of trust, but time was closing in. Once this investigation was over he would admit his desertion to the court of Sweden and take the consequences. Right now, he needed to talk to Zofia about Henrik.

He went to Gunne's room, hoping the dwarf had time to escort him to where Zofia was being held. As he approached, Gunne stepped out.

Johan smiled at his friend. "I see you're leaving. Have time to take me to Zofia's?"

Gunne went back inside, took a key from a peg, and returned. "Sure. Come with me. I was going to the queen mother's rooms. She said she's bored and wants some entertainment. The others will cover for me, but not forever." They walked together to Zofia's small chamber. "Five minutes," Gunne said, unlocking the door.

Johan walked inside Zofia's little room and noticed her pale complexion. The enforced isolation and boredom were taking their toll. Instead of a smile, she greeted him with sad eyes. "Tell me the truth. You cannot find the real murderer. It's all right. I have resigned myself to what may happen. I'll be sent from the castle to be tried at a High Court. After that, I will appeal to the palace authorities, which will most likely be Eleanora, and I'll be convicted. I can appeal to the queen for clemency, but by then she'll have lost faith in me. In a book I asked Sigrid to bring me, I looked up the punishment for female thieves. A whipping and a fine, anywhere from forty marks and more. For murder, they hang men, but take kinder to women. They used to bury them alive, but that's gone out of fashion. Mostly now it's death by stoning or for a lighter sentence, public humiliation and banishment."

"Try not to think about that, Zofia. I have not yet given up, and I won't, but I came here today hoping you could shed some light on something very strange."

"What?" For the first time he saw a spark of interest in her eyes. "I'll help any way I can."

"Do you know any of the entertainers personally?"

"I know most of them, but not well. How would I? Until I was put in here, I spent most of my time in my workshop. Why do you ask?"

"Someone is interested in forcing me to abandon the investigation. Do you know anyone who would think you were a witch?"

Her eyes rounded and he heard her quick intake of breath. "Has someone accused me of that? Who?"

"Forget I mentioned it, Zofia. I just thought—perhaps because you're an alchemist, not a common trade for women— someone might get the wrong idea." Why mention Henrik by name? It would only cause problems. Besides, Henrik's mention of witchcraft was probably an attempt to alarm Johan, or stir up trouble. He groped for words to explain. "Perhaps curiosity might send someone to your workshop. I didn't mean to upset you."

She frowned. "If someone said that to you, they are likely to be spreading the rumor. Not too long ago they were burning witches in the square. They could again."

"You've nothing to worry about on that account, Zofia. You have the protection of the queen."

"Only for a time, Johan. If I am allowed to live, and were I to leave the castle, if word spreads around the town . . ."

Johan's mind raced. How to calm her fears? He met her eyes. "No need to worry, Zofia. You said you were the queen's consultant. You can prove your work has a scientific basis—can't you?"

"You see?" she said, balling her fists and rising from the chair. "Even you have your doubts. I can see it in your eyes. Just because I study the movement of planets does not make me a charlatan. I simply experiment—to see if the movements of the seas or heavenly bodies have any connection with how my chemicals react. Experiment is a process of elimination." She slumped in a chair, looking suddenly beaten. "Go back to your music, lute-player. You don't believe in what I do, I know that now." She looked about to cry, and Johan wanted to gather her into his arms, but at that moment Gunne tapped on the door.

"It's time to leave," he said.

Johan paused. There was one more question he wanted to ask. "Did you know Sigrid is interested in printing methods—and puppetry?"

Zofia sniffed. "No. Did she tell you that?"

Johan shook his head. "She has some books on those subjects."

Zofia drew her brows together. "Strange. She never mentioned that to me. And how do you know?" She shot him a worried glance. "Oh, no. You went to her room." She pushed back a loose strand of hair. "That was a dangerous undertaking."

Johan, surprised at the sudden softness in her voice, swallowed without commenting. Did she truly care? It sounded so.

Gunne stuck his head inside. "Johan, we—"

"I'm coming." He paused at the door and looked back at Zofia. The worried frown, the anxious step forward, the hand she held out, all told him what he hoped. "I'll come back soon, Zofia. For now, trust me."

She dabbed at her eyes with her sleeve. "I do, and tell your informer that I am no criminal, nor am I a magician. I am simply a scientist who happens to be a girl."

"I will." He closed the door softly behind him, hating to go, and wishing with all his heart he had set Henrik straight about the alchemist. What was wrong with him? Truth be told, he had wondered about Zofia himself, wondered why she chose to spend her life in a laboratory with a special lens and formulas and an elaborate model of orbiting planets made from leather balls and twisted wire.

While Gunne secured the door to Zofia's room, Johan waited, his mind in turmoil. If anyone needed magic now it was he, to find the answers that would free Zofia. In spite of her denials, he wished, for the space of a day, that she could actually work magic and divine the truth. Was Henrik behind all this? Who might shed some light on what made Henrik the person he was? And François was another concern. Beaulieu, the dance master, might know something—some little overlooked clue that would lead to an answer before his allotted days were up.

CHAPTER TWENTY-ONE

Desperate to move forward with the investigation before time ran out, Johan set out to find the ballet master. No one knew the dancers like Beaulieu. Perhaps, with some coaxing, he might help Johan tie up some loose ends. After peeking into the performance hall and finding it empty, Johan searched the practice area and even knocked on Beaulieu's bedchamber door, to no avail. He found the dance master in a quiet corner of an empty room, a place where unused instruments and furniture awaiting repair were kept. "Am I interrupting?"

"No." Antoine de Beaulieu laid some papers aside and rubbed his eyes. "I'm getting too old for this. Half blind, and the queen expects me to work miracles." He tapped the papers. "This new ballet requires a much larger stage, and I'm left to work it all out." He ran both hands through his thinning hair, and Johan, in spite of his minor status as a court lutenist, decided he would not like to trade places with Antoine, even considering the honors and good fortune that came with the position.

Antoine locked both hands behind his head and gave Johan his full attention. "How may I help?"

"I'm not sure you can, but it's possible. As you may know, Eleanora is holding the young queen's favorite hunting companion as the main suspect. It's a very weak case, but she's the only suspect so far. That's why I've come to you."

The dance master lost his friendly demeanor. "Just what do you mean?"

Johan hurried to explain. "You are above reproach, of course, but perhaps you could tell me something about the members of your dance troupe."

"Oh, I can tell you plenty about them, but nothing you'd be interested in—like the one who cries when he's corrected. Another sneaks out from rehearsals to be with a girl. And François, a talented young man whose head is in the stars."

"What about Henrik? He's taken a dislike to me, but hardly knows me. And I'd like to know more about François. He befriended me the first day I arrived, and I have played a few games of *tables* with him, but that's all. The others, I barely know."

"That's because they spend their spare time gambling. More than once I have had to loan them money—which I'll never get back. Regarding Henrik, as you may have noticed, he struggles to learn the dance and requires extra practice."

Johan shook his head. "I hadn't noticed, but then I'm no expert."

Beaulieu chuckled. "Watch him when you get a chance. He is sometimes a beat behind and keeps his head down, trying to watch others' footwork. He is determined, and this I give him credit for, but it takes much of my assistant's time. Henrik should have remained as a stagehand." He sighed. "Some royal favor, I suppose, but I do as I'm told. God knows, he is no dancer, and should stick to manual work." Antoine crossed his legs. "On the other hand, we have François. He could rise to great heights—to solo performances, but he seems less interested in the dance than in his books."

"What does he read?"

Antoine chuckled. "I only saw his cubicle one time, when he first came here, but I remember he had a book about alchemy. I asked about it, and he seemed reluctant at first, but then he warmed to the subject, and ended up showing me the text. It had drawings and sketches of rockets, pictures of tubes running in different directions. Funny thing: When I asked later about his scientific study, he said he had lost interest in it. I guess that was about the time you came. Claimed he was concentrating on ballet, but I don't believe that. He's a dreamer, that one. It happens like that sometimes—people with great talent take it for granted. I happen to believe, if one has a talent and lets it go to waste, the talent will be taken from you." He shrugged. "But what do I know? I'm only a dance instructor." He looked down at the papers on his desk and Johan knew he'd overstayed. Beaulieu had problems with the new ballet, and needed time to work on it.

Johan rose and extended his hand. "Only an instructor? The best one in the world, so I'm told."

Antoine laughed, clearly pleased at the compliment. "I hope I've helped in some way."

"You have," Johan said, "maybe more than either of us knows."

Johan stood outside the cubicle assigned to François and called the dancer's name. François peeked past a curtain, then drew it back, revealing a small space, neatly arranged with cot and open shelves. "Johan Sokolewski. Come in." François pointed to a stool. "Have a seat." François sat on the cot. "I don't have many visitors, so I've nothing to offer."

"Quite all right, François. I came to talk, if you have a minute."

"I do. I have only the rehearsal later, but I know the routine well."

"I just spoke with the dance master. He praised your talent and said you learned easily."

"Yes. Well, I suppose." He rubbed his chin, looking uncomfortable. "You were talking with Beaulieu about me?"

"Your name came up, along with others." Johan glanced at the shelves. A costume lay alongside two pairs of shoes. A small wooden clock, a row of hats, and a razor case were wedged between two piles of garments.

"What about?" François seemed to pale, but it could have been the light from the window overhead—the sun had come out briefly, melting the top layer of snow, but the sky had turned suddenly dark moments ago. Another storm was on its way.

"A lot of things. Torelli believes someone tampered with the set."

"Yes, I heard. You could have been killed. Several people saw Henrik around the stage before the performance." He shook his head. "I've never forgotten his rudeness, the day you arrived on the castle grounds. Any idea why he carries such a grudge against you?"

"No. But I'm not here to talk about Henrik. The dance master said you were interested in alchemy. He remarked about your book."

"Oh, that." François waved his hand, as if pushing away a discarded thought. "I've lost interest in reading. Too much to think about, and I'd rather concentrate on the performances."

"Your book—was it costly? May I see it?"

François licked his lips. "I—I gave it away. I just lost interest, like I said."

"So who has the book now?"

"I don't know." He reached to his collar and scratched the side of his neck. "I forget who I gave it to."

"I see." But Johan didn't see—not at all. With the price of books, François must have traded with someone—for something valuable—or else he still had it. But where?

François paused a moment and scratched his shoulder before speaking. "Like I told you before, I knew they had found the guilty party. I know about her father's interest in the Silver

Bible. Who but someone who knows old books, like he surely must, would want something with pages missing? Seems logical he had his daughter steal it for him. He could have it freshly bound and sell it. The right person would pay a small fortune for it. And she was seen near the library about the time that poor man was murdered."

Johan rose from the stool, sensing he was getting nowhere, which left two unanswered questions: Why was François so quick to blame Zofia and implicate Henrik, and where had François's alchemy book disappeared to?

After leaving François's room, Johan set out to confront Henrik one final time. Leaving aside these false leads, which had taken precious time, and curiosities like François's interest in alchemy, everything pointed to Henrik, whose grudge against the new lutenist was now common knowledge.

Beaulieu had hinted that he was pressured to include Henrik in the ballet. Who had intervened on his behalf? Likely someone with power, which would be either a member of the royal family or one of the queen's Privy Council.

Johan found Henrik in the practice room, mending a shirt. Johan cleared his throat. "I hope I'm not interrupting."

"You can see that you are, but what do you want?"

"I'd like to talk."

Henrik clipped a thread and laid the shirt aside. "What about this time?"

"Why are you so quick to accuse Zofia of theft and murder?"

"She has a motive. Besides, you can't trust someone like that. I've seen them on street corners, trying to sell their poisons, promising miracles, but it's not my problem—unless she goes free and continues with her experiments. It's a wonder she hasn't blown up the castle. Did you know, before you came here, she almost caused a fire? Smoke was seen coming from her workshop, and guards helped her somehow, so nothing came of her silly experiment. But it could have been serious. Now, is that all you wanted to know?"

"I thought we might be friends. You know the cast, and the singers and other musicians better than I. How much do you know of François?"

"In the dance troupe? Nothing at all. Why? Is he one of your suspects?" Henrik curled his lip.

"No, I just thought perhaps—"

"I have nothing to say, Polski. Now, if you don't mind, I'd like to get back to what I was doing."

Johan rose to leave.

"And don't be coming around with your questions. Even if I knew anything, I would never tell you. Zofia is in the right place. They have the perpetrator. Leave it be."

As Johan left the room, he thought about Henrik's accusation. If he was guilty, and hoping Zofia would be blamed, how could the man live with himself? But François had said the same thing about Zofia. Why did both feel this way, and was it for different reasons?

Gunne heated a jug of spiced wine on his converted incense burner, poured two cups to the brim, and sat across from Johan. "This is the last of my cinnamon. Too bad it won't grow here. The Dutch are making a fortune importing the spice, while our government pays dearly for it. If I were king, I would establish my own trading company—something big, like the Dutch East Indies Company. Do you know, at one time, cinnamon was worth three times the value of silver in weight?" He inhaled the fragrance, then sipped from the cup. "So, you were saying about Henrik carrying a grudge against your countrymen. But that's no reason to think he has any interest in killing the goldsmith or stealing Eleanora's book."

"I know," Johan said. "And that's what puzzles me. Still, there's the stage accident, clearly deliberate, and one of the dancers was spotted before the performance, hanging around the set. This was one of the nights Henrik filled in for someone."

"Consider this," Gunne said. "If it was Henrik near the set, he could just have an interest in set design, or theater in general. Much like Svante Oxenstiern."

Johan frowned. Gunne was right, of course; there was no proof of wrongdoing. "But the guilty party would have a real reason to want me to stop the investigation—have it over and done with, and let Zofia be blamed."

"You said you spoke with François too."

"Yes, but only because the dance master said François had an interest in alchemy, that he had a book earlier, and then later claimed disinterest in the subject. François never mentioned that before."

"Why would he?" Gunne asked. "Did the subject ever come up?"

"No, but he clearly told me I should stop the investigation." Johan rubbed the rim of his cup. "As did Henrik."

Gunne chuckled. "A lot of people want you to stop. They believe Zofia is guilty, and that you are wasting your own time and everyone else's."

Johan frowned. "It's a certainty she wasn't the one who wrestled with me in her workshop. And that lemon perfume would have alerted the murder victim, especially a man who was considered an expert on fragrances."

"I agree," Gunne said. "But what if the bible theft had nothing to do with the murder?"

Johan rubbed his cheek, resisting the thought of Zofia stealing a book. Was it just that he wanted to believe her? Was he being taken in like his mother had been, wanting to trust, listening blindly? No. That could not be. Someone else wanted access to

Zofia's laboratory, but why? Were they looking for something? If so, what, and who had attacked him in her workshop? Who had run from her room that other night? Perhaps François, with his interest in alchemy, had been snooping around. Even so, did that necessarily connect him to the theft? Trouble was, nothing definitive had been proven—all was conjecture and loose ends, like a giant puzzle where none of the pieces fit.

Johan said, "Zofia is not a criminal, that I am sure of. Somehow I believe the answer is right in front of our noses, if only we could sort it all out."

"You may be right on one point, Johan. The missing alchemy book may hold a clue, since it's the court alchemist who is under suspicion."

That night, lying under a heap of woolen blankets, Johan wondered if he were chasing a ghost. Nothing he had found proved anything. Should he go the other way, and try to prove each suspect innocent, thereby eliminating the suspects one by one? To remove François's name from the long list of suspects, he would have to search his room more thoroughly for clues, especially given Beaulieu's mention of an alchemy book. Why would it just disappear after the bible theft, and François not remember exactly what he did with it? François was hiding something, but did that even matter? Then there was Henrik to think about. Was he simply aggressive by nature or could he murder? As the faces of the suspects crossed his mind's eye, juxtaposed in a mirage that turned into a sea of grinning faces, he turned over in bed and, near dawn, fell into a restless sleep.

The next afternoon, while François took his place on stage for the long rehearsal ahead, Johan decided he'd not have a better chance to search François's room.

He hurried to the dancers' dormitory, and finding it empty, stepped up to François's cubicle and pulled back the curtain.

As he entered the dancer's private sleeping area, he closed the drape behind him and went straight to the shelves. He slipped his hand to the back of each one. Finding nothing of interest, he moved to inspect the cot and looked between the sleeping mat and board beneath. Nothing there. He was about to leave when he realized there was one place he had not investigated. The bed coverings hung to the floor, but the bed board was well off it, leaving enough room for storage beneath. He kneeled, lifted the coverlet, and pulled a box from beneath the bed. He sorted through folds of fabric, costumes and masks, but when his hand hit something firm, he pulled the fabric away. His heart pounded as he saw it was a book and read the title. *The Learned Alchemist.*

He opened the book. There, hidden from prying eyes, lay some loose papers. He took one and saw that someone had written a series of numbers and signs. A secret code? To whom, and for what purpose? This was as puzzling as the sketch from the storage area. He tucked some of the papers in his pocket and replaced the rest as they were, hoping François would not miss these few.

After carefully replacing the book, he shoved the box under the bed and lowered the coverlet, then hurried from the room. Why would François hide the book and lie about owning it, and what were these papers about?

CHAPTER TWENTY-TWO

Puzzling over his latest discovery of an alchemy book hidden in François's belongings, Johan headed to Gunne's room. After sharing the news, he said, "It's clear François lied about losing the book. He hid it purposely."

Gunne took his green satin cloak from a low wall peg and went to the door. "The cleaning lady is coming soon. Let's go to the window seat." He snapped the clasp on his cloak. "Want something warmer to wear? That upstairs hall is always chilly."

Johan shook his head. "Let's go."

Together they went the short distance to the staircase. They were halfway up when Johan saw Henrik rushing down, holding a box, looking neither left nor right. As Henrik reached the step on which Gunne stood, he slipped on the corner of Gunne's flowing cloak. He dropped the box, cursed, and made a quick grab for the banister. The contents of the box tumbled down the steps, landing close to Johan's feet.

Johan bent to retrieve the spilled items. He picked up the nearest one and felt something soft and smooth in his palm. He opened his hand and looked close. This appeared to be a small wax figure. A toy? The figure wore a small yellow surcoat. Johan picked up another. This was a lady, dressed in tiny court finery. She had a thread around both wrists, and the man—he looked back at the yellow surcoat—the man had a noose around his neck, so tight it cut into the wax in one place. Johan stared with horror, hardly listening as Henrik let loose another string of curses, his voice overpowering Gunne's repeated apologies.

Johan went up the steps and laid the dolls in the box. Did Sigrid's wax doll have anything to do with Henrik's collection? Did they practice witchcraft together? These dolls, viewed up close, resembled the wax figures the woman had used at his mother's bedside, except for the clothes. The village woman had arranged them and chanted, chanted. He struggled to erase the image from his mind, but found he was shaking inside. He wiped his face with his sleeve. He had to get hold of himself. One good thing might come of this, though. If confronted about the dolls, perhaps Henrik would hold his tongue about Johan being a spy or deserter. He blotted his brow. What was he thinking? He would never resort to Henrik's lowly methods of blackmail, a dishonorable deed at best. Johan squared his shoulders. Let the truth come out. He could deal with that.

Henrik grabbed the box. "Don't touch my things. Did I ask for your help?" He hugged the box to his chest and continued down the steps.

Johan and Gunne ascended the steps and found their way to the window seat. Gunne climbed up and arranged the folds of his cloak, while Johan studied the landscape below. Not a soul was out, and no wonder. Even with every hearth lit, the palace remained cold.

Gunne patted the window cushion. "Sit down and relax. You know, Henrik's stranger than I thought. And he didn't even thank you for helping him. If he'd watched where he was going, he'd never have slipped. Everyone knows these steps are narrow. What was he thinking?"

"Maybe about his dolls."

Gunne looked up. "What dolls?"

"Wax dolls, like those people use to cast spells. That's what was in the box." Johan sat. "I think I'll confront him directly and ask him what they're for. What do I have to lose?"

Gunne clapped his hands together. "Good idea. Go to his room later. Find out what you can."

Johan raised one eyebrow. "He has his own room? Doesn't he stay in the dancers' dormitory?"

"No. He goes there sometimes to practice, but he's not a regular member of the dance troupe. He's had his own room since coming here." Gunne drew a quick sketch. "Follow this. I'd take you there, but a friend is helping me guard Zofia's hallway and I need to report back."

Later that same day, after a long and tedious rehearsal when everything seemed to go wrong and Beaulieu threatened to give up his position in Queen Christina's court for good, Johan made his way to Henrik's chamber. The lute needed a new string but that would have to wait. Right now, he wanted to question Henrik.

With most of the palace appointees taking part in a backgammon tournament, Johan had the corridor to himself as he headed to that wing of the palace. Henrik had chosen a nap over backgammon, and had left the door wide open. Johan took a deep breath to steady his nerves, then rapped on the door casing.

Henrik scowled and sat up in bed. "What do you want? My head hurts. It was a terrible rehearsal, and Beaulieu was ferocious."

"I heard about that," Johan said, gratified that Henrik seemed merely surly toward him rather than threatening. "Still, can't say as I blame Beaulieu. Missteps, torn costumes—enough to upset any dance master." His thoughts raced. How to approach this now? A spent candle sat on the bedside table. He had a sudden streak of madness. Would it work? He had to try. He strolled deliberately to the table and dug loose the hardened wax. "Is this where you get the wax for the dolls? There's plenty around, what with all those candles in the library and other public rooms in the palace. How do you use the dolls? To try costume ideas, perhaps? Beaulieu has his own designer, but of course there's always the chance that—"

"Is that any business of yours?" Henrik's expression had changed, and Johan could almost see the stagehand's mind working, inventing a lie. "And I resent your nosing around in my personal affairs."

"Are they your hobby, Henrik?" He had a mental image of the sorcerer, the witch who had killed his mother. Anger rose in his chest. "Do they give you personal power? Or do you use them against your enemies?"

"How dare you come here and question my integrity?" Henrik's mouth twitched. "I owe you nothing, but to protect my good name, why don't you ask Sigrid what the dolls are all about?" He wore a smirk now, and seemed to be daring Johan.

"I shall do that, Henrik. I'll ask Sigrid and tell her you sent me."

"Fine. Now leave my room. I should have known you had come to cause trouble."

Johan went out, not looking back. He had confronted Henrik about the wax dolls, and yet Henrik seemed only annoyed, not worried. Surely he realized how this would look should word get out that Henrik had an affinity for wax dolls in tortured positions. Was Henrik bluffing, hoping his nonchalance would send Johan in another direction? Was this a sign Henrik was innocent of any wrongdoing? The investigation appeared to be going nowhere, but he could not quit now. Besides, he had another link to follow, which gave him hope that somewhere there was an end to all this, that he would, eventually, find the murderer and the thief of the Silver Bible. Tomorrow morning he had to question Sigrid, if he could find her.

★ ★ ★ ★ ★

Sigrid pulled back the privacy curtain and peered out from her room. She looked first at Gunne, then at Johan. "You cannot come in."

Johan stood his ground. "We only want to talk."

She uttered a loud sigh. "Very well. I know a place, but you can't come in here again. I can't risk having the queen mother find out." She led them to a quiet antechamber, a space allotted for private meetings, then indicated two straight-backed chairs. While waiting for the fire tender to add new logs to the fire, she poured coffee for Johan and Gunne. Johan, remembering her earlier disdainful looks, wondered if she would divulge anything at all.

She sat in an upholstered chair, its wooden arms ending in lions' heads. "So, I guess you both want information. I should begin by saying that you, Johan, have done nothing but stir up trouble for Her Majesty since your arrival. If you plan to do more of the same, I'll tell you here and now, I have no intention of complying."

She turned to Gunne. "You, on the other hand, are my friend, and a friend of Her Majesty the queen mother. I will speak only with you."

Gunne shifted uncomfortably. "I know of your deep loyalty to the queen mother, Sigrid, and it is an admirable trait. However, I think you are mistaken in your belief that Johan, here, has done anything to harm Eleanora."

"Of course he has. The Silver Bible matter would have been settled long ago had he not chosen to keep the whole castle in an uproar over what was a simple matter. You know Eleanora is sensitive about anything pertaining to the dead king's memory."

Johan leaned forward. "I'm also investigating a murder."

Sigrid narrowed her eyes at Johan. "Bah. That should be left to the authorities, not some newcomer. It's your own fault she saddled you with an unsolvable crime. And all this, while I and the other ladies have tried to keep the queen mother's mind calm, to keep her entertained." She looked back at Gunne. "And you helped this perfect stranger find his way around the castle, and to what end? It has only kept the matter alive in the queen mother's mind. But go ahead. Say what you have come for."

Gunne cleared his throat. "Please, Sigrid, listen to Johan. He saw something firsthand. It's only right that I have him tell the story."

She gave Johan a glazed look. "This had better not be any useless accusation. I'm losing patience."

Johan crossed his legs. "It's no accusation, Sigrid, only a question. I was sent here and told to ask you—"

"By whom?"

"Henrik."

He noticed a sudden change in her demeanor. Her fingers tightened on the arms of the chair. So, she was connected somehow to Henrik, and likely knew of the dolls. Whatever this meant, Johan had to find out. "I happened to see Henrik's collection of wax figures. Being fascinated, as one would, I asked what they were for. He told me to ask you."

She blinked and the blood drained from her face. "I told him this would happen. I warned him—"

"Of what?" Gunne asked.

She took a deep breath and was quiet so long that Johan feared she would not respond, that she would send them from the room. Instead, in a voice so faint he had to lean forward to hear, she said, "He was only trying to help." She lifted her gaze to Johan, and for the first time, he saw a frightened young woman, no longer the haughty lady-in-waiting. "I implore you, do not let the queen mother know this. She has promised to elevate me to senior lady-in-waiting, a singularly important post. I would be in charge of the bedchamber. It's a position I want more than anything. She believes I am the most capable of all her ladies, and I want to keep her thinking so. Henrik is the mastermind behind the puppet show that has brought many hours of pleasure to the queen mother. I constructed the scenery, with the help of the court carpenter. It was the puppets I couldn't get to work. I found a book of puppetry, but it used straw figures. Straw was impossible to work with because it makes me sneeze. Then Kirsten, my friend, mentioned my problem to Henrik and he said he could make the puppets from wax, that it was easy, and that finding spent candles and wax took no time at all. So Kirsten brings me the dolls, and I sew the clothes, while the other ladies do their embroidery. All this was to be a big surprise for the queen mother's fiftieth birthday.

"What frightened me was the possibility of someone finding the dolls and thinking Henrik was involved in witchcraft, which evidently has come to pass." She worried the lace trim on her skirt. "I paid him, though, for his trouble. Not money, but I persuaded Eleanora to promote him from stagehand to entertainer. It hasn't quite worked, because Beaulieu is a hard taskmaster, but Henrik wants to dance and I want to keep people happy."

Johan scratched his chin. In light of all this, a comical situation at best, should he bring up the subject of François and the alchemy books? He decided there was no better time. "One more thing. How well do you know François, the dancer? At one time he was interested in alchemy. To some, that is aligned with magic. Old ideas die hard." He sat back. Where had that come from? It was true, though. Had he not been guilty of the same, lumping all experimentation, even Zofia's medical curiosity, into one? Potions and lenses and wax dolls, they all were used in the belief that man could control what happened in life. Perhaps someday the lines between old beliefs and new discoveries would be clearly defined, but for now, it was all unexplored territory. Was it possible that the woman he blamed for his mother's death had truly believed in her potions? What if she was simply trying to help, and believed, as Zofia did, in what she was doing? The notion caused him to break into a cold sweat. He was relieved when he heard Gunne speak to Sigrid, prodding her for any information about François.

"François is my friend," she said, her voice soft. "Leave him out of this. He has hobbies, like everyone. He has an inquisitive mind, and he's always proposing new ideas. Some of them sound preposterous to me, but he makes it all sound logical. He even brought me a book to read once. It is written in German, but I looked at the pictures. It was about making rockets with fireworks and weaponry."

So, Sigrid knew François quite well. Johan wondered how this fit into the puzzle. He felt suddenly tired and needed time to think. If Sigrid was telling the truth, Henrik was innocent of wrongdoing, and had no sinister intent as far as the dolls were concerned. Sigrid's story was easy enough to check out, especially with Gunne's access to the ladies in Eleanora's court.

Still to clear up was François's denial about the alchemy book, though that was nothing to tie him directly to any crime. Then there were the unexplained papers hidden in the book, rows of numbers and letters that made no sense.

"We should go, Gunne," he said, anxious to pursue the only clues he had left. He had been misled by the wax dolls and spent valuable time with another idea that went nowhere.

After breaking his fast the following morning, Johan headed for Gunne's room. He had almost reached the stairwell leading to the corridor where the dwarfs had their rooms when he met Alexandre Voullon coming his way. Their paths had not crossed since that night Johan had followed Voullon in the cold, only to learn the man had simply gone to Mass, but now, there was no avoiding him. Fine, let him have his laugh and be done with it.

"Bonjour," Voullon said, wearing a casual grin.

Johan returned the greeting, and knew instinctively that Voullon had no intention of bringing the embarrassing incident up.

"Guess you've heard the news," Voullon said.

"No, I've not talked to anyone this morning. What news?"

"Henrik has disappeared. No one knows his whereabouts. I thought you might like to know, since you two weren't the best of friends. I overheard some of his snide remarks. Good riddance, I say."

Johan's mind raced. This put a different light on things. Could Henrik have the bible after all? If he did, and now had fled the castle, he would have taken the book with him, leaving no way for Johan to help Zofia. Without the bible's return to Eleanora, Zofia's name would never be cleared.

Voullon said, "I wonder how Henrik's lady friend is taking the news."

"I know nothing of his personal life, Alexandre."

"Not many people do, but I've known for some time. They pass beneath my window when they can spend time together. There's an old footbridge near the third tower. Lovers used to go there, but it was put off limits. The old queen thought it contributed to low moral standards in the court." He chuckled. "Foolish to think you can stop what's gone on for ages. Anyway, that's how I know about Henrik's affair with the girl."

"Know who she is?"

Voullon paused, as if wishing he had never revealed so much. "Yes, but I don't want to get involved in anything troublesome. I keep to myself and it serves me well."

"I won't reveal your name, but I need to know this girl's name."

"Kirsten. I've heard Henrik say it several times."

Kirsten. That was Sigrid's friend, the one who had persuaded Henrik to make the wax dolls. So, Sigrid told the truth, as he had suspected.

Voullon continued. "Like I said, they stopped not far from my window. I felt like an eavesdropper, but what could I do? Tell them to leave?" He glanced over his shoulder, then leaned closer. "I have something to tell you that weighs on my conscience."

"Yes?" Johan said, wondering what mild-mannered Voullon would have to say that was so secretive.

"I should have told you earlier, but of course there's nothing to link the two together."

"You mean, Henrik and the girl?"

"No, no. That much is for sure. The other, though, is simply speculation. I'm not one to start rumors, but I've had time to think on it, and it's something you need to know. You can decide for yourself. Henrik met the girl there frequently, but one night—I remember distinctly when it happened, because I had to miss playing that evening. My gout was acting up and I could scarcely walk. Anyway, the next day I heard about your accident on the stage. Then I remembered Henrik and what he had said to the girl the previous evening—something about getting even, and revenge. Then he talked about the pulleys and machinery to move the sun. I thought nothing about it at the time, but when I heard about your accident . . . Please, don't mention my name to anyone."

"Don't worry, my friend. Your words are safe with me. This Kirsten, I imagine she has been questioned about Henrik's disappearance."

"I doubt it. Not many knew about her. I'm surprised he even had a girl. Henrik was hard to get along with. Everyone knew that, and left him alone." He shrugged. "But I suppose he was kind enough to her."

"Thanks, Alexandre. I may talk directly to Kirsten."

"Remember, you gave your word. You didn't hear it from me."

Chapter Twenty-Three

Johan rapped on Gunne's door. "Thank goodness you are still here. I ran into Voullon in the corridor. Sit down. I have some news." After explaining about Henrik's disappearance, Johan continued. "That's not all. Voullon overheard a conversation between Henrik and Kirsten, that girl Sigrid mentioned when she spoke about the wax dolls. Seems Henrik hinted of revenge, and referenced the stage machinery. This new development might shed some light on the whole mystery. Can you arrange for me to speak with Kirsten?"

Gunne scratched his beard stubble. "That won't be easy. Those women of Eleanora's are always together, but I'll see what I can do. For now, go and wait near the statuary room while I speak with her."

Later, as Johan sat alone on a hallway bench, he saw Sigrid coming his way. He rose to bow and she snapped his name. "Johan, the self-appointed sleuth."

Johan resisted the urge to point out that he'd been appointed by the queen mother. Why argue with a sharp-tongued lady?

She had reached the bench and stood, arms crossed. "I understand you want to see Kirsten."

"Yes. Is she not well?"

"What do you think? I suspect this sudden interest in Kirsten is about Henrik, am I right?"

"Well, yes, I suppose."

Sigrid leaned to touch the wooden bench with her fingers.

"It's too cold to sit here. I know of a place near the kitchen. Come with me." She took him to a quiet corner next to the wine cellar. "I suppose I can tell you. You'll find out soon enough anyway." She leveled her gaze at Johan. "I'm surprised, with all your snooping, you never knew about Kirsten and Henrik."

"My snooping was only to—"

"Free the alchemist? When will you learn, she is guilty? Before long she will be gone from court."

He decided to ignore Sigrid's prediction, although he feared she was right. "What about Henrik and Kirsten?"

"They met about two years ago—at one of the queen's balls. They danced together, and ever since, they have been lovers. Her heart is broken. She's been crying all morning, ever since getting the news about Henrik. She was the only reason he wanted to stay here, but when it all came apart—"

"What came apart? She fell out of love?"

"No, not at all. Kirsten's father found out. He is the oldest son in one of the richest noble families in Stockholm. He found out about Henrik and offered him a large sum of money to go to Denmark until spring, and when the weather breaks, to the New World. Of course Henrik could not turn that down, being who he is. He took the money and left. Her father broke the news to her this morning, shortly after morning prayers with the queen mother."

"That's the only reason Henrik left?"

She blinked large, luminous eyes. "Does he need more reason than that?" She crossed her arms and regarded him sternly. "I hope that puts an end to some of your sneaking around. Oh, yes, another thing. Before he left, he told me your little secret. If you don't want the queen to know who you really are, a deserter turned spy for the Russian authorities, you will drop this investigation of yours and tell the queen mother she has her thief and it's Zofia."

So, Henrik had told Sigrid everything, and now she was threatening, as Henrik had done, to reveal that he was a deserter. "I was not in the queen's army," he said, hoping he could bluff her into thinking his past would not matter here.

"It makes no difference. The queen would think little of a deserter in any army. She has a special feeling for brave men who go to war and are loyal to a just cause. She values loyalty above everything. I know she exiled two maids of her bed-chamber to their estates. They made disparaging remarks about her femininity, and she considered them disloyal. If you doubt me, ask around. Others know it happened."

Johan swallowed. What Sigrid said was true. The queen would probably see him as nothing more than a cad—indeed, the whole world would. He had a choice to make—drop the search for the thief and let Zofia take the blame, or be exposed for what he was—a deserter.

"I'm going now," she said. "Think about what I said. I believe you'll make the right decision, especially if you want to stay at court."

Johan made no reply. Henrik's departure had changed nothing at all. Sigrid had taken his place, and likely would do anything to guarantee her rise in rank within the circle of the queen mother's ladies-in-waiting. Somehow, Johan had to forge ahead in spite of the obstacles that slowed his advance, blocked his every move like a clever chess opponent. After all, if he had to live his life in the shadow of the past, was it worth living? He had to trust the queen, who seemed fair, should he be branded a deserter. Besides, let the truth come out. He could not run forever. Let him be judged by the way he lived, not how he might have died. Was it heroic to fight when the battle was already lost?

Sigrid had disappeared down the hall, leaving behind her

warning and the smell of her perfume. Her words, instead of unnerving him, had served as a reminder of how little most knew of what war was really like. Once in the battlefield, a soldier soon realized it was not glory and fame, but hardship and pain. He rubbed his eyes, trying to shut out visions of a place he wanted to forget. He saw it all clearly: the tent beneath the stars, and the battlefield, full of injured and dead; heard the sound of muskets in the distance.

A bell rang in one of the towers. Johan drew his coat close against a sudden draft. Zofia had a way of making him forget the bad times. He needed to find Gunne again, this time to escort him to Zofia's room.

CHAPTER TWENTY-FOUR

Johan stood beside Gunne while the dwarf inserted the key and undid the latch. Zofia pulled open the door. "Gunne. I'm glad you . . ." She lifted her head, and seeing Johan, burst into tears. "Give me some news, Johan, any at all. I am going mad, locked into this tiny room. It truly has become a cell, no different from those in the dungeon except for a more comfortable bed. It's the confinement that drives a prisoner to prefer death. I understand that now."

Gunne handed her a clean linen. "Calm down, Zofia, or you'll frighten off your friends." He chuckled and went to the door. "I'll be just outside." He shut the door behind him, leaving Johan alone with Zofia.

Zofia sat on the bed and indicated a chair for Johan. He sat, feeling miserable. He had come here for encouragement, but Zofia needed comforting far more than he. He leaned forward. "I wish I had good news." He stared at his hands, one on each knee, and remembered how Zofia had rubbed ointment on them. But she was waiting for news, and he wanted to take her mind from her predicament, if only for a few moments. "Did you hear about Henrik?"

"No," she said. "Tell me."

"He fled the palace. They think he went to Denmark. He was a lead suspect, and with him gone—"

"Are you sure he didn't leave because he thought you were closing in?"

"No. He had me fooled, though. Here's what I know. He and one of the queen mother's ladies-in-waiting cared for each other. The girl's father, however, had different plans for his daughter. He offered Henrik a large sum of money to leave Stockholm for good. Henrik took the money and bolted. The girl is broken-hearted, but likely better off. Henrik is a bitter man. He blamed me for his father's death, even though I was nowhere around."

"Why blame you?"

"I was in the Polish army, and a Polish soldier killed Henrik's father."

She nodded. "That's not uncommon. I mean, to blame a whole group for what one man did. The past, sometimes, is better left to rest. Why struggle with something you cannot change? No one can change the past, much as we might like to. We have to accept the good and the bad for what they are, and go into the future. Besides, I doubt Henrik's father, if he were alive, would want his son to bear a lifelong hatred for a certain group of people. It just doesn't make sense."

"You are right, Zofia—about the past, I mean. I faulted Henrik, and now I see I was doing much the same—living in the past. I have nightmares. I see the campfires, and hear the dreaded bugle horn calling the garrison to war. It won't leave me alone." He plunged ahead, telling her everything.

She spoke quietly. "How do you know you could have saved your brother's life?"

"I don't, not really. They came from all sides. I suppose I feel guilty because I'm here and he is not."

"Hmm. A bit the way Henrik might feel. I think, in a way, when we lose someone dear, a piece of us wants to be with them. My mother died during an outbreak of the plague. For days after, I wanted to be with her, to lie beside her in the deep, comforting earth." Zofia shook her head. "It was Papa who got me through, and now I know I was mad with grief."

236

Johan's thoughts raced. He, too, was probably crazed. That's why he remembered little of the journey northward—no memories of riding through the countryside on his way to the Baltic. It was as if he'd buried his brother and woken from a deep sleep at the point of a musket, a day's ride from the Baltic seaport.

Zofia put her hand on his arm, a light, comforting touch. "Do you think your brother would have been pleased to see you refuse his command, to see you die on the battlefield? Would that make sense? He wanted one life to be saved, and he cared enough to use his last words to make that happen. Don't twist it around. Let it go, Johan. Your brother wanted it this way."

He locked and unlocked his hands. Zofia was right. He'd worn his sorrow like a protective shield, not allowing his brother to be the hero he was. And now, to make matters worse, he had wanted to comfort Zofia and instead, she was comforting him.

As if reading his thoughts, she abruptly changed the subject. "So you have no other suspects, now that Henrik is gone?"

"A few, yes, and I have discovered some strange things that go on in the palace."

"What, Johan? I may be able to help."

"Well, Beaulieu mentioned Henrik and François both, and that made me start thinking, which eventually took me to François's room to look around. He had a book on alchemy earlier, according to Beaulieu, but François said he had lost interest in the subject and had not kept the book. That was a lie. I found it hidden in his room.

"Then there were the dolls in Henrik's room—wax dolls, the kind used for putting curses on people, or for calling up spirits. His dolls were dressed like regular people, some as courtiers. One even had a tiny crown. When I saw those, I thought perhaps he used them for witchcraft, but I learned it was actually an innocent venture, something to do with puppet shows for

Eleanora. Now, I'm wondering if everything else will lead nowhere, but I wanted to ask what you think. I'd like to know why François would hide an alchemy book."

Zofia seemed about to reply, then rose abruptly. "Would you like coffee? We could have Gunne—"

"No, Zofia. Can we talk about the book?"

She drew her brows together, and in a moment, lifted her gaze. Her eyes, he noticed, had darkened. Or was it the frown that warned him of her anger? "Why would the possession of a book about alchemy make you believe François had anything to do with the theft of the bible?"

"Now who is being irritable?" He added a smile, which seemed to calm her a bit. "No reason, except that François denied having it. For some reason he wanted no one thinking he was interested in alchemy." He shifted his weight and searched for a way to send the conversation in another direction. "Oh, I almost forgot." He reached into a pocket of his coat. "I found these papers in François's room, tucked inside the book. There were others, but I was hoping if I left a few there, he might not notice some were missing. Do you know what they mean?"

She brought the papers to the light, then turned each one, studying the letters and symbols. After a few moments, she spun around to face him. "These," she said, holding the papers tight, "are my formulas—taken from my laboratory."

"You are sure of that? To me they looked as mysterious as the one I brought earlier, the one you didn't recognize."

"I had never seen it before, that drawing, but I can positively identify these as being from my workroom. Ooh, to be kept here while someone comes and goes freely in my workroom." She took a deep breath and leaned her head against the window frame, as if resigned to her situation. A moment later, she straightened. "I'm curious about something. Why did the wax dolls seem more important to you than these formulas?"

He paused, then decided she had a right to know. "I had seen dolls like those being used before. I know the harm they can do."

"Then you believe they can put a curse on someone?"

"No, but it's the belief itself that can harm. It was a sorcerer of some sort who brought potions and dolls to my mother, forestalling any treatment from someone who could have saved her. The woman took the last of our fortune, promising a cure, but in the end, neither her dolls nor chanting nor potions helped."

Zofia had moved to sit beside him. "Is it possible the woman believed she could help? Every day we are learning new things." She tucked a loose curl behind her ear. "That's why I want to get back to my laboratory. All this time I might have been discovering something important. Instead I am holed up here, useless as a worm."

"You are not useless, Zofia, especially not to me. In fact, you've given me something to think about." He rubbed his chin. "I still don't understand why Henrik was so determined to see you blamed for the theft. Any ideas?"

She slowly shook her head.

Johan, puzzled that she seemed not at all surprised, pushed on. "I could tell he holds a deep anger toward you. I know Henrik to be offensive—many cannot get past his brashness when they speak of him—but this seemed like something more. I worried about you, and for your sake, I'm glad he's gone."

Zofia caught her breath, a quick intake of air he almost missed. She pinched her lips together, obviously uncomfortable with what she was about to say. After a brief pause, she met his eyes. "I can take care of myself, but I should have told you earlier about Henrik—and me. I thought it had no bearing on your investigation. Besides, I promised myself I would put it behind me—all of it."

"What, Zofia? What do you know? Do you think he left with the bible? Do you think he's the murderer?"

She shook her head. "This is about Henrik, and something that happened before you came, but he was punished for his misdeed. It has nothing to do with your investigation."

Johan reached out, put both hands on her arms. "I'm listening, Zofia."

She leaned forward, her eyes searching his. "Promise me you'll not repeat this to anyone. It's better forgotten—for everyone involved."

"I give you my word."

She sat and reached for a pillow, then clasped it to her chest. "It was shortly after the queen mother brought them here— from the orphanage, I mean. Sigrid and Henrik both. Sigrid, of course, Eleanora kept for herself, to be raised by her own serving women until Sigrid was old enough to serve the queen mother. Henrik, husky and in good health, was to be trained for the Queen's Guard—an honor reserved mostly for noblemen's sons, but his father had died in the war, and his mother had died in childbirth. Eleanora's heart is sometimes too soft for her own good." She paused, picking at a thread on the pillow.

"Go on, Zofia."

She laid the pillow on her lap and crossed her hands. "It happened about seven years ago. I was thirteen at the time, and Henrik, fifteen. I had just left the queen's chambers after nursing her with one of her—she has terrible pain every month, as some women do. Her ladies had all gone to bed, and as I was leaving, I heard someone whisper my name. It came from further down the corridor. I thought it was one of the women, wanting to know about the queen, so I walked into the alcove. It was very dark, and at first I didn't know what was happening, but then I saw Henrik. We had talked before, even shared a dance, and so at first I was not frightened. He pulled me down to sit on the padded bench beside him. I told him I wanted to go, to get some sleep before checking on the queen again, but he brought me close. He kissed me, a rough kiss, then on my throat . . ." She rubbed her neck as if wiping away the unwanted kiss. "He would not let me go, and then—and then, he pulled at my bodice. That is when I got really afraid. The harder I tried to push away, the tighter he held me. He shoved me back onto the pillows. I screamed, but he clamped his hand over my mouth. He lifted my skirts, and tried—he tried to—" Tears rolled from her eyes, wetting her cheeks, and Johan could no longer stand to see her cry.

"Never mind, Zofia. I think I know. I'm sorry." He held her, letting her tears dampen his shirt, and wishing he had never asked anything about Henrik.

"No, I want to tell you the rest. One of the women told me later that she heard someone scream. That's how she knew to come there. When she saw what was happening she shouted for help. Henrik ran, probably fearful the guards would come, and he was right. They caught him at the end of the corridor. Margit told them what had happened, then she came back and walked with me to my room. She is gone now, retired to spend her last years with her sister, but Margit was kind to me—waited with me in my bedchamber until I fell asleep.

"The next morning, while I was trying to figure out how I could avoid ever seeing Henrik again, Queen Christina sent for me. She made me tell her what happened, although of course, the guards had already told her everything. When I finished, she slipped an arm around my shoulders. Then she said, 'Bring him in.'

"I trembled, because I knew I would have to face Henrik, but I'll never forget the queen's words. 'In my castle,' she said, looking straight at him as he stood between two guards, appearing as though he would rather be anywhere but there, 'no man should ever dare assault a lady. Those who know me well, know that the thought of such a thing disgusts me. I have decided that your punishment is removal from guard training. If you wish to remain here at the palace, I forbid you ever to so much as speak to Zofia again. You will begin training as a stagehand, to assist the ballet director and stage crew in any way you can. Should you ever be brought before me again for a crime such as this, I will send you into the streets of Stockholm penniless, to make your own way.' "

"And did he obey the queen?" Johan asked.

"Yes. He never spoke to me again, but I have always known he hates me. In a way, I feel sorry for him."

"You should not, Zofia."

"I know, but in any other court . . . It's just that the queen is different. She prefers to be around men, discussing the hunt, and government policy, but she has no intention of marrying. She is frightened of childbearing." Zofia put one hand to her mouth. "Oh, please, I should not have told you that. She speaks of it in front of me, and has told Oxenstiern the same, but she would not want it talked about." She heaved a deep sigh. "I always thought it Henrik's bad luck that he was in her court. I know from what her ladies have said that any other royal would not have given a second thought to something like what happened to me."

"I'm sure of that too, Zofia, and don't worry. Nothing you told me will ever be repeated."

She gave him a small smile and wiped the last of her tears. "So, you see now why Henrik would probably be pleased if I were punished. He would think I had it coming to me."

Gunne rapped on the door. "I have to leave," Johan said, "but I'll come back soon, hopefully with good news."

"Be careful, whatever you decide to do. Someone has already

tried to harm you." She touched his arm with her fingertips. They felt like angel breath on his skin. "Take care," she said, her eyes crinkling at the corners.

He wanted to stay, and he wanted to go. He needed no complications in his life. There were too many already. She was dedicated to her work, and so he would be, once this investigation was over. There could be nothing but friendship between the two of them. Besides, there was another pressing problem. He had to confront François and ask about the book. That might change everything. What Zofia had told him tonight explained a lot, about Henrik and also about her, but it brought Johan no closer to finding the murderer. Henrik had been argumentative and evidently acted before thinking of the consequences, but it did not make him a criminal. François had taken papers from Zofia's room, but did he murder the goldsmith?

Later, Johan made his way to the secluded alcove where he did his best thinking. He had a slim lead, but a lead, nonetheless. François was in Zofia's workroom and had taken some of her formulas. What else was in his room? It deserved a closer look.

CHAPTER TWENTY-FIVE

As the last of the ballet dancers left the dormitory and headed to rehearsal, Johan fitted his lute into its case, stored it on the shelf next to his belongings, and went into the adjacent dormitory. He stepped inside François's cubicle, one of the small rooms divided by wooden partitions and curtains, a clever and inexpensive arrangement intended to give each member of the ballet troupe a sense of privacy. Johan worked quickly, sorting through costumes, looking in boxes, just as Zofia had asked him to do. He checked the shelves again, moving items and looking behind them. Giving one last swipe to the back of a shelf, his hand hit a pot, too heavy to be empty. He pulled it forward to the light and saw he had almost overturned a mortar and pestle. He'd missed it before. Or had it been put there more recently? Was François hiding some spice concoction?

Half amused, Johan's thoughts went back to his childhood, the oft-told story of Baba Jaga, the old woman who lived in a house that stood on chicken legs. She flew through the air in her mortar, using the pestle to steer, and swept behind her with a birch broom. He shook his head, wondering how old he had been before finding out it was only a legend. Smiling to himself, he lifted the pestle. A thick, gummy substance with what looked like metallic specks in it dripped from the end of the pestle. Was this something Zofia would recognize?

Reminded of where he was, and the danger of being found there, he decided to go straight to Zofia with his find. The rehearsal would go on for hours, so he had plenty of time to return it before François came back—at least, he had to hope so. This new discovery might explain why François had taken the formulas from her laboratory.

Johan hid the mortar and pestle in the folds of his cloak and left the room. Gunne, his self-appointed lookout, waited in the corridor. On the way to Zofia's little room, Johan showed Gunne the strange mixture.

"Looks like some kind of experiment to me," Gunne said. "But I suppose as long as he doesn't set fire to the place, he's doing nothing wrong."

After a quick knock and a twist of the key that hung from Gunne's belt, the door creaked open. Johan set the gummy mixture on Zofia's table.

She lifted the pot, tilting it from side to side, watching the contents as if she were seeking the future in a scrying mirror. Finally, she turned to face him. "Just as I thought. My formulas were not the only thing he took from my laboratory." She turned back, lifting the pestle from the pot of thick liquid. "This is probably from my supply. It's gum arabic, used as a thickener. He mixed it with something else. I was experimenting with herbals, and used gum arabic as a binder."

"Do you suppose he is trying to concoct medicinals?"

"Who knows? The gum arabic is useful for other things. Painters use it, it's used in making ink . . ."

Gunne, who had been silent until now, spoke up. "But the formulas, Zofia. If I had to guess, I would say he was trying to use your formulas for some concoction."

She shook her head and cupped the pot in one hand. "This is nothing like my formulas. It has some kind of ground metal in it. Others have experimented with using precious metals as a cure for certain ailments, but I have no such formula. It's too risky, and I serve the queen. I'm not even sure which metal this is. Perhaps the queen's art curator would know. He restored some of her Titians, damaged in transport from the palace at Prague, so he is knowledgeable about mixes like these."

Gunne slid from his chair, and Johan knew his friend was as anxious to find the curator as he was. Besides, it was getting on toward dusk, and François would return to his room before long.

They found the curator hunched over a painting. He fixed a stare on Johan. "Aren't you the one who's investigating for the queen mother?"

Johan nodded and showed him the mixture. "I hope you can identify what's in this."

The curator took the pot and pulled a lamp closer. After poking one finger in the pot, he rubbed the gum on a rag and picked at the particles. "Can't say as I know. Some kind of metal. It's strange, though. It looks like a powder I found on the frame of a Holbein in the queen's gallery. That was a real mystery. How did a ground metallic substance get on a picture frame? Someone must have had the dust on their hands and handled the frame." He handed Johan the pot. "Sorry I can't help. If you find out, I'd like to know."

Johan thanked the man, left the curator's small workshop, and headed back to the dancers' dormitory. While Gunne waited near the door, Johan returned the pot to its owner's cubicle. Back in the hall, he walked swiftly and spoke low, keeping an eye out for anyone who might overhear. "Gunne, do you recall Zofia saying that François had likely spent hours in her laboratory? That would have to be at night, when no one would see him." He paused and looked down at the dwarf. "Remember the paper I found in a box in the dancers' dormitory? That wasn't Zofia's. In fact, she didn't know what the symbol meant. Do you suppose there is any connection between that symbol and Zofia's formula?"

Gunne shrugged. "There could be, but that first paper you found might be nothing—or it could mean everything." He chuckled. "What a puzzle." He folded his arms and looked suddenly thoughtful. "Tell you what. Bureus might be able to help you decipher that symbol. He considers himself a scholar of the Rosicrucian documents, and they're full of symbols. Don't know why I didn't think of it sooner."

Johan resumed walking. "Bureus? Ah yes, the mystic. Matthiae's drinking companion and alibi. I'll pay him a visit. It's worth a try."

The room in which Bureus lived and worked looked to Johan like a drawing from some medieval stage play. "Sit down," Bureus said, lifting a stack of papers from a high-backed chair and giving the seat a swipe. A cloud of dust filtered upward. Johan coughed. How did Bureus sleep in such a place?

Spent candles and empty cups lined the sill of a window, boarded up now for winter. A fire burned in the hearth, and Johan knew, after a moment's glance, that the room was a hazard to the entire castle. Fire could erupt at any moment, making an inferno of all Bureus's possessions.

Bureus shooed a cat from a worn upholstered chair and sat. "I get few visitors, now that I'm old, and that suits me fine," he said. "The chambermaids used to clean my rooms, and in the doing, I lost many old manuscripts. I have a rule now, and they respect it. They may come once a week, when I am here to guard my belongings. Now, how can I help?"

"I understand you have an interest in Rosicrucian documents."

Bureus's brows lifted. "Oh? Do they interest you?"

Johan smiled. "I know nothing about them. That's why I came here. As you may know, the queen mother has the court alchemist secured in a room. I'm sure you know about the murder investigation. The girl is the chief suspect right now."

"I heard something about all that, though I stay away from court politics."

Johan noticed the cat eyeing the only empty chair. He'd best sit while he could. "I don't blame you," he said, easing into the chair. "However, I'm hoping you can help. Perhaps you can decipher this for me." He handed over the drawing. Would Bureus laugh at his pitiful attempt at finding clues?

Bureus examined the paper. "Does this belong to your suspect?"

"I'm not sure. If you think it relevant, I can find out whose it is, and possibly make a connection to the theft and murder."

"I see why you think this might be important, but it is nothing but a poor attempt to draw an illustration in the documents—the way one would sketch something that was on their mind. I wonder, could this belong to François, a member of the French dance troupe?"

"That is possible," Johan said, his heart pounding. So, there was some connection. The next moment, he remembered he'd secretly removed the paper from a dancer's box of personal possessions, and hoped Bureus had no interest in reporting his guest to the royal guards. "What makes you think it belongs to François?"

Bureus scratched his chin. "Because he came here weeks ago and asked to see the documents. He had the mistaken notion that the manifestos had practical secrets, like formulas, such as a scientist would use. He did not understand that the documents are sacred texts explaining secrets of the universe—an insight into nature and the spiritual realm.

"But on your question as to whether or not the texts relate to alchemy, there is another text in the manifestos. I'm attempting to find a copy, but François may have heard of it—*The Chymical Wedding*. It is full of alchemical symbolism. I always thought it might be an allegory of an alchemical process, but I seriously doubt it would be anything a French ballet dancer would be reading, let alone understanding.

"So you see," Bureus said, "I doubt there is any clear connection between this drawing and the murder or the theft." He leaned back and crossed his arms on his chest. "I am curious as to why anyone would want that bible, aside from its value as an artifact. Especially puzzling is why someone would kill to get it."

Bureus was interrupted by the cat as it jumped into his lap. He stroked the cat and continued. "The book is incomplete, you know. The missing leaves have never been found, and probably never will be, which lessens its value, in spite of its age. In addition, there is this to consider—the book may simply have been removed for religious reasons, with no intent to sell it at all. And I'm sure you've considered that the murder may not be connected in any way to the theft. We are in a time of turmoil. I can imagine a Catholic not wanting that book in the Swedish queen's possession, and I can see why a Lutheran would also want it removed. What I don't understand is why anyone would murder a goldsmith and leave the coins untouched."

Without giving time for Johan to answer, Bureus smiled and continued, obviously enjoying the conversation. "Did you know that *The Confessio,* part of the Rosicrucian documents, was possibly written by a Lutheran preacher? The writer implied that the Fraternity is Protestant, and said the pope is an Antichrist." Bureus chuckled. "And how you would sort that out to help your investigation, I have no idea, but perhaps begin with the foreigners—all papists."

Johan stifled a smile. That's what he had done, which had led him into this circle with no way out.

Bureus folded his hands together. "But back to the mysteries of the Rosicrucian documents. Who exactly wrote them and what they are about are open to wide interpretation. All scholars have differing views. There are secret symbols, and all the texts were heavily influenced by alchemy and magic. Therein lies the fascination for those of us who would decipher the secret mysteries. However, the Rosicrucian movement is supported by learned men—the Englishman Francis Bacon, for instance. He is a thinker and scientific investigator—no magician, I can assure you. So you see, your suspect, with his interest in alchemy, most likely hoped to find something useful in the manifestos. That is absurd, of course. Great minds have puzzled over the meaning of the documents. Sorry, but I see no way this poor drawing can be connected with the theft of the Silver Bible or the murder."

Johan rose. The meeting with Bureus, while interesting, had produced nothing useful. He thanked the mystic and left the room, wondering if what he had in mind to do that evening was a foolish venture. No matter, time was running out for Zofia. He had to make a last desperate effort to find the murderer, and right now it looked like he needed a miracle, or divine intervention, to solve the crime.

That night, while the castle slept, Johan made his way to Zofia's laboratory. Here in the shadows he would never be seen, but the half moon cast a soft light from a high window, enough to illuminate the door to her workshop. If François had something to do with the theft and murder, perhaps they were linked to his visits to her workshop.

He wrapped his cloak tight and sat in the shadows. From his vantage point, he would be able to make out the face of anyone entering the room. He had only to use patience, his supply of which was running low. If someone came in the night to her room, should he be so lucky, that someone would likely be the same man who had attacked him, and who had led him on a futile chase through empty corridors before disappearing from sight. François's formulas, Zofia insisted, were hers, straight from her laboratory, but with her in virtual seclusion, he needed to find proof, beyond her word, that François had been in her workroom.

All through the night hours he kept watch. At daybreak he rose, discouraged, and stiff from the cold. Was he being a fool? Something told him he was very close to making a keen discovery, else he would have heeded Gunne's words that he was wasting his time. He yawned, then headed for his cot in the dormitory for a much-needed nap.

That evening, after a hearty meal and two hours of poetry recitations, he returned to the dormitory with the other musicians. Later, satisfied that his companions had fallen asleep, Johan rose from the bed and tiptoed out. Walking down the corridor, empty now except for sleeping dogs, he headed for his hiding place across from the door to Zofia's laboratory. Once seated in the shadows, he huddled inside his cloak as he had the previous night, waiting for someone who might never come. With his head against the cold stone wall he fell asleep, dreaming he stood beside Zofia in her laboratory, mixing, mixing, but the mixture never changed and she insisted he stir it more.

Sometime in the dark of night, a sound close by jolted him from his dream. He opened his eyes, trying to orient himself to wherever he was. *Flap, flap.* Those were footsteps, coming his way. He tensed as the steps grew louder and a figure moved from the shadows and approached the door of Zofia's workshop. A moment later François's face appeared, clearly outlined in the moonlight. Johan's heart pounded. Now what? Follow him in? Grab him from behind, and what then? François was clearly trespassing, but with no other witnesses, it would be one man's word against another's as to who was doing what.

When the door closed behind François, Johan rose from the icy stone, no longer feeling the cold. If he went inside and confronted François, what would that prove? François would probably run, as he had before, and would hide in one of the many ancient corridors. Besides, a scuffle would bring the palace guards at night, and who would they believe? No, he had to think. If he decided to confront the man, it must be planned in advance, when there was no possibility François could slip from his grasp again. Besides, if Zofia's lens got broken in a fight, there would be hell to pay.

As he turned to leave, he heard the door open and close again. François stepped into the moonlight and walked quietly away. Johan watched him retrace his steps, but near the end of the corridor, instead of turning right into the hallway leading to the dancers' dormitory, François kept walking.

Johan followed, grateful he had on his thick fur boots, silent on the wooden floor of the passageway. Keeping to the shadows, he realized his heart was thumping wildly. Where was François heading this time of night?

When François turned down another corridor, Johan hurried to keep pace, fearful he would lose the dancer in one of the dark hallways. Moments later François entered the queen's art gallery, a large room filled with paintings where the doors were never locked, a practice the queen insisted would encourage her courtiers to study the masterpieces.

Johan kept to the darkest shadows, afraid to move and risk hitting a statue, which would alert François to his presence. Instead, he waited, listening. He heard a bump, then a curse, coming from the right side of the room a good distance back. After what seemed like an hour, but in reality must have been only a few minutes, he heard something grating against the stone wall. François retraced his steps and headed for the door.

As François passed by, Johan froze against the wall, not daring to breathe. Once the sound of the dancer's footsteps had faded, Johan left the gallery and hurried down the corridor to keep the dancer in sight. When François entered his dormitory, Johan knew he would have to wait until tomorrow to explore the gallery closely in order to discover the truth about what he had just witnessed.

CHAPTER TWENTY-SIX

Johan sat next to Gunne on a bench not far from a window, where a stream of sunlight promised a bit of warmth. After telling Gunne about last night's puzzling experience with François in the royal gallery, he turned to face his little friend. "So what are you thinking? Should I watch another evening? Explore the gallery this afternoon? Today's the twentieth day of the queen mother's directive. This means we have to make every hour count. Can we afford not to go to the gallery right now?"

"I vote to wait until tonight," Gunne said. "Everyone knows by now that we're deep into an investigation. Why would we suddenly decide to view some works of art? Prowling around in broad daylight, studying the queen's art collection, may look a bit curious."

Johan nodded. He wanted to laugh at the image Gunne painted, but the seriousness of Zofia's predicament sobered him. "All right, but this morning at breakfast I heard someone say scaffolding was being built in a field behind the stables. A carpenter said it was for the murderer. I know it was gossip, but still, it alarmed me that Zofia might hear the same. She'd be frightened to death. I'd like to move this whole thing along, but you're right. I believe the real mystery may have more to do with the gallery and what goes on there in the dark of night, and less with Zofia's laboratory."

Gunne brushed ash from his boots and crossed his ankles. "True. This might lead to real proof of her innocence."

Johan grimaced. "We've thought that before. Perhaps this time, with luck . . ." His voice trailed off.

Gunne gave Johan's knee an encouraging pat. "Remember the Greek slave's story, that persistence wins out."

"Ah yes, but François is no hare, and I've not the patience of a tortoise. However, we do have the musicians' ensemble rehearsal today, and I have missed too many already."

"Then it's settled. Go on to the rehearsal, and tonight, why not wait outside the gallery and see if he comes again? In the meantime, in case this new lead goes nowhere, and François is only guilty of using the court alchemist's laboratory without permission, be thinking what we can do next."

That afternoon, sitting idly through a long rehearsal while the wind players struggled with a difficult passage, Johan reviewed what he knew so far. Some of those at court had never been suspects, mostly because of Gunne, who knew palace routine. Ordinary workers had been cleared, along with the queen's Privy Council, all of whom had been gone to Uppsala Castle during that fateful night. Svante Oxenstiern had a reliable alibi. The royal treasurer had probably been the intended murder victim. Henrik, as it turned out, had more to worry about than stealing a bible, but his involvement in this affair could not be ruled out, not yet, until the guilty party was found. Even now, Henrik might be halfway to Denmark with the bible. But was he the murderer? Would François be vindicated, and if so, what then? It looked more and more likely that Zofia, even if granted leniency by the queen, would soon find herself back in her father's book binding shop. What would happen to her work here at court? The queen would just bring in another alchemist to replace her. Who would not leap at the chance to have the Swedish treasury willing to pay for the newest tools used in experimentation, to say nothing of being patronized by a royal? Was this what François hoped for? If this was his only ambition, that might mean he had nothing to do with the theft or the murder, eliminating another suspect. And what then?

With the rehearsal finally over, Johan hurried out, avoiding any possible confrontation with François. Later that evening, after his favorite meal of herring and mashed turnips, but one that tonight held no appeal, he made his way to the window seat, his sanctuary, and waited. Fresh snow covered the ground and stable rooftop. A lone wolf howled in the distance. At last, when he knew the entire palace slept, Johan made his way to the shadowy darkness outside the queen's art gallery and sat on the floor to wait. His thoughts tumbled and twisted, a myriad of images forming a collage of his life—his mother, his brother as he raced into battle with the red pennant flying, the farmer with the musket, and the courtiers—so many he had come to know and like. He envisioned the queen mother and her ladies and dwarfs, Torelli and his rotating stage, his insistence that the rope had been deliberately cut—and as the heavy weight came hurtling downward, Johan woke with a start. Those were footsteps in the corridor.

He straightened, trying to focus on the rectangle of light from the window, where he hoped to see François's face. He eased to a standing position, intending to bring François to the ground before he had a chance to go inside the gallery, but when he caught sight of an object in François's hand, all thoughts of an attack left his mind. A book, small and bound with metal clasps, made his heart race. It looked like Gunne's description of the Silver Bible. Why would François be carrying it around in the dark, and why bring it here?

He could jump François now and take the bible, but what would that gain? Better to see his intentions. Johan decided to bide his time, remembering Gunne's words, the reminder of the fable. If ever something called for patience, this was it.

Evidently, whatever François's business was in the gallery, it would not take long; he had left the door standing wide. Johan crept inside the room, grateful for the little moonlight. Tonight he could see more plainly what François was about, but it meant staying in the shadows to remain undetected himself.

He watched the dancer make his way to the same section he had gone to the previous evening, a place near the back. In the darkness, Johan could see little of what was happening but from here it looked like François was doing something to a painting. A frame hit the wall, and a moment later the dancer headed toward the open door.

Johan decided it was now or never. He leaped from the shadows and lunged at François. They fell to the ground, struggling in the dark. Johan felt a blow to his ribs and tried to return the punch, but François was no easy match. A crash sounded not far away, and Johan realized something in the queen's art collection had shattered. A fierce determination overrode caution, and he made one last attempt at pinning François down. "The book. Was that the Silver Bible? Where is it?"

He heard a guttural laugh. "You wouldn't dare, not if you're smart. They would never believe you—no one would. Besides, I have the queen mother's favorite lady willing to swear my innocence." He laughed again and landed a blow to the left side of Johan's head that sent him reeling. Before he could regain his balance and his breath, he realized the room had come to life. Through a haze of pain he glimpsed Gunne standing nearby, holding a lantern high to illuminate the room as guards closed in.

Two of the guards, burly Swedes wearing the uniform of the queen's own guard, hoisted François between them. One shook the dancer's shoulders. "Where is it, François? We know you had it."

François, struggling to free himself from the grip of the guards, made no reply.

Johan wheezed, still reeling from pain. "Look near the paintings, back there." He pointed to the wall near where François had paused. "One of those. I'm sure of it."

One by one, the other guards examined the back and front of each painting, and when they came to a large Holbein, one called out. "It's here, cleverly hidden in a back corner of the frame. There's a leather strap . . ." The guard swiveled one end of the strap loose and held the Silver Bible up for all to see, then stepped close to François. "You're under arrest for crimes within the palace."

As the guards led François away, followed by the guard carrying the Silver Bible, Johan made his way slowly out, walking beside Gunne. "How much did you see?"

"We were never far away. I summoned the guards after talking to Zofia. She reminded me that if anything happened, you would likely get the blame, and who besides me would know the truth? I told the guards something strange was going on at night near the gallery. This way they kept their distance."

"Then I should thank both you and Zofia. The bible is found, and they know the real culprit. When we struggled tonight, I knew François was the man who attacked me in Zofia's laboratory. You're right, of course. They needed to catch him with the evidence, and this they did." He rubbed the place on his head where François landed the blow. "For a dancer, he sure has a powerful right punch."

Gunne examined the bump. "You should be better after a night's sleep. Speaking of that, we had better go to bed. When the queen mother finds out what took place, there will be a trial and we'll both be called as witnesses. A murder trial will last for days."

Johan gave a deep sigh. He dreaded tomorrow, but he had not let Zofia down. It had been a long time coming, the pride of a job well done, but most important, he knew that tonight he had acted with courage. Courage ran in their family, and he would follow that model for a lifetime. Right now, though, he had to get some sleep for what lay ahead.

He climbed into bed, rolled onto his side, and stared into the dark, reliving all that had happened. The theft of an ancient book, then threats on his own life. Still, nothing compared to the murder of the innocent goldsmith. Johan scratched his head. Somehow, he was missing something. Yes, the bible thief was caught in the act, but did he have blood on his hands? Blood. The victim's garment, stained with blood.

Johan blinked, sat upright in bed, his thoughts racing. How could he have missed such an obvious clue to the murder?

CHAPTER TWENTY-SEVEN

Twenty-one days after the queen mother's challenge to Johan, a guard delivered a formal summons to him in the musicians' dormitory. Court would be held in her antechamber when the tower bell rang the hour. He wrapped a wool scarf around his neck, warding off the ever-present chill of the palace, and went to the dining hall to break his fast. To his surprise, Svante Oxenstiern rose and extended his hand. "Let me be first to congratulate you for a job well done. Here, there's room at my table."

Surprised by the welcoming smiles, Johan took a seat. Evidently word had spread through the castle overnight. Gabriel Oxenstiern leaned close to Johan's ear. "I am glad to see the culprit brought to trial. A pity Eleanora will sit in judgment. She has a soft heart." He reached for a loaf, broke it in half, then handed a half to Johan. As Johan ate his meal, Gabriel continued. "The king always knew about his queen, and when he was away, he cautioned his councillors never to include her in their deliberations. Now, though, our good-hearted young queen, who has her eye on acquiring more riches and learning ancient languages, allows her mother to handle matters like these. I wonder what punishment she'll impose for the murder."

Johan felt a twitch of indecision, knowing the investigation was not quite finished. For now, though, with everyone looking on, he decided the less said the better. After all, Gabriel's cousin Axel, one of the most important men in the country, was here at the table and no telling how he felt about all this. Besides, Johan had a fondness for the old queen. At least she had given him the chance to prove Zofia's innocence.

He rose from the table. There was one last thing he wanted to do before appearing at Eleanora's court, and that was to speak with François. In spite of all that had happened, he felt sorry for the dancer, a man caught up in a profession not to his liking, and having to hide his real passion.

Johan followed Gunne's directions, taking a dark hallway that led to the ancient dungeon area Gunne had shown him earlier. After passing a row of empty, windowless cells, Johan approached a lone guard. "I want to visit François, your new prisoner."

The guard picked at his teeth and rose from his chair. "He's our only prisoner right now." He reached for a ring of keys at his waist. "He's in the end cell. We gave him the only cell with a window."

Johan followed the guard, acutely aware of their footsteps echoing in the cold, empty underground space. He shivered. Poor François. What to say to a man condemned to—what? He hated to think of what lay ahead for the dancer.

The guard stopped at the last cell, inserted a key, and then pulled the iron door open. Johan stepped inside. "François?"

François lifted his head and looked at Johan through swollen lids. Johan felt a surge of pity. The dancer had been crying, and no wonder. There was no way of telling what punishment Eleanora would mete out for the crimes he had committed. "I wanted you to know, I said nothing to Eleanora about those times you went to Zofia's laboratory, and I will not, if you tell me why you were there. It was you who took me on that chase through the old part of the castle, wasn't it?"

"Yes," François said, his voice breaking. "I should have stopped then, should have given it all up, but it doesn't matter now. I've lost everything."

"The formulas? Why did you steal her formulas?"

François lowered his head again and ran his hands through his hair. "You'll find out soon enough. They'll all find out."

Johan pressed on. "And I have to ask—did you foul the stage equipment?"

"No. That was Henrik. I saw him in the act, but he didn't know that. After it happened, I was too afraid to say anything, knowing I was at fault for not reporting it to Torelli before the show."

"And the lute strings?"

"Lute strings?" François turned his swollen face to the light. "I know nothing about any lute strings. But I lied to you about the alchemy book. I had it all along."

Johan looked down. "I knew that. I wanted to speak with you before the trial begins. Did the goldsmith interrupt you? Is that why you had to kill him?"

François turned a tear-stained face to Johan. "I thought perhaps I had one friend, someone who knew me better than that. I could never kill anyone. Besides, I had no reason to."

Johan met François's gaze. "I want to believe that, but I need proof." He experienced a moment of conflicting emotions. If François was cleared of the murder, what then? Would Zofia still be held?

The tower bell rang and a guard opened the cell door. He met Johan's eyes. "You'll have to leave now. It's time for the prisoner's hearing."

Johan nodded to François and left the cell. What would François's punishment be? The question of why he had taken the bible might never be revealed. That was something only François could answer. And if the queen mother still believed that the theft and the murder were committed by the same person, François would be punished for both crimes.

As Johan entered the corridor leading to Eleanora's apartments, he considered how best to test his theory of François's innocence in the murder.

Inside the queen mother's antechamber, Johan signed the recorder's book and was shown to a chair. His head still hurt where François had dealt him a blow the previous evening.

Shortly after the dwarfs took their seats, two guards brought François in, releasing their hold on his arms only long enough for him to record his name. They led him to a chair directly across from Johan. François stared at the floor, his shoulders hunched forward like a man on his way to the gallows.

Johan shifted his weight, wondering what thoughts were going through the dancer's mind. Would he claim innocence of the theft? How could he, when the royal guards themselves had heard and seen everything?

The door opened and Zofia entered, flanked by two of the queen's ladies, evidently sent to escort her here. Johan watched as she made her way to a row of chairs set aside for interested courtiers. She sat, thanked her escorts, and cast a glance around the room. Seeing Johan, she gave him a tenuous smile. He returned the smile, and she winked. He hid a chuckle. There was nothing timid about Zofia.

Eleanora strolled in, surrounded by the ladies, and all eyes turned respectfully to the queen mother. She sat, and her ladies took seats around her. Sigrid, Johan thought, looked particularly wan, but maybe that was the light. "We will begin," Eleanora said, her voice filling the room. He noticed she held the Silver Bible in her hands, carefully, like a treasured relic, and he was reminded, in spite of her voice, that the queen mother was no longer young and vibrant. Likely it was the recovery of her book that had cheered her.

As the trial progressed, with one after the other of the guards telling their story, the queen finally allowed François to speak. "And you, the accused. What have you to say for yourself?"

He shook his head.

"You waive the right to speak? Have you no excuse for your crimes? Let's begin with the theft. Why did you steal my book?"

"I needed it to match the ink."

"What? Speak up. Did you say link? What link?"

"The ink, Your Majesty. I wanted to duplicate the silver ink. I was so close, but it was not quite right. I believe it has something to do with the paper on which they wrote."

"Ah, yes." Eleanora opened the bible and rubbed a finger along the edge of a page. "A light purple, some of them are. That is part of the book's appeal." She blinked and closed the bible. "Tell me, François, if you had managed to make an exact match, what then?"

"Why, I was—I was going to sell the formula. It would make me rich enough to court one of your ladies openly. I wanted to ask your lady, Sigrid, to marry me."

The courtiers surrounding the queen mother, the dwarfs seated in judgment, gasped in unison, but Johan's thoughts were on Sigrid's books about printing. Of course. She had been trying to help François. Had she known all along about the theft?

The queen mother's eyes were on Sigrid. "How much did you know of this?"

"Nothing, Your Majesty," François shouted. "She knew nothing. I swear on the Silver Bible itself. If she knew I was the cause of your unhappiness, she would never have spoken to me again—as I am sure she won't now. My love of discovery has ruined me, but I pray you not blame your lady."

Eleanora cleared her throat. "I will take this matter up with her later." She tapped her nails on the arm of her throne-like chair. "For now, though, this is about the theft. Now that you have told me why you wanted the bible, I see our court alchemist was wrongly accused—kept from her work for days." She leaned back and crossed her arms. "You owe her an apology. And now we come to the matter of the murder." She narrowed her eyes and stared at the accused.

François shook his head. "I know you won't believe me, but I am not the murderer. I did take keys from your hiding place. I had seen you slide the key beneath the cabinet. It was easy. I opened the cabinet door, found the book, locked the cabinet and replaced the key. No one saw me come or go. I—I took no notice of anyone else. I assumed the library was empty that time of night—though I recall seeing faint candlelight above the partition that sets the reading area apart. I thought a candle had been left burning. I meant to check, in case of fire, but changed my mind. The flame would likely die in a puddle of wax anyway. I hurried back to my room with the book."

François paused, looking down at the floor.

The queen mother leaned forward. "Go on. Tell me everything."

François looked up and continued. "Once I discovered a mixing pot was gone from my shelf, I knew I would have to find a place to hide the book. The gallery was the perfect place. No one goes there at night because candlelight does not do justice to the paintings or statuary. They need the light of day. So you see, I had no reason to kill anyone. It was all very easy—until the lutenist discovered my hiding place."

The queen mother frowned and called her small, curly-haired dog to her lap. "Do you have any oath-maker to speak on your behalf in the matter of the murder?"

François shook his head.

Johan squirmed, hoping someone would step up. When no one did, he rose. "I will speak for François. While he took your book, I don't believe he is capable of murder. His heart is in the world of science."

The queen mother leaned forward. "But you can't be sure, can you?" Her voice had risen, frightening the small dog, who burrowed into the voluminous skirts of its mistress.

Johan's thoughts raced. If he revealed the reason he believed François was innocent, the real murderer could hide the evidence. However, if Eleanora judged that François was guilty of both crimes, Johan would simply have to divulge his theory, and the real murderer would never be found. He made a quick decision, praying it was the right thing to do. "I am convinced of his innocence. That is all I have to contribute."

Eleanora turned to Zofia. "And you, alchemist? What say you?"

"I have nothing to say, except that I share François's interest in the silver ink. I, too, would like to discover the formula used by the ancients."

Johan swallowed, feeling suddenly proud to have saved the reputation of the court alchemist. Still, no one was clear of the murder, not yet.

When Eleanora yawned, Johan knew her patience was wearing thin. She leaned forward. "We will recess to discuss the matter at hand." She indicated the two rows of judges, sitting in their miniature straight-backed chairs, newly built especially for them by the palace carpenter. "Come with me. All of you." The dwarfs rose and followed her out.

The minutes ticked by. In spite of all the trouble François had caused, Johan hoped the queen mother believed the dancer. How different would the man be now, had his parents allowed him to pursue his interest in science, a field on the edge of new ideas? What would the world be like without men like Copernicus and Galileo, who searched for answers? He crossed his arms, wondering what François might have invented had he been free to pursue discoveries.

By the time the queen mother returned, followed by the dwarfs, Johan had begun to sweat. Across the way, a courtier had fallen asleep, lulled by the crackling fire in the queen mother's porcelain stove. In contrast, Her Majesty's ladies fluttered like birds, all but Sigrid, whose expression puzzled Johan. The poor girl was probably torn between having the matter settled and over for the queen mother, whose health was not the best, and concern for François, whose fate was as yet undetermined.

The bell tinkled again. Eleanora cleared her throat and patted her knee. The dog jumped into her lap. "After consulting with my court," Eleanora said, "I have decided only to hand sentencing down for the theft of my bible. The innocence or guilt of the accused I will leave to a higher court. As for the theft, I have settled on an appropriate punishment, one I think fair for all. François, considering the serious crime of stealing from the royal treasury, the inconvenience you have caused to be settled on both the lute player and Gunne, one of my most trusted advisors, to say nothing of the grievous harm visited upon Zofia, the court alchemist, while at the same time recognizing your past service to my daughter the queen, and your contribution to court entertainment, but most of all, taking into account what I have heard today from those most inconvenienced by the theft, I sentence you to six months servitude in the court laboratory, during which you will serve as Zofia's aide in an apprentice-style arrangement. At the end of that period, she can make the decision as to whether you may continue, or if you should return to France. In nine months the last ship will be crossing the Baltic. Whether or not you will be banished from Stockholm forever is up to the court alchemist."

François raised his head. "May I speak?"

"What?" Eleanora said. "My punishment, considering your grievous crime of theft, is most generous. But if you have something to say, yes. I always allow the accused to speak."

François stood. "Your Majesty, may I serve in another capacity? I mean, working under a lady's supervision, that's quite, um, unusual."

Eleanora rubbed the dog's ears and smiled. "It's your sentence. There are no options. As for your marriage to Sigrid, I will allow the marriage, should she agree, once you have completed your obligation, and provided the queen lets you live."

Sigrid handed the queen mother a cup. She sipped, blotted her lips, and continued. "Court is adjourned. Everyone is dismissed, except for Gunne and Johan."

When the oak door closed and they were alone, Eleanora leaned forward. "So, if you're so convinced François is not the murderer, who is?"

"I have a new lead, Your Majesty. I would like your permission to continue."

"Well, I want nothing more to do with it. I have my book back. If it were up to me, I'd turn the information we have over to the town authorities and let them work their will. However, the queen may have other ideas, once she knows the outcome of this trial." Eleanora stroked the dog's fur. "You are dismissed for now. I may require your services later. I'm impressed with your sleuthing abilities, lutenist."

Johan bowed, wondering what else the queen mother had in mind. For himself, he wanted nothing but to get back to playing his music, but Eleanora sounded as though she had something else in mind.

CHAPTER TWENTY-EIGHT

Johan sat next to Gunne on an upholstered bench in Queen Christina's anteroom, puzzling over why the queen had sent for them. He crossed his legs and tried to get comfortable. Since there was no set time for the meeting, he'd just have to wait until she appeared. To pass the time, he studied his surroundings.

As the minutes ticked by, he leaned to speak with Gunne. "The room hasn't changed much since the last time I was here, the day the queen appointed me to be court lutenist." He rubbed his forehead. That day now seemed a lifetime ago for him, but apparently nothing had changed in the queen's life. Evidence of her scholarly leanings, her fondness for learning and the excitement of the hunt, all were visible here. Leather-bound books lay atop three different desks. Some of the books were open, a gold braid marking the pages, signifying an item of interest she wanted to further explore. Stacks of papers and an assortment of writing paraphernalia lay among the papers. On a marble pedestal, the sculpture of a horse commanded attention, centered as it was in a large window surrounded by blue velvet drapes. Across the room, two scribes sat at either end of a gleaming oak desk, evidently waiting for the queen's appearance.

Gunne sneezed, breaking the silence in the room, but made no reply to Johan's observation. Instead, he blew his nose.

Johan resumed studying the architecture. This must be part of the new palace, built within the confines of the old fortress.

High ceilings, gilded columns, and ornamental moulding were obviously new additions. Some of the dark corridors through which he and Gunne had walked could use the queen's decorator, he thought, hiding a smile. Here, instead of cold stone, heavy tapestries covered the walls, a colorful display of battle scenes and mythological creatures. In opposing corners, two porcelain stoves, decorated with floral designs, helped dispel the seasonal cold.

A guard appeared, his red and blue uniform designating him as one of the royal ushers. "The queen just returned from a ride. She'll be here in a few minutes." He disappeared as quickly as he'd come.

A short time later, Queen Christina entered, a bit breathless. Johan jumped to his feet, and she held out her hand. "Be seated. We need to talk."

As she crossed the room, he took note of her stride—self-confident and bold—something she'd probably learned as a child, being raised by her father to someday rule the kingdom. Her thick wavy hair stood away from her face as if an unexpected wind had blown through her chambers. She wore a coat and doublet of deep blue. Beneath the doublet a white buttoned shirt, fastened with a black tie at the neck, looked much like the one Johan presently wore. When she turned her back to address a servant, Johan saw that beneath her masculine attire, she wore a *devantiere,* one of those riding outfits popular in France. Barely visible below her coat was the modest split in the back of the voluminous skirt of the *devantiere,* making it possible for a lady to ride astride.

She dismissed the servant and turned back to look directly at Johan, her large blue eyes still holding the excitement of the ride. "I asked for chocolate—the perfect answer to a cold morning, don't you agree?"

Without giving him time to answer, she spoke again. "I called you and Gunne here because I feel responsible for law and order within the palace. I hoped, of course, that my mother would handle this to the end, as she was determined to find the thief who stole her book. However, the investigation has taken a whole new turn, now that the dancer seems to be cleared of murder. I understand you vouched for his innocence on that count. How are you so sure?"

Johan hesitated. Guards waited at the door. A servant stoked the fire. Could these people be trusted to stay silent? How could he explain his reasoning without jeopardizing the investigation? "Your Majesty, may I reveal it to you in private?"

The queen waved her hand and smiled. "No need. I trust you and Gunne as well, and respect your instincts. After all, you found the thief and Mother is relieved. But if the dancer didn't commit the murder, that means we still have a killer loose in the castle. Who knows when she or he will strike again?"

A serving girl appeared with a tray holding a silver pitcher and goblets. After serving the hot drinks, she removed the tray and left. Queen Christina wrapped her long, slender fingers around her cup and leaned against a cushion in her high-backed chair. "It's not only the worry of that, it's that soon the townspeople will get wind of all this, if they haven't already, and will say that the queen cannot even manage her own castle." She sipped from her cup and set it aside, then leaned forward. "Lutenist, I'd like for you and your assistant to continue the investigation for another week. See what you can find. After that, I suppose there's nothing to be done but call in the local authorities." She sighed. "The Town Council would take great pride in solving a mystery the queen's own sleuths could not solve."

Johan tasted the chocolate—rich and dark, like Zofia had fixed. The queen had thrown out a challenge—and a plea. How could he turn her down? "Very well, Your Majesty. We will begin

271

at once. I do have an idea as to what should be done next."

Christina rose from her chair. "I need to leave. I am already keeping my sketching teacher waiting."

Johan and Gunne hurried to rise. She gave them a smile, and Johan thought, except for her large blue eyes, her mouth was her best feature.

She fastened the clasp on her riding cloak. "Johan, you'd best start right away. Remember, you have a week. Don't let me down."

Johan and Gunne bowed low. Once she was out of sight, they quickly finished their chocolate and left the room. Making their way in the corridor, Gunne looked up at Johan. "You did an admirable thing, swearing to François's innocence and telling the queen you had a lead. It will give us more time to find the murderer. Quite a brave move."

"Gunne, we need to talk about that."

"Sure, but for now, there's something we should do while we have the chance."

Johan raised his brows. "What's so important it can't wait?"

Gunne breathed an impatient sigh. "Earlier, you said you wanted to look closer at that image on the sketching teacher's desk. Now may be the perfect time. You heard what the queen said. She has an art lesson now. I'm guessing it lasts about an hour, so Marin's room will be empty."

Johan nodded, feeling suddenly weary. Gunne seemed determined to follow every clue, no matter how minor. Or was the dwarf only hoping to keep Johan's spirits up? No matter. He remained curious himself about the framed sketch on the teacher's desk. Besides, explaining his conviction about François's being innocent of the murder could best be done with a demonstration.

★ ★ ★ ★ ★

After knocking at the art teacher's room and getting no answer, Gunne used the key he claimed would open almost any door in the castle. The lock released with a click and they hurried inside, closing the door behind them. Darkness surrounded them. Johan blinked. "Just our luck. He's pulled the drapes tight." He eased toward the desk, feeling his way along. Once there, he continued to the window. He pulled back the drapes, flooding the room with a cold, grey winter light.

Gunne crossed to join him. "Nice view of the courtyard. I see it's beginning to snow."

Johan returned to the desk, lifted the framed drawing and brought it to the window. "It's only a sketch of the exterior of some building." Scrutinizing the drawing, he noticed a signature, written in tiny letters. "Look, Gunne. Is this the artist? Looks like S . . . Simon de la Vallée. I'm sure of it."

Gunne looked up. "Hmm. Certainly not a plan of the palace. So much for that idea. And this is outside the castle walls. I don't recognize it." He handed the drawing to Johan. "We should leave before someone comes. The name sounds familiar, but it may simply be a friend of Marin's. Still, he seemed a bit secretive about the sketch."

They stepped into the hall, Johan closing the door behind them. "All the more reason to come out and ask him directly."

Gunne hurried to keep up as Johan moved off. "Now, what's this idea of yours, about solving the crime? You mentioned it to Eleanora, and then to the queen."

Johan tucked the scarf tighter around his neck. This part of the castle was always the coldest. "I'll demonstrate. Let's go to your room."

Gunne nodded. They were partway down the hall when Gunne stopped. "I remember now. I knew that name was familiar. Simon de la Vallée was a Stockholm architect. He was killed in the town square a few years back. I didn't pay much attention to the whole thing. That's about the time I discovered my wife with another man. But I remember there was a lot of discussion in town about it—who killed him and such. People talked at the market, anywhere they congregated. Nothing much was said in the palace, but I guess that's because it happened in town. The case would have been settled in public court."

Johan resumed walking. "I'd like to learn more. Who could we ask?"

"Queen Christina's librarian, Freinsheim. If he can't recall details, he knows where to get answers."

A short while later they sat in Freinsheim's office next to the library. Freinsheim greeted them warmly. "Congratulations on solving the theft. But I heard he was cleared of the murder. Makes me a little uneasy, knowing someone got away with killing a man, right in the palace library."

Johan took the indicated chair. "Not yet. And that's why we're here. This may be nothing, but can you tell me about Simon de la Vallée? Anything about his death?"

Freinsheim stared in disbelief. "That was years back. What does that have to do with anything?"

"Possibly nothing. Please tell me what you know."

"Not much, only what I heard. I didn't know the man personally. Others may have known him better. He was a popular architect in Stockholm. Came from France highly recommended. He had several of his buildings actually built, such as those around the castle you see now. But back to his demise. Seems he was walking home one evening at dusk, minding his own business. Erik Oxenstiern, a well-known troublemaker, rode up for no reason, slammed the flat of a blade on his head, and rode off."

Johan's mind raced. "This Erik—a relation of the chancellor's?"

"Yes, a nephew, but he was an embarrassment to the whole family. He'd been known to get into fights for the fun of it. Once he attacked some men on General Horn's own property. Erik is no longer here, though. Left town, probably under pressure from his relatives. You can imagine, a family like the chancellor's."

"He was never convicted?"

"Funny thing, poor Simon lived for nine days. He had doctors day and night, but they couldn't save him. During the trial, one of the doctors said the blow to his head was not severe enough to kill him. The others agreed. So Erik was fined for assault and physical maltreatment. I don't know the fines, but the money would have been distributed mostly to Simon's family, with a portion going to the town of Stockholm, and some to the royal treasury as is the general policy with fines."

"So the fines were paid, I suppose."

Freinsheim chuckled. "It's that or suffer another punishment, like exile, stoning, something like that. But of course Axel, and his cousin Gabriel, both of whom had sworn not to help the young man again, paid the fines. Erik had little money of his own. What he had was spent in taverns."

"Was this architect married?"

"Oh yes, he left a widow and several children behind. His mother lived in the household too, and he supported her, of course." Freinsheim leaned forward. "That's all I know of Simon. It was a public trial, so there are written records. You could go into town and search those if you like."

Johan paused. Searching through unfamiliar records, with nothing more than a name to go on, would take weeks. "Any idea of a trial date?"

Freinsheim drew his brows together. "Let me think."

Gunne spoke up. "I recall the year. It was two years ago, in the winter, I think."

Freinsheim leaned forward. "Hmm. Two years back." He scratched his chin. "Let's see." He rose, went to a shelf, and brought down a heavy ledger. After thumbing through several pages, he replaced the book and returned to the seat at his desk. "Yes, the trial began shortly after I finished helping Axel Oxenstiern write terms of a treaty. I recall he wanted to be here for the trial but had to negotiate with the Danish." Freinsheim chuckled. "We did manage to secure new lands for Sweden, though." He beamed, obviously proud of his part in the treaty. "So you'd be safe looking at records between August and December of that year."

Johan rose, relieved that they'd pinned down a date. He rose and extended his hand. "You've been a big help."

"Anytime," Freinsheim said, shaking hands with him and with Gunne.

Once they were gone from the room, Gunne said, "I don't see any clear connection between Marin and this architect— although that sketch on Marin's desk was definitely a drawing of a structure."

Johan spoke, half under his breath. "I think we're getting close to something, Gunne, I just don't know what." He paused. "You know, Freinsheim's mention of General Horn reminded me of something else. We dismissed the general earlier because of his age. We knew it was a younger man running from Zofia's workshop. So Horn wasn't the thief, but his age doesn't prevent him from being a murder suspect."

Gunne clapped a hand to his forehead. "Of course. I quite forgot. We should leave nothing to chance, and an interview with General Horn is overdue. But first, why don't you come to my room and tell me this secret card you hold in your doublet— the reason you believe François didn't kill the goldsmith?"

Johan grinned. "Sure, but after that, I'm eating dinner in the main dining hall." He patted his stomach. "Going without meals the way we've been doing, eating the extras the cook happens to have, is no way to keep warm."

A short while later, Gunne sat on his child-sized chair across from Johan, who had taken the upholstered wing-backed chair reserved for company. Gunne crossed his arms and waited.

Johan stroked his beard. It needed a trimming. "I have a theory, but I'd like to see what you think." He kneeled on the floor. "Pretend I'm the goldsmith." He leaned forward a bit as if to write. "Now, you sneak up on me, stab me in the heart from behind. I never hear you coming. Go ahead."

"You mean . . ."

"Try to think like the killer. You have a blade in your hand. You want to put it into my heart."

Gunne lifted a quill from beside his inkpot. "Very well. Hold still."

Johan waited. Nothing. He turned around to see a puzzled look on Gunne's face. The dwarf held the quill aloft. "Something's not right. I'd have better luck stabbing you in the ribs, like this." He went for the spot beneath Johan's right arm.

"Why there, Gunne?"

"Because if I go for your heart, I'd have to move to your left. You'd see me before the deed was done."

"Why move to the left?"

"So I could get my arm over your chest in the right place."

Johan rose to his feet. "Exactly. The blade is in your right hand. A killer would use his sword arm for sure advantage. It's my belief the murderer is left-handed. That's why I was sure François was not the killer. I watched him sign the record book at the trial. He's literate and has a fine script, and he's right-handed."

Gunne slapped his thigh. "By all that's holy, I think you're right. Besides, you said the blood on the goldsmith's cape was on his left shoulder. The killer removed the blade, brought his hand across the victim's left shoulder, and fled the scene. So now all we have to do is determine which of our suspects is left-handed."

Johan frowned. "I'm not sure that would be enough evidence to convict a man of murder."

Gunne nodded agreement. "True, but at least we'd have a place to begin, which is more than what we have now."

Johan smiled. "Well, we have a motive for General Horn. We know he disliked the French and resented them being brought here. The goldsmith was French, but that's the only connection. We'd need more evidence—like maybe Horn is left-handed, but even that wouldn't be enough to arrest him for murder." He rubbed his temple. "Let's pay a visit to the general—either learn something meaningful or scratch his name from our list."

CHAPTER TWENTY-NINE

Johan followed Gunne down a corridor, grateful that this visit to General Horn's room would not require taking the back way, through slippery tunnels and bat-infested catwalks. Instead, they had asked for an appointment and Horn had agreed to meet with them.

Shortly after Johan knocked on the door, the general greeted him with an outstretched hand. "Come in." He bent to shake hands with Gunne. "You too, of course." He indicated two of three straight-backed chairs. While the general questioned Gunne as to the queen mother's health, Johan sat, remembering his last time here—snooping around, looking for early leads.

The general's room had changed little since that day Johan discovered the unfinished letter, written to Horn's brother, in which he confided his disapproval of the queen's obsession with the French, and how the French Catholics would take over the Swedish government.

Now, the desk held only books, a quill and ink, and some maps lying alongside a stack of fresh parchment. Heavy old tapestries still covered the walls. The modest furnishings evidently suited the general's style, because his clothes, although made of the finest fabrics, were long out of fashion. His greying hair was trimmed neatly just below his ears. A neat, short beard and greying moustache reflected grooming expected of an officer in the queen's army.

General Horn sat in the only other chair and leaned back,

looking at Johan with dark, unreadable eyes that seemed to bore into Johan's soul while revealing nothing of the general's. Horn crossed his legs. "I understand you found the thief." His moustache twitched. "I figured one of the foreigners took it. I can read men pretty well. I've told the queen not to be misled by the ways of the French." He raised one hand into the air, a mocking gesture. "But what does an aging general know?"

Johan changed the subject, thinking the best way to learn anything from this man was to gain his trust. "From what I've heard, you know plenty. I understand you were the king's top man in the long war, commanding the troops skillfully."

"Yes," Horn said. "I'd have done anything for King Gustav. When he died at the Battle of Lützen, Sweden lost a great king. Brave, too. He was killed while leading a cavalry charge. Smoke and fog covered the field, separating him from his fellow riders. We didn't know, for a while, that he'd died, but when we saw his horse standing alone, we knew the worst had happened." General Horn rubbed his eyes, then looked up, seemingly eager to continue the story. "You've met Jakob Fabricius, the royal preacher? Well, he was there. When the king died, Fabricius gathered our officers around him and started singing psalms. For a while, the fighting ceased, but later it started again. By dusk, both sides had lost too many men, but the king's death— well, it kept us going. Men died all around me, but I was only wounded. Catholics took me prisoner, but later they had to retreat to Leipzig. Before they put me in prison, I learned that the Swedish army had prevailed. I rotted in a Catholic prison for almost three years, but our alliance with Saxony was intact. We won the battle but lost our king."

"An amazing story," Johan said. "I can understand why a man like you might resent the French coming here." He searched his memory. He should have learned more about the goldsmith, and if he was Catholic or Protestant.

General Horn grunted a reply. "Yes, I do resent them, with their bibles and papist views. Of course I do."

"And you were wounded. That would make anyone resentful."

The general shrugged. "I've grown used to my wound. Keep it hidden for the most part, so people don't ask. Men died out there. I was lucky. I only have this." He took his left arm from the pocket of his cloak. Johan tried not to stare, but evidently, the bone had been broken—by a bullet? It must never have been set. The hand hung useless and shriveled.

While the general tucked his left arm back into the pocket, Johan exchanged a look with Gunne. So much for this lead. General Horn had not killed anyone with his left arm, not since the battle that killed the queen's father. What's more, he didn't hide his disdain for the French. No, Horn was an honored general who apparently would live out his life serving the royal family.

As Johan rose to leave, thanking the general for his time, he realized with a sinking heart that they had wasted an afternoon chasing another false lead. All that was left, right now, was Marin's secretive nature about a drawing done by an architect, which might have nothing to do with the murder. What possible link could an architect have to a goldsmith?

CHAPTER THIRTY

The evening following François's trial and sentencing by the queen mother, a heavy snowfall raged through the city, piling snow roof high and keeping everyone in the palace for three days. Johan kept to his room, alternately practicing his lute and trying to devise a way to observe who in the palace might be left-handed. This morning, though, the sun shone, and by noon, word spread through the musicians' dormitory that a celebration was imminent. At one o'clock, all courtiers and staff were expected to attend a banquet in the dining hall.

Johan dressed in warm clothes, wondering what this meant for palace entertainment, and if the musicians' ensemble would be called to extra rehearsals. This would delay his investigation.

Leaving the dormitory, he bumped into servants carrying piles of linens. As he approached a narrow corridor, he was shoved aside by a group of palace guards carrying banners. He entered the dining hall and saw the room was filled with strangers. Where was Gunne in all this pandemonium? Was there even a vacant seat to be had?

While making his way through the crowd, he passed groups of dignitaries dressed in fine clothes. Interrupted by a nudge on his knee, he looked down. Gunne crooked his finger and Johan bent to listen.

"You're staring," Gunne said, pulling him from the crowd and into a quieter corner.

Johan chuckled. "Sorry, but who are these people?"

"Visitors. Some of them have been in Stockholm since the snowstorm started. A few were lodged in the palace, but most stayed at the palace in Uppsala." With a nod of his head, Gunne indicated a group by the door. "They are English gentry, here to escape the turmoil of the civil war in their homeland across the channel. They arrived last night, but most of these visitors are here by invitation. See those men to the right?" He lowered his voice to a whisper. "Louis XIV's representatives are easy to spot. Note the short doublets."

Johan nodded and hid a smile. In contrast to their short fitted doublets, the French visitors wore full, long breeches, well past their knees. The breeches, mostly silk, were decorated with lace ruffles and small ribbon bows. He estimated the bows on one man's outfit had taken a tailor several weeks to tie and sew on. "So what are we celebrating?"

Gunne took Johan's hand. "I'll explain, but come with me. Voullon is saving our seats." They wove through chattering ladies to a table not far from the dais. Once they were seated, Gunne poured their drinks and continued. "One of the queen's ships, the *Swan*, has returned from New Sweden, crossing the ocean in five months. They were gone for over a year. The queen's ships always bring treasures from the New World, and these men know of Queen Christina's generosity." He sipped from his beer. "Just this morning, after workers cleared some of the snow, crates of beaver pelts were delivered and taken to the palace storage room. From there, the queen can distribute the furs to these visiting dignitaries. It's a way to get political favors."

Johan drank from his cup. "I saw some guards with banners. They almost ran me down."

Gunne smiled. "By now, those banners will be hanging from the precipice. That way all the residents of Stockholm know that dignitaries are in the city. If there is a street brawl while these men are here, the fines are doubled." He laughed. "Keeps the streets peaceful."

Trumpets blared and Queen Christina entered, dressed in a flowing green gown trimmed in ermine.

Silver dishes piled high with steaming meats and vegetables circulated through the hall, now filled with guests and the entire crew of the *Swan*. Johan poured another beer and waited for their table to be served the main dish. He looked down the long table. Not far away sat Marin, the queen's sketching teacher, with a subdued François on one side and Beaulieu on the other.

Johan cut a slice of cheese from a platter and saw that the cook's helpers were approaching their table, carrying trays of food. They set down steaming bowls of pea soup, with alternating dishes of herring and eels floating in an egg broth. Good. He had built up an appetite.

The roast mutton was served, the best he'd ever tasted, and stewed apples were the perfect complement. When Beaulieu and Voullon began discussing music, Johan looked up. He caught sight of Marin, knife in hand, reaching for a slice of meat. Johan continued chewing the mutton, intrigued with what he'd just seen. Now, as the others enjoyed the same dish, Johan kept his eyes on the sketching teacher.

Gunne reached for a ladle and took more vegetables. "You're quiet. Don't feel well?"

Johan looked back at his own serving dish and kept his voice low. "Don't let him see you looking, but watch Marin. Tell me what you notice."

"He's drinking wine."

"Not that. Watch him with the eating utensils." Johan reached for his cup, trying to hide his rising excitement.

A few moments later Gunne drew an audible breath. "You don't suppose—"

"Could be. But we need more proof."

All through the extended speeches, the exchanges of gifts, Johan's mind raced. Here it was, in front of him all the time. As a last resort, if unable to determine whether Marin was left-handed, Johan had planned to ask the queen, but this was a gift. Questioning the queen about one of her teachers was not to his liking. He wiped his hands on a linen. Wouldn't it be something if a piece of mutton was all it took to solve a mystery?

Suddenly, the thought of questioning a lead suspect reminded him of how careful he had to be. If Marin suspected his left-handedness was all the evidence Johan had, he might laugh them from the room. Or he could lie or find an excuse, saying the dining table was crowded, or any number of things that might come to his mind. The more Johan considered the issue, the more worried he got. In truth, the evidence was too flimsy to accuse a man of murder. Besides, the table where Marin sat *was* crowded. Much as Johan would like to solve the case, he didn't want to accuse an innocent man.

Queen Christina rose, interrupting his musings. A horn blew, and the room fell silent. Her low, clear voice carried to every corner of it. "I have invited a choir of Italian madrigal singers to entertain you this afternoon. I hope you enjoy them."

Gunne leaned to speak with Johan. "I guess we need to ask Queen Christina."

Johan nodded. "I was hoping it wouldn't come to that, but yes, I suppose we do."

Queen Christina looked up from her desk. "I only have a moment, Johan. The doorman said you had a question." She laid her quill to the side. "How can I help? Is this about your investigation?"

"Yes, Your Majesty," Johan said. "We will only take a moment. You may recall—"

"Go ahead with your question, please." She smiled, softening the sharp interruption.

Johan decided brevity was best. "Your sketching teacher, Marin de Courlas. Does he sketch with his right or left hand?"

She drew her brows together, then shook her head. "What an odd question. Surely he's not a suspect."

Johan chose his words carefully. "Your Majesty, we can overlook no one."

She leaned back and crossed her arms. One corner of her mouth turned up, and Johan wondered if she was going to laugh him out of her room. Instead, she smiled. "I like a man who considers all sides of an argument. Very well. I'll answer your question. He sketches with his right hand."

Johan swallowed and was about to back away, begging her pardon for the interruption, when she held up her hand. "That is not to say he never uses his left hand to sketch. He does at times, when he's in a hurry, or gets upset with my poor attempts and tries to correct. But he always begins with his right. Does that answer your question? I suppose one could say he uses both."

Johan bowed low. Gunne gave an exaggerated curtsy, and together they retreated toward the doors. Once outside her chambers, Johan said, "Let's go up to your reading nook."

Gunne grinned. "Yes, we need a quiet place to talk." He hurried to keep up with Johan's long strides, and after climbing two sets of stairs, they reached the window alcove, Gunne's private place.

A ray of afternoon sunlight shone on the red velvet window seat. Johan remained standing, looking outside, his gaze on the winter-scorched pasture, the stables, and the outer edge of the cook's garden, brown and waiting for spring. "I still think we're getting close to something, in spite of this latest setback. If Marin sometimes reverts to his left hand when sketching, why wouldn't he use it for other things?"

"Like killing the goldsmith, but still, we have no motive."

Johan nodded. "Yes, but I'm thinking we should do as Freinsheim suggested and make that trip to look through the records. The fact that Marin has some connection to the murdered architect, and the trial concerned a member of the Oxenstiern family, has me baffled."

Gunne rubbed his knees. "My legs hurt when the weather changes like this, but I agree, the trial records need examining."

"Then let's go first thing tomorrow."

Johan paused at the entrance to the Stockholm court, a century-old stone structure that held trials and meetings of the city council, and was also a depository for all public records. After stomping snow from his boots, Johan opened the door for Gunne, who looked like a forest animal from the back, encased as he was in fur from head to toe against the weather. For Johan, two sets of woolen breeches, boots that reached to his knees, a fur hat, thick gloves and a fur-lined coat had kept him warm on the way here.

Once inside the building, Johan blinked, allowing his eyes to adjust to the dim interior after the bright glare of the snow. An arrow pointed to a desk some little way from the door—perhaps a place for visitors to ask for information. A bespectacled clerk with stringy dark hair rose from behind the desk as they approached. "How can I help?"

Johan removed his hat and tucked it in the waistband of his breeches. "We're here to examine records of a trial. Where are public records kept?"

The clerk tilted his head, scanned Gunne, and looked back at Johan. "That depends on the date. A current trial?"

"No, two years back. Sometime between August and December. We're not sure of the month."

The clerk waved them down a hallway. "That long ago, the records would be bound by now and put downstairs." He led them to an arched opening, pushed back a curtain, grabbed a lantern from a hook, and started down a set of steep steps. Johan trod carefully after him, his wet boots slick on the narrow wood planks, and Gunne followed behind, complaining of the cold.

The clerk set the lantern on a table and pointed to some shelves. "There you are. Help yourselves. You should find what you want somewhere in this area. The bindings are clearly marked with the months and inclusive dates, but inside the bindings, the trials are in no particular order." He turned and hurried up the stairs, as if lingering might bring another request.

Gunne braced his hands on his hips and looked up at the shelf. "This will take days."

Johan pulled down one of the heavy bound ledgers and laid it on one end of a long table. "Not if we get started. Here, you take this. It's August." He reached for the next. "And here's another—the same month."

Gunne climbed onto a stool and opened the book. "Hmm. A farmer's cows ruined a widow's newly planted garden. The case was dismissed because the plaintiff and defendant married before the scheduled date for the hearing."

Johan pulled a stool next to Gunne. "Never mind that. Look, at least the pages are numbered. Keep going until you get to another trial or we'll never finish."

Gunne pulled the lantern between them and gave a loud sigh.

Johan smiled. Gunne was right. This would likely take days.

On the morning of their third day, when Johan was wondering if they would ever find what they were looking for, he turned a page and saw, in careful script at the top, the words he hoped for. *Trial of Erik Oxenstiern for death of Simon de la Vallée.* "Gunne, here it is." Johan pushed back the lamp and moved the book closer to Gunne.

The minutes ticked by as they read together, the trial unfolding before their eyes, including witnesses' and physicians' names. But nowhere did they find any mention of Marin de Courlas.

They reached the last page, and Johan's heart sank. They'd spent three days chasing the wind, accomplishing nothing. He was about to close the book when he saw, below the neat text of the court scribe, a complete list of trial witnesses. He looked at the names. Nothing meaningful there. Then, at the bottom of the page, he read: *Benefactors of the Settlement.* He scanned the list. Two of the names made his heart leap: Pauline de Courlas and Maria de Courlas. Were they relatives of Marin? If so, where exactly would this information lead?

CHAPTER THIRTY-ONE

Johan passed through the castle gates and went with Gunne to the side entrance. "At least," Gunne said, "thanks to the court records, we have a connection between the architect Simon de la Vallée and the queen's drawing teacher."

Johan nodded. "The last name is the same, but we need to look at every angle. If members of his family were beneficiaries of the fee paid by the Oxenstierns, that means they had a loss—or so it was determined by the court. So it's easy to understand that Marin could have carried a grudge these last few years, especially if he thought an Oxenstiern got away with murder. But why kill the goldsmith? Because one of them hired the man to value some coins?" Johan shook his head. "I'm convinced the goldsmith was in the wrong place at the wrong time. Marin, intent on the crime, didn't look close. He thought he was killing an Oxenstiern."

Johan opened the kitchen door, waved to the cook, and walked ahead of Gunne. When he spotted an empty meeting room, he motioned the dwarf inside.

Gunne hunched his shoulders and pulled his cloak close. "It's as cold in here as it is outside." He hooked the clasp at his neck and sat. "What now? I agree we have no direct tie to the murder, but there's something about Marin . . ."

Johan loosened his scarf. The room was freezing, but his skin was beginning to itch from the wool—a scratchy fabric, but warmer than anything else except fur. "I think the only way to handle this is to confront Marin. Mention what we found. Let him think we know more than we do."

Gunne shrugged. "Let's go and get this over with."

A few minutes later, Johan knocked on the door of Marin's room. The sketching teacher opened the door a crack. "Go away. I'm taking a nap. Besides, I have nothing to say to either of you."

Johan pushed his way in, with Gunne beside him. "But we have something to tell you."

Marin's eyes widened. Then, evidently realizing his actions could give him away, he crossed his arms defiantly. "Go ahead. I'll give you two minutes." He slumped into a chair, leaned back, and pushed hair from his face. "What's all this about?"

Johan sat on a stool across from Marin, while Gunne sat on the end of Marin's cot. Only the sound of a ticking clock broke the silence. Johan noticed the framed sketch was still face down on the desk. He clasped his hands and leaned forward. "I'll be direct, Marin. You are the prime suspect in the murder of a village goldsmith. All the evidence points to you. So you can either explain to us, or to the queen, why you did it." He shrugged, hoping he looked confident, though he felt anything but. "We know the murder was committed by someone left-handed. The queen confirmed that you use both your hands well."

Marin's face turned red. He rose and crossed the short space between the two of them. "How dare you accuse me of such a thing? Bah. You imply I killed a man I didn't even know?" He was shaking, whether from fury or fright, Johan had no idea. "I am not left-handed," he raged. "I sketch with my right hand."

"You can claim whatever you like, but no right-handed man can handle a knife with his left hand the way you did. The mutton gave you away."

"Lies. All lies. You need to solve a case, and I'm a good target. I'm a newcomer to the palace, hired from the city. This way, you have a scapegoat. None of your precious courtiers can be blamed, especially none of . . ."

"Of whom, Marin? Go on."

"Nothing. I've said all I'm saying. I'm not your man." He crossed to the door and then turned back, his features hardened by anger. "If I were you, I'd look first at the men closest to the queen. They may have had a motive. I didn't. I didn't even know the man." He turned away, but not before Johan saw a shadow of pain cross Marin's features.

Johan rose and stepped forward. This might be his best chance. "And we know about Pauline and Maria de Courlas."

The blood drained from Marin's face. A muscle beneath his eye twitched. "Wh—how do you know of them?"

"The trial records, Marin. We know everything now."

Marin backed away and groped for the desk, his hands shaking. He braced himself to keep from falling and made it into his chair. "The records prove nothing."

"On the contrary, we learned what we needed to know. Do you want to talk with us, or to the queen?"

"No. Not to the queen. She believes in me, she gave me a chance. I can't face her, not now."

"Then tell us," Johan said. "It will be easier on you if you confess. I can understand how you must feel about the Oxenstierns." Johan held his breath. He'd done everything he could. The rest was up to Marin.

The art teacher lowered his head between his hands. "It's almost a relief to be discovered. I'm afraid to go to sleep because of the nightmares."

Johan felt a pang of pity for the broken man in front of him. Guilt was a wound that never left, not until it worked its ugly way to the surface to be confronted like the enemy it was. "Go ahead, Marin. Who is Pauline to you?"

A sob came from the lowered head. "Pauline was my mother.

She's gone now, died last Advent. Everyone's gone. My sister Maria too; she died in childbirth." He picked up the framed drawing and brought it close. "Even my half-brother, Simon. One of the best architects Stockholm ever had. Killed by Erik Oxenstiern, who never spent a day in prison for his crime. He would have, if not for Axel and Gabriel, his rich uncles. They're guilty, too. If not for them and their money, Erik would not have gone free."

Marin wiped his tears and looked up. "Simon was a real brother to me—taught me drawing, taught me how to sketch a building, or a face." He gave Johan a bitter smile. "He made me use my right hand. At first I was uncomfortable, but he persisted. Said some people still believed left-handed people were dim-witted, or cursed. Things like that. Said if I wanted to draw professionally, I needed to use my right hand. Still, as you noticed in the dining hall, I frequently use my left. Sketching is about the only thing I do right-handed." He set the frame on the desk. "He was a great man, my half-brother. I still miss him."

Johan leaned forward. "What did you have against the goldsmith?"

Marin's face crumpled in defeat. Tears poured down his cheeks and he choked on a sob. "By all that's holy," he said, wiping his face on his sleeve, "I never meant to kill an innocent man. I wanted to avenge my brother's death, but I should have known something would go wrong. Nothing is right since Simon died—nothing." He pulled out a linen and blew his nose. "In a way, I'm glad you found out. Ever since I learned what I did, I can't sleep." A fresh wave of sobs wracked his body. His stooped shoulders shook uncontrollably. A few moments later he lifted his head, eyes streaming tears. "I'll never forgive myself. From the back, he looked just like Gabriel Oxenstiern. Or even Axel. They all look alike." He was shaking uncontrollably now. "As

God is my witness, I never meant to kill him. Had I known . . ."
He lowered his head again and sniffed. "Gabriel was there every
night, counting, counting. Oh, those Oxenstierns know how to
count money. And then that night . . . I killed the wrong man."
He gave a bitter, twisted smile. "The irony is that an Oxenstiern
got away again." Marin's shoulders drooped and he rubbed his
reddened eyes, then pointed to the framed sketch. "I had a feeling, the day you asked about this, that you would somehow
learn the truth."

Johan's voice softened. "He gave that sketch to you?"

Marin nodded. "It's all I have of him now. Simon raised me
after our father died. He spent a lot of time with me. Said he
would show me how to draw great buildings when I was good
enough." Marin wiped a tear away and continued. "And he did.
He taught me everything I know. There was a time people cared,
about him and his work, but they've all forgotten. It's as if he
never lived."

Johan took a deep breath. "Tell me more about the trial."

Marin clenched his fists. "Erik Oxenstiern got away with
murder. Those lying doctors said that since Simon lived nine
days after the attack, it wasn't the blow that killed him. The
whole town knew the truth, even the doctors, but they lied."

Johan pressed on. "But Erik was fined for the crime."

"Ha. What's a fine to an Oxenstiern? Besides, Erik's uncles
paid the fine." Marin scowled. "He killed my brother and got
away with it."

Johan met Marin's eyes, hating to go on, knowing he had to.
"So you decided to get even. An eye for an eye."

"Something like that. I thought about it a long time, that I
was the only one who could bring justice for my brother's
death." He shook his head. "I've learned a lesson. Not that it
matters now, but what I did was as bad as what Erik Oxenstiern
did—killing an innocent man. That's why I don't care what

happens to me now." He blew his nose again and coughed. "What will they do with me?"

Johan rose from his chair. "I don't know. That's not up to me."

Marin tried to stand, nodding, the tears still flowing. Johan slid one hand beneath Marin's arm. "Here, I'll help. Gunne, open the door. We need to get this man to the guard commander."

The following morning, while breaking his fast, Johan received a summons from the queen. "You too," the page said, looking at Gunne.

Johan nodded and rose from the bench as the page left the room. Gunne took another cake from the platter of sweets. "What do you suppose now?"

"Perhaps a trial will be set. We will be witnesses."

Gunne dropped his chin. "I feel bad for a murderer. Something's not right about that."

Johan chuckled. "I feel the same, but it's out of our hands."

When they were shown to the queen's antechamber, Johan saw that Marin was already there, standing between two guards. The queen sat not far away, riding crop in hand. Johan swallowed. He wanted none of this, but there seemed to be no way out.

Queen Christina turned her large blue eyes on Johan. "Ah, you're here. I'll keep this short. The guard commander alerted me to what happened. Marin de Courlas has already pled his case. He explained everything to me, and begged for mercy."

She looked at her Privy Council, seated around her. "My learned advisors say one thing, but my good sense says another." She ran one hand through her thick hair, then stroked the riding crop. "Lutenist, I wanted you to hear my decision, since I understand it was you who solved this mystery, you and Gunne."

Johan looked over at Marin, who seemed to have shrunk since yesterday. From here, Johan saw that the man's limp was caused by one leg being shorter than the other. He was visibly trembling, and no wonder. The whip looked ominous.

Queen Christina looked directly at Marin. "As the ruler of Sweden, I can grant clemency, or pronounce death. In the case before me, I have decided to take the middle ground. All involved, beginning with you and your half-brother's death, have lost something dear—a life, or trust in our system of justice. After weighing the facts in the case carefully, I have decided to grant you clemency—in spite of the unlawful act you admitted. I am assessing the fine at one hundred fifty marks. I understand the victim had no living relatives, so the fine will be paid to the orphanage I am establishing here in Stockholm." She lowered her gaze. "In addition, Marin de Courlas, you will help clean the stables for a period of six months, after which we will resume the sketching lessons." She raised her head and looked around the room. "Commander, the man is released under his own recognizance. I imagine he will need time to sell some of his property to pay the fine." She stood, still holding the riding crop. "Lutenist, the queen mother wants to see you. Now, everyone is dismissed. I am riding out. It's too nice a day to be in." She turned and left the room, followed by her Privy Council.

The commander led Marin away, and Johan and Gunne left by another door. Once in the hall, Johan looked down at the dwarf. "With the crime solved, I'm wondering what Eleanora wants with us now."

Chapter Thirty-Two

Johan sat on a bench in the queen mother's salon, the same room in which François had been tried. Was Eleanora planning some new scheme? Why exactly had he been summoned here? Across the way, Zofia sat calmly, arms folded.

Johan tilted his head to study her face. She lifted her chin and met his eyes, then smiled broadly, putting him at ease. If she was content, so was he. Because of her, he had learned to accept without guilt the gift of his brother's courage. Perhaps someday he would get to thank her properly. For now, though, a few well-spoken words were all he dared. The best things were worth waiting for.

Not far away sat François, deep in thought. Johan knew from the look in the dancer's eyes that he bore a love for Sigrid strong enough to carry him through life, wherever that might lead.

A curtain slid back, exposing a side entrance, and a line of Eleanora's dwarfs came out and took their seats along one wall. This was no trial. It had the feel of a lecture.

Eleanora's ladies filed out, taking their places on stools surrounding the queen mother's high-backed chair, all but Sigrid, who headed straight for Johan. *Now what?*

She sat next to him on the bench and surprised him with a gracious smile. "Eleanora will be here soon, so I only have a moment. I want to thank you for what you did for François, standing up for him the way you did. Without you, I don't know what he'd have done." She took a deep breath and continued.

"I spoke with Zofia today too." She licked her lip. "I apologized for what I did to her."

"What was that?"

"I tried to get her to admit to a crime she didn't commit."

"Yes, she told me about that. Why did you encourage her to do such a thing?"

Sigrid lifted her chin. "Kirsten is a nice person. Others are jealous because I'm Eleanora's favorite, but Kirsten has always been kind, and it's partly because of her that Eleanora is considering making me Lady of the Chamber. Kirsten loved Henrik, though I don't know why. He's the only person I know who seldom smiles. I guess that's why I thought he might have committed the crimes. He angered the queen years back—none of us know what that was about—and I knew that if he had stolen the book, she'd send him away forever. Kirsten's heart would have broken." She shook her head. "But that makes no difference now. He's gone anyway. I know, it's unforgivable, what I did—protecting someone I thought was a criminal. But Kirsten is my best—my only real friend, except for François, of course."

"No need to thank me, Sigrid. A lot of us will do most anything for a friend. Anyway, here comes the queen mother."

Sigrid spun around and rushed to her place.

The queen mother entered in a rustle of skirts. When she took her seat on the gold-upholstered chair, Sigrid arranged the folds of Eleanora's outer robe. Her dog jumped to the royal lap. She stroked him and rubbed his ears.

Johan crossed his legs and waited. There was no hurrying a royal.

Eleanora cleared her throat. "I thought it fitting to bring all of you together today as we bring this unpleasantness to an end. My daughter, the queen, has made a decision this morning with which I agree. Now that all this is behind us, there is another issue that must be addressed."

Eleanora turned to Johan. "Lutenist, I am impressed with the work you and Gunne did on this matter. I had my doubts, with time running out, but you surprised me. You are a good team together."

The dog jumped down and headed for Sigrid's arms. The queen mother shook her head and smoothed her skirts. "Johan, I am sure you know of my German roots, of the family I left behind. Oh, I don't regret leaving there—my years as King Gustav's wife were the brightest years of my life—but I love my family, too, and have kept in touch through the years."

Johan shifted his weight on the bench. The fire was going out and the room was no longer warm. He heard the queen mother's next words through a haze of disbelief. "There is trouble at court in Brandenburg," she said. "Intrigue and bad dealings run rampant, or so I am told. I am recommending you, Johan, and Gunne, to go there and discover exactly what problems they are having and what is going on.

"You may remain here until spring, of course, as travel is impossible in this weather."

Johan leaned forward. "Your Majesty, you mentioned problems in Brandenburg. What problems, if I may be so bold as to ask?"

"Oh, some valuable paintings missing—a murder—who knows what goes on in a court that size? The city is growing too fast and is overrun with foreigners. But I assure you, it will test your abilities as a sleuth far more than the hunt for the Silver Bible has done. Now, it's time for the noonday meal. You are all dismissed."

She left the room, followed by her ladies. Zofia rose and walked to where Johan stood, still pondering what had just taken place. She gave him a broad wink. "You will love Bran-denburg. I'll write and tell you of my first major discovery." She smiled, and he noticed how her bow-shaped lips turned up at the outer edges. He winked back, wanting to kiss her, and deciding now was not the time. Anyway, it was months until spring, and anything could happen between now and then.

AUTHOR'S NOTE

The precise year in which the Silver Bible was written, as well as where the book lay hidden for centuries, is unknown. In the sixteenth century, the bible was discovered in a Benedictine monastery. Scholars believe the manuscript dates from the sixth century, and was probably transcribed for the Ostrogothic king, Theodoric the Great.

In the seventeenth century, the book was in the possession of Emperor Rudolph II at his castle in Prague. At the end of the Thirty Years' War, it was taken to Queen Christina's palace in Stockholm, and gradually made its way to Uppsala University, where it now resides.

ABOUT THE AUTHOR

After a brief teaching career, **Joyce Elson Moore** turned to writing full time, and has since reached a widening audience with her books, most of which reflect her background in music.

Among other awards, Joyce's medieval romance, *Jeanne of Clairmonde*, won First Place in the FWA Royal Palm Literary Awards. Another novel, *The Tapestry Shop*, (Five Star/Cengage), won a medallion in the Popular Fiction category from Florida Book Awards, sponsored jointly by Florida State and the Humanities Council of Florida.

The Stockholm Castle Mystery is the first in a three-book series featuring Johan, a seventeenth-century lute player appointed by an eccentric queen mother to solve a murder mystery.

Excerpts and reviews of Joyce's books are on her website: www.joycemoorebooks.com.